THE ANCIENT TERROR

Bedford turned from Kalissae and walked to the face of the mine wall where bits and pieces from the rock bore still lay entangled with debris from the blast. He bent over and with light, dancing movements of his fingers began touching everything. He immediately picked up a resonance beneath the rocky surface—a pulsing resonance that threatened to overwhelm him.

Bedford! Stop! whispered Issykul in his mind. *Pain you cannot feel! We will die! Stop!*

As though hit for an instant by a million volts of electric current, Bedford's body stiffened and froze. He hung suspended in time and space, paralyzed, yet aware of everything around him. The only thing he wanted to do was scream.

An instant later his knees buckled and he fell. The swirling black quicksand of unconsciousness quickly swallowed him in its mindless embrace.

THE SEREN CENACLES

Warren Norwood and Ralph Mylius

BANTAM BOOKS
TORONTO · NEW YORK · LONDON · SYDNEY

THE SEREN CENACLES

A Bantam Book / October 1983

All rights reserved.
Copyright © 1983 by Warren C. Norwood & Ralph W. Mylius.
Cover art copyright © 1983 by Barclay Shaw.
*This book may not be reproduced in whole or in part, by
mimeograph or any other means, without permission.*
For information address: Bantam Books, Inc.

ISBN 0-553-23574-5

Published simultaneously in the United States and Canada

PRINTED IN THE UNITED STATES OF AMERICA

H   0 9 8 7 6 5 4 3 2 1

For Nina and Margot

ONE

"Ground floor, real world," the mechanical voice droned. "Family, friends, and associates. Going up, please. Going up."

It always began the same way. When Theeran prepared herself for an Isoleucine-graphite Ore Pocket Reversal, she imagined riding on an automatic elevator as it passed through the infinite layers of memory in the center of her mind. It was a discipline she had learned as a novice, and it always worked to clear her thoughts and intensify her concentration. Her imaginary elevator was programmed to stop periodically at levels where she could drop off a few of her conscious distractions and concerns. Thus, as she reached each higher plateau, her focus on the task ahead narrowed and sharpened.

"Level six, please. Level six, fears and anxieties," the voice purred as the shimmering doors of her elevator opened.

Theeran stared across the threshold. The blurred image of Euphrates mine manager, Kalissae Boristh-Major, smugly stared back. How could someone with my mother's blood

1

in her veins be such an unsympathetic bitch, Theeran wondered?

"It's a silly fear, Theeran," Kalissae's image whispered. "The scans show only a minor aberration, nothing to be so frightened about."

"How would you know? You're not a psychominer anymore. You probably can't even remember what it's like to turn an ore pocket inside out." Kalissae's image dissolved into a shapeless, green haze, but Theeran's mind kept shouting as she had to Kalissae so many times before. "You can't remember, can you? You can't even do the slamball trick anymore. Some of the fuzz still stays on the outside of the ball when you try to reverse it." The elevator doors silently slid shut.

"Level nine . . ."

"Damn her! And damn the Helical Minerals assignment computers for sending me to her mine," Theeran cursed softly.

"Level twelve . . ."

Again Kalissae's image appeared. Her silver eyes glowed with anger, and her cheeks flushed to a pale blue against the pastel green of her face. Theeran forced her mind to close the doors and move upwards. She had to clear away the memory of the argument, or she would never be able to reverse the ore pocket.

"Level twenty . . . thirty . . . forty." Higher and higher her elevator rose, but still Theeran could not rid herself of her half-sister's image.

"I don't know what it was like for you, Kalissae, but for me it is like having the label of my mind soaked off the body of my physical reality. Any reservations, any small doubts about my ability to put my label back on once I've finished the Ore Pocket Reversal could destroy my sanity. *My* sanity, Kalissae! That's what we're talking about." The words echoed back in Theeran's mind, hot, angry, frustrated. Her inability to clear her emotions and begin the second phase of O.P.R. tore at her self-confidence like a twin-edged razor, slashing the fabric of her trust in her own technical skill.

"This pocket is no different than any other, Theeran."

"But . . . it is. It's altered somehow, not like any pocket I've dealt with before."

"You will perform your job."

"But—"

"You *will* do what you have been *trained* to do. Saints of Vantrul! You're a professional, Theeran. Your natural talent has been sharpened into an exquisite skill—at great cost to Helical Minerals, I might add."

"I know what I cost."

"And you know what the company pays you. So don't give me any more of this whimpering. You will make every effort to reverse this ore pocket, or"—Kalissae paused, her eyes narrowing—"or I will have you reassigned to one of the remote exploratory mines, where you will live and work under the crudest of conditions. Is that clear, Theeran?"

Theeran shuddered. She knew what Kalissae meant by crudest of conditions. It meant living and working in an intravivo pressure suit, all day, every day for a six-Standard-month tour of duty. Reluctantly she nodded her head, her eyes burning with anger. "Yes, high-sister," she said as evenly as she could, "that is very clear."

"Level one hundred. Level one hundred. Insertion, insertion, insertion . . ." the mechanical voice in her brain insisted. As Theeran eased her mind through the narrow door the voice added, "and too high for your talents." She shut off the echoing whisper and pulled herself into phase two.

Theeran stood in a large room with mirrored walls of thick, smoky glass. It was like standing in a fog, yet still being able to clearly see everything in the room. The familiarity of the setting reassured her enough to proceed. Imbedded deep in the reflective surface of the mirror, she could see tiny bits of phosphoresence glowing like thousands of unblinking eyes. Her own image floated on top of the mirror, blotting out the small pinpoints of light where its frail woman's body slid over the cold surface of the walls.

Her training told her not to pause too long. Instinctively she began a grid-pattern search of the glassy walls, looking for the brighter telltale glow of the Isoleucine-graphite deposit. She was not far into her search when she spotted it. Six meters up the wall on her left a large pulsating spot glowed with the characteristic violet color. "Steady for the hard part," a new voice whispered in her mind.

She had learned as a novice that the hardest part, the real trick of psychomining, was to loosen the glue which held her mind to her body and to slip her noncorporeal Self through the mirrored walls of the abstracted ore pocket. It was like trying to penetrate an eggshell without breaking it and without letting the shell break the surface tension of her extended mind. With a slow, deep breath Theeran repeated the litany of her training.

"First, NEVER lose sight of your body. It is your only path of return. Without it you will die."

Faint heat waves shimmered from the image of her body in the mirror.

"Second, bond your mind to the outer surface of the Isoleucine ore pocket."

Her image in the mirror imperceptibly stiffened as her psyche's inner surface touched the cold outer layer of the ore pocket and held fast.

"Third, flow like thin oil and envelop the pocket."

As Theeran let her mind flow over the curved surface of the ore pocket, the last threads connecting her psyche to her body broke. They shattered like a million crystal shards, releasing her, setting her free from corporeal limitations. Her mind swelled with confidence, the center of its focus rising like a slow bubble through a dark heavy liquid. The ore pocket sparkled and flared in myriad shades of purple vermillion. The richness of it filled her with joy.

Reaching, probing, feeling, Theeran poured her mind

over every amorphous hill and valley of the pocket. At
each new crevice she annealed the point of contact with
the concentrated kinetic energy of her willpower. At first
slowly and carefully, but then with an increasingly eager
pace she sealed herself over more and more of its surface
until all but the last few square meters of area were en-
cased within the essence of her Self.

As she stretched to close the remaining gaps, the ore
pocket lurched with a brief, painful force. Theeran had felt
containment reactions before, but never one so strong.
She shivered with a fear which her training immediately
dispelled.

"Do not deviate from the plan. There will always be
some resistance. Close the gaps."

Self touched Self, and the last surface area was covered.
Again the ore pocket lurched. The pain was more intense
and felt like tiny bits of glass being ground into her
unprotected nerves.

"Fourth," the insistent litany continued, "compress the
massless energy of your psyche into a sphere with a
diameter equal to zero."

For Theeran this had always been the easiest part to do
and the most difficult to explain. It was almost as unconscious an act as blinking an eye. The facile and judicious
use of direct control on the process was what made it
different. Once when she was talking about it to the
Euphrates novice, Friesh, she described it as switching
from an infrared C minor to an ultraviolet C minor. It
crossed the spectrum of visible phenomena even to a
physically detached mind, yet retained its static reality in
a constant underlying sound. Her explanation made no
more sense to Friesh than it did to anyone else. But the
important thing was that she could do it with no trouble.
In an instant she compressed her psyche to a sphere with
no dimensions. It was an imaginary point in space which
existed solely because she willed it to exist. Infrared
turned to ultraviolet, but the C minor wavered.

"Fifth, your psyche is one with the ore pocket, and it is

one with you. Zero equals zero equals unity. Hold the interior surfaces of mind and pocket together and decompress."

With a mental sigh of relaxation caused by her anticipation of successful completion, Theeran began the decompression. Or tried to. Something was wrong. Instead of uniform expansion, bulges and depressions formed in the fabric of her psyche. Instinctively she checked her physical body. It stood glistening with sweat on the floor below her. As she fought to control the distortions of the decompression, her body jerked with pain. The C minor warbled toward C major.

"Steady. Steady," the voice whispered.

Like icy water seeping through freeze-ruptured couplings, panic soaked into her mind. Her concentration was breaking up. Her body was suffering. She was losing control of the situation. She had to hang on. But she couldn't. If she let the decompression continue as it was, all would be . . . what? Theeran didn't know what.

Anger burned out the panic with a hissing steam of determination. She had to get back to her body. The ore pocket was out of control. It was time to save herself.

Theeran struggled against the forces of dissolution and tried to pull herself away from the ore pocket. The harder she tried to disengage, the weaker she felt. But the sight of her pain-racked body spurred her efforts with the energy of desperation.

With a rippling explosion of raw determination, Theeran tore herself from the virulent pocket. A thousand cracks appeared in her psyche. The seams of her control split open, and the oily essence of her Self spilled out in hot, viscous streams.

For the first time she heard herself scream. She desperately tried to hold herself together. Nothing else mattered. Nothing. But in an instant she had lost. She knew she was going to die.

At that moment of realization, her pain stopped. Her body held a reserve, some secret, healing source of energy.

It could not keep her alive, but it would enable her to direct one brilliant flash of self-made light upon the mystery which was destroying her. There would be no surrender. She would know why.

In an instant she sucked up all her remaining energy, concentrating it all for one brief moment. Releasing it in a single, glaring burst of white luminescence, she looked upon her enemy.

Kalissae threw her clenched fists up to her ears, shielding them from the penetrating scream which blasted the water-slicked grey-green walls of mine level eighty-seven. Her body stiffened involuntarily. Her pale blue teeth gnashed together with a low grinding noise. The muscles on her neck bulged out like the roots of some massive green tree. Unable to avert her eyes from the psychominer, she watched Theeran's skull rupture like a germinating seed. Kalissae's knees locked, and she stood frozen in place as the now lifeless body slumped in slow motion to the damp, cool floor, streams of red, hissing liquid spewing from her half-sister's head.

"Saint Gunson, what have I done?" Kalissae rasped as the O.P.R. crew chief rushed to Theeran's side. Slowly lowering her fists from her ears she asked again in a lowered voice, "What have I done?"

Mental images of Theeran clicked through Kalissae's brain like rapid-fire still pictures. She desperately sought release from the feelings of guilt which flooded her mind. Theeran was only a half-sister, of course, and deserved no special consideration. Her blood was impure. But could Kalissae justify forcing Theeran to proceed with the ore pocket reversal? Yes.

"She's dead, Manager," the crew chief said as he looked up from the body toward Kalissae. She stared right through him, her body still frozen, her eyes focusing narrowly on the corpse beside him.

"Manager?" Chief Stancell asked with a heavy, bone-

weary voice as he rose from the body and faced his
superior. He had been in the pits a long time and realized
that what had happened could mean big trouble with the
plush-carpet boys at Helical Minerals. In his twenty Standard years as a professional miner he had seen more than
his share of psychos blow out, but none had gone quite so
violently as Theeran. There's something wrong with this
ore pocket, he thought as he approached Kalissae, and
she'd better be damn careful about what she does next.

"Manager, Theeran is dead."

"Why did this happen?" Kalissae asked in a barely
audible whisper. She wasn't talking to Stancell. She wanted
the answer from herself.

It would have to wait. Now she had to pull the safe
shroud of discipline down over her emotions. There was
still a mine to run and Isoleucine to ship to a hungry
galaxy.

"I depend on you, Chief," she said as the stern realist in
her began to take over. "I know you realize the potential
seriousness of this situation." She paused, looking into
Stancell's eyes for some sign of affirmation. He only stared
straight back at her, tense, alert, and noncommittal. "I
want you to get this area cleaned up, Chief. Quietly. And
with as little disturbance to the rest of the complex as
possible."

Kalissae knew that without Stancell's help she would
have a hard time dealing with official inquiries about her
competence. But those same officials would expect her
mine to continue making shipments on schedule. She
could order Stancell to assist her, but that was too risky.
Better to secure his complicity in her actions and insure
his cooperation on the basis of vested self-interest. Stancell
was an old-timer. Kalissae knew he understood the delicate
politics involved. The problem was finding a deft way to
maneuver him into sharing the responsibility for any decisions she had to make.

"Chief, how long have you been with Helical?" Kalissae
asked in an authoritative voice.

A frown added a new set of lines to the wrinkles on Stancell's face. The obvious change of focus in the conversation caused the zero-g atrophied muscles in his legs to ache. When he answered, he was thinking about the body that lay on the floor behind him. "Twenty Standard years, Manager."

Kalissae gave him a broad smile that revealed her canines. Involuntarily he flinched away from her. It still unnerved him when Pflessians grinned. Though most of their powder blue teeth were smaller than those of homo sapiens, Pflessians had long pointed canines. For Stancell they never failed to bring up visions of ancient legends about vampires. It was a foolish notion, but the sight of those narrow, blue stilettos set in a green-complexioned face always caused a shiver of repulsion to run up the middle of his back. "Twenty years," Stancell repeated as he regained his composure. "Why do you ask?"

"I just wanted to know how much longer we could have your good services. You'll be able to retire next year if you want to, won't you?" Kalissae gave him another of the canine smiles.

"That's true," he said quietly. Stancell had not missed the double meaning in her question about retirement. His leg muscles began to hurt worse.

"It would be hard to get along without you, Chief. Very, very hard." Stancell flashed his eyes at the mining crew standing well away from the two of them, and stole a quick glance at Theeran's body before returning his look to Kalissae. He has gotten the message, she thought. That is enough for now. The power of her position implied the action she could take if Stancell did not cooperate.

A man will mourn the loss of his property more than the death of his father, and the seed of the thought that his retirement might be jeopardized would ensure his assistance long enough for Kalissae to analyze her position. Then she could take the appropriate steps to insure her survival in the hierarchy of Helical Minerals, with or without his help.

Running her long fingers through the ringlets of her close-cropped auburn hair, Kalissae spoke with an intimate sigh. "Chief, I'm going to depend on you in this." Encircling his bicep with her long fingers she looked straight into his eyes, hoping her need for his help would come through over her implied threat. "Let's send the body up to the cyb lab. I'll go to Admin and make the loss report to corporate. You can take care of the cleanup operation down here. Then, if you can assemble a new crew by fifteen hundred hours, I'll get Friesh prepared for another try at the ore pocket."

Stancell frowned. "With all due respect, Manager, Friesh is only a novice. Should he tackle a pocket that has killed an experienced psychominer?"

Kalissae held her tongue. Under ordinary circumstances she would not have brooked Stancell's questioning of her directions. But these were not ordinary circumstances. Still, her aristocratic upbringing had not prepared her to stand insubordination for very long. "I know the capabilities of my personnel, Chief," she said with more force than she meant to.

Born to the high caste on Pflessius, the hyphenated suffix behind her surname reflected the pride her ancestors took in the racial purity of their forebears. Relationships with those of lower castes had to follow prescribed forms, forms which did not allow for unnecessary questions from those who served. But what she was doing now with Stancell, and would have to continue doing, was complicated by the fact that it was her low-caste half-sister who had died because of her orders. On Pflessius it would not have mattered. Theeran would have been considered no more than a servant. But this was not Pflessius.

"Chief, we'd both better get to work. I'll be in Admin if you need me for anything."

As Stancell accompanied her to the elevator, his face became set with a look which showed he understood the position they were both in, but it did not assure Kalissae of his acquiescence to her future orders.

"If it's all right with you, Manager, I'll seal this level off to any unauthorized personnel. The operation can be kept more secure that way." He tried not to let his voice betray the queasiness he felt about the whole thing. Unresolved questions were turning him inside out, but there would be time enough for them later. Right now it was important to keep the manager happy.

"Good idea, Chief," Kalissae said as she turned and punched the floor-indicator button for the Admin level. She paused for a moment, held the elevator door open with her left arm, and stared into the old crew chief's eyes. "I think we'll work well together on this," she said softly, her voice resonating against the shiny, plasteel walls. Stancell disappeared as she released the door, and the soft grey seals thumped together with a faint hiss.

After a momentary pause, the elevator gave a gentle lurch and began the fifteen-hundred-meter journey up to the Admin level. Kalissae sagged against the walls of the cubicle, suddenly fatigued from all that had happened in the last few hours. The muscles under her breasts twitched with spasms that pinched her external aortic membranes causing intense, stabbing pain. She lifted each breast in turn and tried to massage away the tension with her thumbs. "Damn you, sister," she said in a half moan.

The spasms grew stronger and fought her rapidly rubbing hands. "Damn you," she repeated in defiance of the pain. She forced herself to straighten up and pressed her shoulder blades flat against the elevator wall. Reaching into a pocket of her baggy, orange coveralls, she withdrew a small vial of white tablets and slipped one under her tongue. The effect was almost immediate. Her breathing leveled out as her muscles relaxed and the constriction on her aortic membranes eased. By the time the elevator decelerated to its destination, Kalissae's body had returned to normal. The same could not be said for her mind.

❃   ❃   ❃

The intersystem vidicom sputtered to life with an orgasmic display of random, jagged black-and-white lines intermingled with bright flashes of pastel colors. Kalissae sat in the padded chair behind her massive pearlite desk and stared impassively at the flickering screen. With a practiced gesture of her hand she punched the cracked yellow button in the upper left-hand corner of the vidicom's console. A staccato pattern of light from the screen reflected off Kalissae's bronze-patinated face, and she narrowed her eyes with a squint of disapproval at the slowness of the system to come on-line. Finally, a very long five seconds later, a snap of discharging static electricity signaled the appearance of READY-TRANSMIT on the screen.

Kalissae flipped open the cover of a small receptacle on the right-hand side of the unit, inserted her scramble-code key, and turned it until she heard a metallic click. A short sequence of four audible beeps announced the acceptance of her key, but before the sound registered in her brain, she had already started typing.

DATE: 2107 A.H., 12 Octerra
TIME: 1146 L.C., 0146 G.S.T.
TO: Nicholas Malvin, Director, Sector Operations
ADD: 531181-229-eqn77
FR: Kalissae Boristh-Major, Manager of Mines, Euphrates Planetoid, 109459-883-bbe60
A/C: 12 Imperial, EYES ONLY
SUB: Report of Fatal Accident

MESSAGE:

1. At approximately 0922 L.C., Master Psychominer Theeran Silet, I.D. P–1797, suffered severe physical trauma while attempting to perform O.P.R. on level 87, this station.

2. Trauma was of unknown origin, and resulted in the death of subject employee.

3. Suspected cause: Extreme, unjustified apprehension on the part of the employee with respect to this particular ore pocket which prevented her from maintaining the appropriate level of concentration.

4. Preliminary adjudication: Employee negligence.

Kalissae paused to look at the last entry. That won't do at all, she thought. She deleted the line and began typing again.

4. Preliminary adjudication: None.

5. Employee's final salary and entitlements are effective this day. Please transmit same and all terminal benefits to next of kin along with standard condolence notification, C-5.

6. This station will proceed with mineral extraction efforts using Novice Psychominer Carrol Friesh, I.D. P-2093, under rules 23A through 46 of Corporate Fringe-System Operations Manual.

7. Please advise status of replacement Master Psychominer ASAP.

Signed: KB-M

Two careful readings of what she had written satisfied Kalissae that the message was more than adequate. That prick, Malvin, would have a hard time finding fault with it, she thought. She punched the SEND button and watched as a yellow asterisk appeared in the upper left-hand corner of the vidicom, and she checked the text codes while the computer link-up verified her access numbers.

"I hope the bastard appreciates all the credits I'm saving the company by not sending this in real time," she said under her breath.

MESSAGE TRANSMITTED flashed on the screen, and Kalissae flipped the power off. The machine stuttered for an instant then sighed as its screen faded to darkness.

Kalissae slumped in her chair. Why, Theeran, why? No matter how she tried to understand it, the accident made no sense. When you were good—and Kalissae remembered when she had been good—when you were good, O.P.R. just wasn't that difficult. It was a game, a mental exercise which psychominers performed so easily they often reversed ordinary objects just to entertain themselves.

Theeran's taunt came back to her, and Kalissae was tempted for a moment to find out if she *could* reverse a slamball. She could get one easily enough from Recreation. Then all she would have to do would be to turn the fuzzy ball inside out. She could do it in her quarters, alone, and no one would ever know if she still had any O.P.R. talent left.

Simple. Just turn the ball inside out. Put the fuzz on the inside and the slick inner surface on the outside. And not break the ball. Or her mind.

Kalissae dismissed the idea with a sigh of resignation and turned to the mine com located on the oversized arm of her plush chair. "MZ Jones?"

"Yes, Manager," a somewhat breathy feminine voice responded in the characteristic telltale tone of synthesized speech.

"MZ Jones, would you kindly inform our Novice Psychominer, Sr. Friesh, that I require his presence in my office within the half hour."

"Immediately, Manager."

"Thank you, MZ Jones," Kalissae said, smiling to herself at the intimacy with which she interacted with her computers. Crazy. But no crazier than her interaction with the biological members of the staff of her mine.

TWO

The old Yendo trawler looked just like many other space-scarred workships. A rough ovoid thirty meters long, its dull, pockmarked skin was relieved only by the teardrop-shaped extrusion of the life-supporting bridge compartment which bubbled out from its leading edge. The Yendo design had been around for so long that few people could remember just when it had begun to appear in the galaxy. And no one really cared because the Yendo ships had earned a good reputation for dependability and durability even when they were subjected to great abuse. The fact that they could warp when necessary and cruise at a slow but honest two-point-seven-light added to the affectionate regard with which they were held by their owners and crews.

Officially designated Y-Class Ellipsoid Nuclear Drive Orra Trawlers, they were the product of a technology which placed its faith in aesthetically lean, efficient, and reliable machines. That Bedford Odigal preferred to travel in them rather than the faster, more sophisticated ships available, revealed much about his philosophical approach to life.

Bedford had purchased his Yendo shortly after he had been appointed a Free Syndic of the United Federal Margin District. The income, prestige, and almost unrestricted power of his new position would have allowed him to buy almost any of the more modern stellar cruisers, but as he had laughingly told the curious agent who had arranged the purchase, the stark, utilitarian nature of the trawler was more compatible with his concept of a Free Syndic. He had left him shaking his head in bewilderment.

Yet it made perfect sense to Syndic Odigal. He felt so at home on the bridge of the vessel that the only concession he made to the personalization of the ship was to rename her the *Lady Victoria* in honor of a long dead Terran monarch. The new name conferred a certain sense of romanticism on the burly trawler, and was certainly preferable to the previous Central Registry title, Y–06039. Bedford liked to describe the new name as giving his ship the enigmatic purpose of title. He joked to friends that those people who did not understand what he meant actually understood better than anyone else. The sales agent was not the only one left bewildered by his choice of transportation.

The *Lady Victoria* had cleared Center System traffic control and was twelve Standard days into a leisurely return passage to the Margin District when the coded message arrived. In a security cipher usually reserved for military transmissions, the curiously worded communication requested that he make for the Helical Minerals mining planetoid Euphrates as soon as possible. Though the cryptogram gave no further details as to why he was needed there, it somehow conveyed a sense of urgency which puzzled Bedford. Oddly, it also requested that he not acknowledge receipt of the transmission or notify anyone of his intended destination. In effect, it left him no option to deny the request.

"Strange, 'eh, Issy?" Bedford asked without expecting an answer after reading the message a second time. "Guess we'll comply and see what this is all about."

Reaching up to a shelf over the *Lady Victoria*'s main helm controls, Bedford pulled down a large, blue-bound volume entitled *Sector Coordinates: Margin Districts A to K*. Although he had the information stored in the on-board computer memory, he liked the feel of books in his hand, and whenever possible he preferred using them.

"H . . . Helical . . . yes, Helical Minerals. Mmmm, seems that the shortest course to Euphrates should take about three Standard days if we stay sublight." He paused as his pale, silver-flecked eyes briefly scanned the instrument panel in front of him. "Tell you what, Issy," he muttered. The stubby fingers of his left hand wandered through the maze of buttons and switches on the off-white surface of the nav-control. "Let's get there a little faster than that," he said, punching in data by touch as he located it in the book. After several minutes of intense activity he looked up from the text, checked the series of numbers which appeared on one of the digital readout screens, and snapped the book closed with a flourish of his wrist.

"Well, that should do it, Issy. We should arrive at Euphrates in approximately thirty-four G.C.U.'s at warp one-point-nine." He flipped a final, conspicuously oversized toggle switch and sat back into the cushioned confines of the command-console seat.

Lady Victoria's main thrusters flared into life, shaking off millions of shards of frozen hydrogen from the cooling coils of the nuclear engines. When measured against the sparkling background of stars, the ship made a painfully slow arcing turn and came about exactly one hundred thirty-five degrees to the right of its previous course.

"Steady, *Lady*," Bedford said as he watched the stars out of the forward view screen begin their juxtaposition. As soon as the ship came into position a sudden surge of acceleration forced Bedford back into the command-console seat. His head and upper torso pressed hard against the pilot station braces, and the stars, once distant pinpoints of light, became a mass of streaming colors.

"That-a-girl," he said as he held his open hand over a square red button on the navcomputer. "Coming up on one-point-nine-W right . . ." He slapped his palm down on the button. "Now!" The buoyant force of acceleration ceased, but the ship continued to bore through space at a steady pace. Bedford eased himself up out of the command-console seat, stretched, flexed the heavy muscles of his biceps, and stared into the silent wilderness which lay before him. "Nothing to do now except wait," he said softly as he headed for his bunk and some much needed rest.

The sign on the door read: Nicholas Malvin, Director. The letters on the sign were big, bold, solid silver castings done in a florid, neo-rocco style. Someone had once described them as archetypical manifestations of Nicholas Malvin's real personality, an assertion which the director considered applicable only to his personal life. When it came to business, he saw himself as a single-minded predator in a galaxy which rewarded the pragmatic realist more than the romantic philosopher.

"What the hell is going on out there?" Malvin boomed from the center of his office. "And who is this Kalissae Boristh-*Major* anyway, Rosey?"

Arter Rosenthal, Malvin's private secretary, looked at his boss without expression. "Pflessian, female, been with the company three years, eight months, Standard. Exceeds her quarterly and annual mining quotas by all measures of competence. Performance indices rank her as an extremely effective manager," he said in a flat, almost mechanical tone.

"Then why has she killed a valuable psychominer?" Malvin's words were harsh and unforgiving.

"There is no evidence to support the position that MZ Boristh-Major is respons—"

"Green," Malvin said, cutting his secretary off mid-sentence.

"Sir?"

"Green, Rosey. Green. If she's a *Major* Pflessian, she's got to be green." Malvin paused, squinted his eyes at Rosenthal, and continued. "I don't like green, Rosey. Never have. Never will. The color makes me ill. Besides, those Pflessians, with all their inflexible codes of social behavior and whatnot, can get to be real pains in the ass. What I don't need is trouble from a damn *dash-Major* greenie." It was not anger which boiled in him. It was his frustration with the unpredictable nature of corporate existence which caused the hot words to flow. "How old is she?" he said, addressing a problem which was probably going to take valuable time away from his other duties.

Rosenthal flipped through his notes. "Thirty-three, Standard, sir."

Malvin shook his head with a sigh. "Rosey, do I ever ask for ages in anything but Standard? Never mind. We've been through this before." He turned his back on Rosenthal and walked back to his desk. Moments later he pulled a large bottle of amber liquid and a glass from a lower drawer. "I'd offer you one," he said as he filled the glass, "but you don't drink this early in the day, do you?" With one quick swallow he downed the drink then held the glass admiringly in front of his eyes. "A pity, Rosey. A real pity. A good snort of real whiskey before breakfast never hurt anyone." Almost reluctantly he put the bottle and glass back in the drawer.

"Sit down, Rosey," he said as he settled himself into the plush, russet-colored leather chair behind his desk. The warmth of the liquor made him feel better. He leaned forward, planted his elbows on the desk, and placed his chin on top of his folded hands. A hard-copy of Kalissae's message lay precisely centered on a square, green blotter in the middle of the desk. He silently reread the words of the dispatch, closed his eyes, and began mentally sifting through the various courses of action open to him in regards to the Euphrates mine problem.

Rosenthal had seen his boss do this same thing so many times before that Malvin's silence seemed perfectly natural. He slipped into his own meditative state, but when Malvin started talking almost twenty minutes after sitting down, Rosenthal had the first word on his dictapad almost before it was completely pronounced.

"Rosey," Malvin said. "I want you to get this down in the exact order that I give it to you."

Rosenthal, ever the attentive secretary, got every word.

The glass wall of Kalissae's office lost its silvery blue luster and cleared to a light grey transparency. "Do you see all that?" she asked, pointing out the window to the wide expanse of domed buildings, skeletal towers, and freight-docking facilities which constituted the miningplex of Euphrates. "Those structures were built with the hard work, self-denial, and lives of over three hundred men and women from all parts of the galaxy."

Carrol Friesh, Novice Psychominer, lowered his head in deference to his superior's words. At twenty-four years old he was a tall, lithe, blond man who was usually very self-confident. But at the moment he was very nervous and unsure of himself. His summons to the manager's office had turned into a confrontation of large proportions, one for which he was ill-prepared, yet one his stubborn resolve would not let him avoid.

"And do you know why so many gave so much of their time and blood to turn this sterile little planetoid into a living, productive operation?" Kalissae paused to let her question sink in before she continued. "Because without the Isoleucine-graphite we mine here, a great many sentient beings in our galaxy would go hungry. It's unfortunate, Carrol," she said more softly, hoping the switch to his first name would help her appeal, "but the galaxy is protein poor."

Kalissae stopped and looked at Carrol to see if her words were having any effect. It's a pity he won't listen to reason, she thought. It would be so much more simple that way. She wanted Friesh to perform the O.P.R. willingly, without coercion, because if she ordered him. . . . What? Because if she ordered him, she ran the risk of another Theeran debacle? And? Kalissae could not define just what her feelings were.

"You can't remember the days before the first Leuci deposits were discovered," she said, trying to add moral weight to her argument. "They were brutal. Whole races were wiped out in food wars. Star systems were destroyed because of hunger and starvation." Friesh sat placidly unmoved as Kalissae continued. "My own home planet was so depleted of resources that there were secret societies which practiced cannibalism—and those societies were supported by the military, which, of course, had to eat well in order to protect what few food resources we had left.

"Think, Carrol, hunger so fierce that a society would tacitly condone the killing of some of its members so that the others could eat." Kalissae shuddered. The memories were still strong. "It's too horrible a concept to think about. But it happened. And it could happen again were it not for these mines. Can't you see that?"

Friesh raised his down-turned eyes and stared at Kalissae while he searched for some concrete way to formulate a rebuttal. He refused to give in to her emotional appeal. "I'm fully aware of the terrible excesses of the past," he said with forced, cold detachment, "but those days are over. We have a problem here which cannot be analyzed in the light of that part of history. There is something wrong with the ore pocket Theeran tried to reverse, and all this talk about cannibalism isn't going to make me change my mind." With a quick pause to catch his breath, he rushed on, realizing even as he spoke that he had probably gone too far with his superior, but deciding to finish what he had started. "Until further investigation reveals the cause of Theeran's death, and the anomaly in the pocket, I must refuse to attempt a reversal."

"I could order you," Kalissae said, dropping all pretense of wanting to settle the matter without force.

Friesh knew there were rules which would allow him to resist her orders, but if he used those rules, he also knew it would cost him his career as a psychominer. Better to play the immature novice, he thought, and at least have some chance at salvaging his life's work.

"Order if you must, Manager. I will still refuse. It's my life we're talking about."

Kalissae didn't speak for several minutes. Finally, realizing that Friesh would remain obstinate regardless of her efforts to persuade him otherwise, she said, "Very well. Consider yourself relieved of duty, effective immediately. You will confine yourself to the residential sections until further notice." She felt sorry for him. His job at Helical was over. She would see to that.

Friesh stiffened. "Yes, Manager," he said, realizing he had overplayed his hand. With a quick turn he walked out of the room and slammed the door behind him.

"Damned fool," she said through clenched teeth as she slapped the mine com. "MZ Jones." Her words were hard. "MZ Jones!"

"Yes, Manager." The computer voice showed no reaction to Kalissae's angry summons.

"MZ Jones, get me Chief Stancell on the scrambleset immediately."

Logic circuits closed in less time than it takes a light-speed vessel to cross the distance between two hydrogen atoms. The perfectly modulated, totally synthetic voice of MZ Jones announced the mine manager's request through all one hundred twelve levels of the complex. The only slow part of the process was the eight minutes it took for Chief Stancell to reach the nearest scrambleset and respond to the call.

While she waited, Kalissae paced the length of her office, counting the bare, flush rivets which dotted the metallic floor, and cursing Friesh. Part of her knew he was right. She had already caused one death. No! It had been Theeran's fault. Why in the name of Saint Gunson had she been so stupid. She knew better than to let her emotions get in the way of her job. Still, if there was something wrong with the pocket, if Theeran was right and—

The buzzing of the scrambleset interrupted her thoughts. "Chief?" she said, snatching the unit's transceiver and activating it with one quick motion.

"Yes, Manager." Stancell's voice was higher pitched than usual and he sounded like he was wheezing.

"Is there anything wrong?"

"No. Caught me down the chutes," he said, referring to the utility core shafts which ran down to each mine level from the solar reactors on the surface. "No elevators down there. Had to run up six flights of stairs to reach the nearest scrambleset. Sorry."

"No apology necessary, Chief."

Kalissae immediately addressed the problem with Friesh. "Chief, we've got a slight hang-up."

"Oh."

"It seems our Sr. Friesh has decided to refuse my orders. He says he will not attempt the Ore Pocket Reversal."

"And what's his justification?"

Stancell's voice had lost its breathy quality. Kalissae thought she detected a slight sneer in the way he asked his question, but was unsure if it was meant for her or Friesh. "I'm not sure, Chief, but I think the talentless fool is just frightened. He thinks there's something wrong with the pocket. An excuse for his own cowardice, I'm sure."

Even as she spoke, Kalissae knew there was more to it than simple fear. Friesh was young and a novice, therefore his judgment about the ore pocket was suspect. But novice or not, he was a fully qualified psychominer. Just how much Theeran's death had influenced Friesh's decision Kalissae did not know.

"Regardless of Sr. Friesh's refusal, Chief, we'll just have to work around him. How long will it take to set up a standard bore platform with impact lasers?"

Totally unprepared for the question, Stancell involuntarily sucked in his breath. He hoped Kalissae would think he was still trying to recover from his run up the stairs. It had been more than half a career ago when he had last supervised a laser attack on an ore pocket, and he wasn't in any hurry to rejuvenate those rusty skills. It was dangerous work, yet it was obvious from the Manager's tone that hers was not a request, but an order. "A day," he said hesitantly, wishing he could retire from Helical immediately.

Kalissae heard his hesitation. "I think we can do better than that, Chief." Her tone came out harder than she meant it to. "What are the chances of getting it set up by the beginning of the second shift?" she asked more gently.

"Well, I suppose it could be done that fast." Stancell knew he could stall her, but he also knew that it wouldn't take her long to figure out that he was doing it. "Of course, we'd have to divert some of the surface power from the pockets we're working on now and—"

"Good. Do whatever has to be done. Pull people on the second shift early if you have to. Will you have any trouble linking up?" Kalissae hoped that by rushing into the details of the project Stancell wouldn't ask the obvious question about whether they should even continue the extraction attempt.

It did not work. Stancell didn't ignore the question, he just set it aside as being moot. It did not matter whether they should or should not attempt to drill into the pocket. His job was to supervise the mining, not second guess his superior's decisions. "No, I don't see any problem with a linkup. I'll transfer some surplus optic cable over and hook it to the bore's energy control console. Once we integrate into the surface power feeders, we're in business." He was already plotting the schematic in his head.

"I'll leave it to you, Sr. Stancell." Kalissae was relieved

that he had come around so quickly. Two flat refusals to obey orders in one day would have been disastrous to her already bruised ego. "It will be ready by the start of second shift then?" she asked, reemphasizing her need for fast action.

"No problem," he said, surprising himself at how easily he had become an accomplice to an action which his instincts told him was crazy.

"Good. I'll see you down there. Oh, and Chief, thanks." Kalissae's voice dissolved into static.

Stancell held his line open for a few moments before he realized she had closed her connection. "You're very welcome, you frigid offspring of a Pflessian frog," he said as he flipped off his own scrambleset. "I only hope that brain inside your green hide knows what it's doing."

"The platform's in place, Manager," Stancell said with a tight smile as he greeted Kalissae at the doors of the mine shaft elevator.

Well behind him there stood a large, metal-framed structure that still retained vestiges of the battle weapons from which it was derived. Mounted in the middle of a six-meter-square platform which sat on three heavy, articulated legs was a Magnum Model Four-T rock bore. Its dull grey power unit rested on two massive shock-absorbing pistons. Stretching out from the pistons toward the ore pocket was the three-meter barrel of the helium/argon gas-laser. With its clear, plasteel ricochet shields bolted onto the front of the platform ahead of the power unit, the rock bore really did look like an artillery piece.

Kalissae paused for a moment and watched the bore's three crew members as they ran through their checklists and made last minute adjustments to the equipment. "Very good, Chief," she said finally. "You may begin whenever you are ready."

Stancell turned to his crew and yelled, "Status?"

"One minute," came the quick reply.

With a wave of his hand Stancell acknowledged the crewman, then motioned Kalissae toward a smaller ricochet shield set up close to the wall beside the elevator doors. "Observation point," he said quietly. After making sure that she was properly seated on one of the small, cushioned chairs behind the shield, he turned back to the rock bore crew. "Initiate when ready," he called out.

Moments later the three crewmen nodded to each other and took their positions at the firing controls, one on each side of the laser behind the shields, and one at the rear of the power unit. "Standby! Standby! Preparing to fire," a voice boomed from the loudspeakers on the platform. "Power sequence ready. Standby."

The overhead lights in the mine shaft dimmed as the rock bore sucked up power from the main generators. The brute force of concentrated electrical energy was so thick in the air that Kalissae could feel her hair rising and taste the unique acrid flavor of her static-charged saliva.

Suddenly the barrel of the rock bore snapped into life with a fluxing, pearl-white luminescence that rippled along its length. The light trapped in the barrel slowly intensified and shifted in color through a series of deepening pinks. Each hue lasted for a few distinct seconds before the next, brighter, more robust shade took its place. Finally a true red appeared in the barrel. It too shifted in hue until a throbbing vermillion coursed through the laser.

Kalissae had seen it all before, but it never failed to awe her. With practiced hands she flipped the sonic dampers over her ears and in the same motion darkened her goggles. She knew it would only be seconds before the laser fired.

The pent-up atomic fluid burst from the end of the barrel with a thunderclap as its fiery tongue ionized the surrounding air. Rock exploded under the impact. The shattering fragments hissed as they were vaporized by the laser's intense heat. Nothing could withstand such punishment. The laser chewed through rock as though it were sponge foam, cutting, melting, vaporizing everything in its beam, the magic of coherent light waves which did all that man and physics asked it to do.

Suddenly Kalissae saw thousands of twisted images projected on the tunnel walls. For an instant she thought she saw Theeran dancing grotesquely in the shadows.

Then in a blinding flash everything went wrong. Even the dark goggles weren't enough to keep Kalissae from squeezing her eyes shut. The air roared. A hail of rock and metal tore at her shield. The force of the explosion threw her from the chair. For the first time in her life she was afraid she would die. She curled her body tight against the ricochet shield and prayed without words that she would survive.

As quickly as it had happened, the sound subsided to a low grinding noise which filled her head. A rough hand probed at her neck. Cautiously she opened her eyes. Blackness. It took five full seconds for her to remember the goggles. Before she could move, the rough hand at her neck had brushed up her sonic dampers.

"Manager?"

Kalissae swallowed hard and tried to speak. The grinding noise stopped. The ache in her jaw told her why: She had been grinding her teeth. "I'm all right," she said weakly as she sat up with Stancell's assistance and adjusted her goggles for normal light. Only then did she taste the burned dust that clogged her nose and coated her tongue. "I'll be all right, Chief."

"Just sit still for a minute," he said in a thick voice. "The fire and med teams will be here shortly."

It took more than a minute. The elevator doors had been forced inward by the blast, and the rescue teams had to come down an emergency shaft. By the time they arrived, Kalissae had satisfied herself that she was physically unharmed. Despite Stancell's protests she stood up and moved from behind the relative safety of the shield to survey the wreckage. What she saw almost made her knees buckle, and she had to lean on Stancell for support.

The rock bore was little more than a glowing heap of twisted metal that leaned at an odd angle on its one remaining leg. Charred and smoking pieces of cable twisted their way through piles of rock and rubble like grotesque serpents. As they cooled and contracted, they twitched convulsively in the dim glow of the remaining overhead lights. Smoke and dust swirled in slow, meaningless patterns that choked the air with acrid fumes.

Out of the grey fog of destruction a dark, suited figure moved toward her, the green med-light on his helmet shining eerily through the shadows. In his arms he carried the body of one of the laser-bore crewmen, its legs and one arm no more than oozing black stumps that glistened under the green light.

Suddenly Kalissae was on her hands and knees. Rolling spasms racked her body and she vomited. She emptied her stomach quickly, but she could not stop. Even as she heaved and gagged, she knew she could never fully purge herself of the sight of so much death and destruction. Guilt, like a giant hand, squeezed and twisted her insides.

Stancell's written report was brief, concise, and bloodless. The laser beam for no known reason had been reflected back from the ore pocket. It had passed through the transparent ricochet shields and killed the two forward crewmen instantaneously as it burned its way back into the power unit. Considering the force of the explosion, damage was minimal. Stancell had listed the losses neatly at the bottom of the page like an inventory check sheet: one rock bore, so many meters of cable, x-number of safety breakers, miscellaneous equipment, two crewmen.

Miraculously, the third crewman had survived. He might even live long enough to tell them what went wrong. It was the final comment on the report that stuck in Kalissae's mind. Stancell had noted the probable cause of the accident as simply: "Faulty equipment."

Oh, she wished it were true. She wished she could

blame the accident on faulty equipment. But Friesh had been right. And if Friesh was right, then Theeran's unwillingness to reverse the ore pocket had been justified. It was not the equipment which had caused disaster to befall Euphrates. It was her own refusal to listen to the warnings of her subordinates which resulted in so much blood on her conscience, and a mystery which she now had to address. She was sitting on top of a mine that contained something that killed without notice or reason, and she was going to find out what that something was.

With a narrow, grim smile Kalissae turned on the vidicom and prepared to send another message of death to Helical headquarters. Long after the READY-TRANSMIT flashed on the screen, she sat unmoving, her eyes focused far away on a dark infinity she had never known existed. She thought of Theeran and all that had happened since her loss, and as she began to type, one small tear stained her palid, green cheek.

THREE

"Pink! Pinka-pink! Pink, pink, pink!" The Warpulsar's alert signal jolted Bedford awake. Moments later, still groggy from sleep, he stood over the machine's Spherical Image Constructor.

"Pinka-pinka-pinka!"

"Shut up," he said, thumping his fist down on a large red plunger switch. "I'm awake." Having effectively silenced the machine's electronic voice, Bedford wished he could go back to the warmth of his bunk and forget the danger signal the SIC had given him. But he knew that either the *Lady Victoria* had reached its warp exit point, or that she was within the collision-alert parameters of some uncharted space object.

Bedford stared intently at the SIC. Inside its clear plastic globe multicolored pinpoints of light stared back at him. A holographic image of the time-space through which *Lady Victoria* was passing burned away the last vestiges of sleep which fogged his mind. He looked more alertly at the center of the sphere. An orange dot representing the *Victoria* moved slowly along a crisp blue line which the navcomputer projected through a maze of bright yellow splotches of varying sizes and intensities. As the ship moved physically through time-space at warp speed, the warpulsar's photon sonar simultaneously verified its position and made the necessary corrections to the SIC's image.

"Red," he mumbled. "Look for the red." Bedford's eyes scanned the display for a few moments. Then he saw it. Roughly one Pole's Factor ahead of the ship a ruby-red pinpoint of light glowed ominously. Instinctively he checked the SIC's cartographic scale. At their current speed and heading, they were within a point-three probability of collision with the object. Strange, he thought, point-three is too high for a random encounter. Bedford tensed.

He double-checked the various coordinates on the warpulsar's instrument cluster. "Okay, Issy," he said quietly. "It's time for you to wake up and give me some assistance."

I've been awake, your eminence.

"Cut the sarcasm," Bedford said, rolling his eyes in exasperation. "See the red?"

I could if you would look at it.

Issy's words angered and embarrassed Bedford simultaneously. Bringing his eyes as close to the SIC as his nose would allow he asked, "Can you see the red now, your omnipotence?"

Shut up, grouch.

Bedford impatiently stood watching the collision probability read-out climb to point-three-seven. He knew that Issy had seen enough to form an opinion, but was waiting until he received an apology before he spoke. "All right, I'm sorry. I'll try to be more cheerful the next time I'm dragged from a deep sleep for such an emergency. Now, could you please give your thoughts as to what evasive maneuver we should take?"

There once was a man from this sector
Who demanded of me the right vector.
As he dodged the red he didn't think
Of how to avoid all the purple and pink.

If he'd heard what I said,
He wouldn't be dead:
"A red ball so close to our brink?"

Bedford abandoned the tack of calm diplomacy. "Dammit, Issy! I don't need your doggerel. What I need are some hard, concrete solutions. Fast. Are you listening to me?" He clenched his fist into a tight ball and punched it several times against the SIC's hard plastic surface.

That hurts!

"Didn't hurt me," Bedford said. He relaxed a little and allowed himself a slight smile and shake of his head about the vagaries of his relationship with Issy.

One-seven-seven-point-nine-six-nine.

The rigid brace of tension across Bedford's shoulders shattered and fell away as the numbers spilled into his consciousness. Quickly he punched them into the navcomputer. The *Lady Victoria* responded a few seconds later with a gentle surge of power.

For the first time since he had awakened, Bedford felt secure enough to sit down.

Aren't you even going to thank me?

"Thanks," he said absently as he plopped into a chair beside the warpulsar. The navcomputer shaped a crisp green line through the SIC that represented the new course Issy had provided. After a momentary pause in which Bedford critically examined the new line, he reached out and pushed the SAVE button. The green line turned blue and the first blue line disappeared. Bedford grunted his approval, leaned back in the chair and closed his eyes.

Zygore.

"What in the twelve Arturian Bell Pools is that supposed to mean?" Bedford said, recognizing an element of reproach in his ideographic companion's one-word comment. Zygores were tenth-cycle creatures. Their response to stimuli took ten times the galactic norm. To be called a Zygore was to be called extremely slow at recognizing the obvious. Had he missed something? Bedford thought as he sat up in the chair and looked again at the SIC.

See it, partner?

Bedford studied the display and immediately saw that the red point of light which had been vectored out of the danger zone by their maneuver had adjusted its course and was obviously following them.

"No one is supposed to know we're here, much less be following us."

Following us. Issy's words echoed Bedford's suspicion.

Bedford scrutinized the SIC's instrumentation for a possible rebound-effect malfunction. Satisfied that the readings were correct, he shifted his position to the ship-to-ship commgear. After pausing a moment to compose a short inquiry, he activated the standard merchant vessel hailing transmitter and said, "This is the Yendo *Lady Victoria* requesting that you please identify yourself, over."

The yawning enigma of subspace gobbled up his transmission and returned nothing but interstellar static as a response. He repeated the message. Nothing. Again. Still nothing.

After twenty minutes of saying the same thing over all the FedStandard frequencies, he asked, "What do you think, Issy? Could it be a malfunctioning drone-freighter?"

Possible, especially in this sector. They are programmed to latch-sync with any passing vessel in case of major breakdown. Keeps them from getting totally lost. Still, let's play it safe. Turn on the mag-tow.

"Mag-tow," Bedford said, pondering the request before taking any action. "If that is a derelict ship out there, the mag-tow would confuse its homing equipment. We'd lose it, but it might pick up someone else just as easily as it picked us up. At light speed that could be fatal."

Bedford, we are a Free Syndic on a mission. We cannot compromise our primary obligation to the duties of our office. Unhindered and direct travel is essential. Please, turn on the mag-tow.

Issy was in a strange mood. Why all the hurry to get to Euphrates, anyway, Bedford wondered as he activated the mag-tow and adjusted it to a sufficient three-quarters power. He had been putting up with Issy's idiosyncrasies since they had both been children. Well, Issy had never really been a child. But as far back as Bedford could remember, the benefits of their relationship had far outweighed the occasionally annoying side effect of Issy's disconcerting behavior. Besides, when it came to questions of priority, Issy was usually correct.

"As you wish, my friend."

The *Lady Victoria* buzzed with an almost imperceptible vibration as the mag-tow's magnetic cone enveloped them. Bedford watched as the red dot in the SIC floated out of range of the photon sonar.

"Guess it was a drone-freighter, Issy."

The silence which greeted him was punctuated by the squeak of dry bearings in a ventilator fan. Bedford sighed and headed toward the maintenance locker. It was better to keep busy while Issy was thinking.

"Bring your vessel to bearing two-two-niner," ComRelay Specialist Jay Hanssan said. He covered the microphone with his hand and turned to Chief Stancell. "What's a Free Syndic doing out here?"

Stancell furrowed his brow as he took a quick glance at the minimum range radarscope. With a shrug of his shoulders he said, "Don't know. Maybe the new king of the sector is just paying a call to see what kind of people he's got to deal with. In any case, I think we'd better handle this as formally as possible."

"Chief?" Hanssan hesitated. "Could this have something to do with level eighty-seven?"

Ignoring Hanssan's question, Stancell rose and headed for the bulkhead door. Could indeed, son, he thought to himself as he started through the door.

"Chief?" Hanssan asked, his voice stronger, pressing as much as he dared for an answer.

"Only the manager knows the answer to that one. You just bring our visitor in nice and safe like, while I go down and get a reception committee together." Before Hanssan had a chance to try another tack, Senior Mining Operations Chief Theodor Stancell was through the communications compartment bulkhead and on his way to the manager's office.

"Welcome to Euphrates, Syndic Odigal. I trust all is well at Helical headquarters?" Kalissae Boristh-Major's greeting contained all the friendliness of a Strawn whipviper's preliminary strike, and even less subtlety as to who she thought had sent Bedford to the mine.

"Thank you very much, ah?" Bedford said as he extended his right hand to the woman.

"Mine Manager Kalissae Boristh-Major, Syndic."

"Pleasured to meet you, Manager," Bedford said clasping her hand and shaking it while he studied her face. She had a striking sort of beauty. The delicate features of her narrow face were accentuated by the pale patina of her complexion, and the shocking blaze of red hair which curled randomly atop her head gave her a no-nonsense look which Bedford found suitable for a female mine manager. A pity she's not my type, he thought as he turned to the row of mine personnel behind her.

Well, she certainly is mine.

—Not now, Issy. We're working.— Bedford hoped his subvocal message would quiet his friend long enough to allow the formation of unbiased first impressions to be completed.

Kalissae was slow in responding to Bedford's obvious gesture indicating he was ready to be introduced to the rest of her senior staff. She could not take her eyes from the Syndic's face. Still gripping his hand tightly, she tried to make sense of what she saw.

Running from his hairline down the right side of his cheek and straggling down his neck into the high collar of his dress tunic was a mottled, dark scar. It seemed to pulse with an obscene life of its own like knotted blood vessels, and destroyed whatever might have been considered handsome in his tanned face.

Given the fact that modern surgical techniques could have removed the scar totally, Kalissae was at a loss to understand why someone as powerful and influential as a Free Syndic would keep such a monstrous deformity. Whatever his reason, she knew the purple, wrinkled rope of flesh would make the task of guiding him through his investigation all the more difficult. His disfigurement was repulsive both to her eyes and to an aristocratic instinct which told her that all powerful people should be physically attractive. Bedford Odigal would never have reached the position of Syndic if her home planet had ruled the galaxy.

Bedford sensed Kalissae's discomfort and tightened his grip when she tried to remove her hand from his. With a grace born of long practice, he bent low and kissed her pale green knuckles, deliberately grazing his scar across her fingers as he released his hold. Tough, but not as tough as you pretend to be, he thought as he brought himself upright and smiled at her.

Not now, Bedford, we're working. Issy's words were full of sarcastic venom. *She hasn't done anything to us. You know we're not physically attractive to most humanoids, so don't push it. Give the woman a chance.*

—Stow it,— Bedford said subvocally. —I don't need your input right now.— He was surprised at his words even as he spoke them. It was just something he sensed, a feeling, a gut reaction which said this woman was going to be trouble. It was also clear that Issy felt differently. Time for a talk, he thought as he looked at Kalissae and said, "Would it be possible, Manager, for you to arrange for my quarters as soon as possible?"

"Certainly. As you wish, Syndic Odigal," Kalissae said with an air of uncertainty in her voice. Who in Saint Gunson's galaxy had Nicholas sent to her mine, she thought. This man shows up unannounced, says a brief hello, and asks to be given his quarters. No mention of why he's here or comment about level eighty-seven. Kalissae's distaste for Bedford turned to distrust. "Certainly," she repeated. "Please follow me."

In the elevator on the way down to the residence section neither hostess nor guest said a word. Each resisted the inclination to ask the other questions.

Humanoids, Issy hissed sarcastically.

Bedford ignored him. As the minutes dragged on in the descending elevator he caught himself stealing examining glances at Manager Boristh-Major. Once he caught her glancing back and immediately looked away, but not before a faint warmth touched him.

Damn, she thought while trying to untangle the contradictory signals she was picking up from the Free Syndic. *He seems as confused about why he's here as I am.* She glanced back at him and caught him looking at her again. This time she held her stare and so did he.

That's better.

When the elevator hissed to a stop at the residence section Kalissae motioned Bedford through the open door without breaking her stare.

"Please," he said, waving her ahead of him.

After a brief moment's hesitation, she stepped out of the elevator and strode purposefully down the carpeted hallway.

Knew you could be a gentleman if you tried.

—Enough.—

She sure walks nice. Good pelvic rotation.

"Your quarters, sir," Kalissae said as she stopped in front of a closed door. She slipped a plastic card into a slot beside the oval depression and the doorway flared like the iris of a huge camera. "Your access key," she said, handing Bedford the card. "The only duplicate is in my security vault. Should you need anything, please use the service-com mounted beside your sleeping foil." As he took the card from her she made sure their fingers touched, almost as though she wanted to reinforce her initial feelings of revulsion. Nothing happened.

"Thank you, Manager. I appreciate your attentions. And I apologize for the delay in discussing the problem you have on Euphrates. I shall look forward to a long conversation with you tomorrow." With a slight bow he stepped past her and entered the compartment.

"Syndic Odigal," she said as she reached out touching his arm, and stopping him in midstride. "Please excuse my bluntness, but your last comment has me totally confused." She lowered her arm and hesitated for a moment, then continued, "I'll make it simple. Why are you here?" She felt a release of tension as soon as she had asked the question.

The lady has courage too.

"Well," Bedford said, raising his eyebrows and clearing his throat. The sense of confusion was now mutual. "I'm sorry, Manager, but I had assumed that you would tell me the answer to that."

"I don't understand. Why did you come here?" Kalissae was beginning to suspect a bureaucratic foul-up had sent the Syndic to her mine, one of a purposeful nature, done to deliberately put her off guard.

"A blind, high priority message just said I was to come to Euphrates as soon as possible. No signature or indication of why I was needed. I presume you do have a problem here?"

Kalissae debated with herself over the advisability of telling the Syndic about the accidents just yet. If she gave him the bare outline of the problem, then she would have time to construct a better description of the incidents for him by tomorrow. "Yes, Syndic Odigal. We've had two fatal accidents down on one of our new mining levels."

"I see," he said. "Well, we can go over the details once I've had some rest." Bedford knew he needed to clear up some things with Issy before the investigation got started.

"As you wish," Kalissae said, relieved that he was not

going to press her for further facts. "Sleep well then." She turned and started down the hallway for the elevator.

I haven't seen such good posture on a woman since your father first . . .

"We need to talk, Issy," Bedford said as he walked into the compartment and stood with his back to the door until he heard it close behind him.

The room was typical abso-ordinaire. Eclectic in its use of randomly available materials, it projected the uninspired utilitarian design of contemporary industrial architecture. Roughly seven meters square, it contained all the necessary elements for living, sleeping, cleansing, and waste disposal—nothing more. Only the indirect lighting, which softened the room's barren walls, gave it any kind of warmth.

Bedford set his shoulder bag on the floor and flopped into one of the two chairs. "Okay, let's have it," he said quietly.

What?

"You know damn good and well what. I realize she's not a bad-looking woman, but—"

Do you?

"I just said it, didn't I?"

I know you said it, but do you realize it?

"Come on, Issy, this is no time for games. She's the top executive of this complex, and we're here to investigate. Don't you, my usually rational partner, think it would be better to keep a certain distance from this woman?"

No.

Bedford waited for more, but got none. "What do you mean by *no?*"

Just no. Simple. No.

"Issy? What's the matter with you? I haven't seen you this emotionally worked up in a long time. And never while we're on a job."

You. You're such a zealot sometimes. While I'm perfectly willing to admit that my response to Kalissae Boristh-Major was partly emotional, I think I'm quite capable of

*maintaining my detachment. I'm not sure about you.
Besides, a little feminine symbiosis is necessary now and
then.*

"It's not symbiosis, and you know it. We real people call
it companionship."

*You real people call it a lot of more descriptive things
than companionship, but whatever you want to call it, I
think we could achieve it with this woman.*

"Dammit, Issy, don't go sensy on me."

Frustrated, aren't you?

"Of course I am. But we're here to do an investigation,
and all you seem to be concerned about is satisfying your
primitive sensory needs." Bedford got up from the chair
and moved over to the sleeping foil. After testing it with
one hand, he eased himself gratefully into its softness and
let its warm fabric caress the contours of his body. He was
more tired than he had realized. "You want me to allow
you to—"

Allow?

"Yes, allow. Unless you're changing the ground rules on
me, I thought we did these things by mutual consent."

*Mutual consent is different than the boss allowing the
slave a little pleasure.*

"Don't give me that drickle. You know what I mean. You
were supposed to evaluate Borisht-Major's galvanic response to our first meeting. Instead, you defend her, drool
over her, and—"

*In the whole history of my existence I have never
drooled.*

"You did today," Bedford sighed. "Why can't we get this
straight? We're here to investigate what we now know
were two fatal accidents in a mine run by a beautiful
woman, a woman who would send us back into subspace
in a millisecond if she thought she could get away with it.
Doesn't that seem more important than glandular and
sensory needs?"

*Save the duty-and-justice-before-pleasure lecture. I taught
it to you, remember?*

"How could I forget?"

Sometimes I think you do. I think you forget that I really am a separate entity. You take me for granted. You disallow any needs I have that are different from your own as somehow less meaningful.

"I don't mean to."

I know that. But you still do it. Turn it around, partner. It's like those times when you really need me to work out a problem for you. You NEED me then. You need my mental powers to work for the sake of your well-being. Well, sometimes, I need your body for the same reason. I need you to do certain physical things for the sake of my well-being. And in both cases, we're doing it for OUR well being. Right?

Bedford smiled and shifted slightly on the foil. "Right, my friend. Think with me." For Issy's sake, and perhaps for his own amusement, he tried to conjure a picture of what Kalissae Boristh-Major's sleek green body might look like naked. He couldn't get the picture to hold still, then realized that Issy was tampering with it.

"I wonder if we'll ever truly understand each other?"

We might, partner, but I wouldn't bet on a date. So I'll tell you what. I'll control my emotional and physical reactions to the lady in question if you will relax enough to let whatever happens, happen naturally.

"Sounds like a deal to me," Bedford said sleepily. "You want me to dream about her for you?"

No. You just rest.

" 'Nother deal," Bedford mumbled moments before sleep pulled him down into its warm darkness.

There were occasions when Issy envied Bedford's sleep cycles and wished he too could slip into that realm of subconscious delight and rest. But those occasions were rare, and this first night cycle on Euphrates was not one of them. He was too busy evaluating information and ordering it into files for immediate access should he and/or Bedford need it.

Once Issy satisfied himself that all the data he had

accumulated had been properly dealt with, he directed his thoughts back to Kalissae and began a series of speculative fantasies that Bedford probably would not have approved of. But Bedford would never know about them, and Issy did not need his approval.

What Issy did need, however, was something that even Kalissae Boristh-Major could not give him. It was something only he expected to ever understand, and a need he never expected to have fulfilled. Neither pressing nor dire, it was always there just below his consciousness. A tiny grain of irritation that could never quite be scratched away. As far as Issy knew he was the only member of his race left in the galaxy. And his one need that would never be fulfilled was to meet a member of his own race.

FOUR

Bedford awoke in the darkness and realized he had fallen asleep with his clothes on. He got up and undressed mechanically, taking the opportunity to relieve himself at the waste disposal unit. Falling heavily back into the sleeping foil he began to use his favorite technique for going to sleep quickly.

He imagined himself holding a soft rubber ball in his hand. He squeezed the ball as hard as he could and held it there. Inevitably, as his grip slowly began to loosen, the expanding ball pushed away both tension and consciousness. Like the five uneven petals of an Arturian pentarose opening to the morning rays of Cygil's tertiary sun, each of his fingers separately uncurled itself from around the ball. Once his hand was fully open, the ball rested motionless on his palm. Then as the gravity of sleep pulled against his outstretched hand, the palm tilted and the ball rolled off into the gentle coma of nothingness.

Bam! Bam! Bam! Each time the ball hit the floor, the sound jolted Bedford one more step toward consciousness.

Bam! Bam! Bam! He opened his eyes, fully awake as the knock on his compartment came again.

"Syndic Odigal," a muffled voice called, "may I enter?"

The barely recognizable male voice sounded like it was coming from the depths of a tunnel. Bedford reached over his head and flicked on the doorcom. "Who is it?" he asked with a tone of annoyance in his voice.

"Chief Stancell, sir. May I please enter?"

"Stancell? Hmmmmm? Do we know a Stancell, Issy?" Bedford whispered as he yawned. He reached for his tunic then pressed the doorcom again. "Just a moment, Chief."

Stancell. Senior Mining Operations Chief on Euphrates. You remember, we met him this morning.

Of course. Stancell had been part of the welcoming committee. Bedford quickly pulled on his pants and buttoned his tunic. He ran a brush through his curly hair, made a final inspection of his appearance in the tiny mirror over the sink, and reached over to push the door control. The iris flared open with a burst of yellow light from the corridor. Just outside the door stood the dark, husky figure of Chief Stancell. Bedford squinted against the bright light. "What can I do for you, Chief?"

"Syndic Odigal, I apologize for the early hour, but I was sent by Manager Boristh-Major to request your presence down on mine level eighty-seven as soon as possible."

Rude lady, Bedford thought.

Don't rush to judgment.

"Level eighty-seven? That's the level where the accidents occurred? Right?"

"Yes, sir," Stancell said formally.

"Come on in, Chief, while I get my boots on," Bedford said, noticing that Stancell had not moved from the position he had held since the door was opened.

The Chief took four measured steps into the room and stood in a stance that any good military man would have described as parade rest.

Strange, Bedford thought as he found his boots and sat

in the chair to put them on. Someone with Stancell's experience and seniority should be used to dealing with officialdom. He was obviously using strict protocol as a means to mask the fact that he was ill at ease. "I hope there hasn't been another accident," Bedford said, trying to probe the reasons for Stancell's behavior.

"No, sir. No more accidents."

"Are there any other problems then, Chief?" Bedford took his time adjusting the snaps on his boots. He was irritated enough about being rudely awakened and called into the mine without having a chance to clean up and eat something. The least he could do was get some answers out of Stancell as a way to balance the account. "Well, Chief?"

Stancell shifted slightly and stared at the wall over Bedford's head. "None to my knowledge, Syndic Odigal. The Manager went down to eighty-seven early this cycle and soon thereafter asked that I come up and personally escort you to that level."

He's scared. Issy had detected tension behind Stancell's inflectionless reply.

Bedford finished adjusting his boots and leaned back in his chair. "Won't you please sit down, Chief Stancell?"

"I'm fine, sir."

"Good, then I'd like your opinion about everything that has happened . . . before we go down to eighty-seven."

Stancell twitched nervously, and answered only after a long pause. "No opinion, sir."

"Not even off the record?"

"Sir?" The question was rhetorical, Stancell's attempt to buy some time as he considered how much he could tell the Syndic without jeopardizing his position.

"Sr. Stancell, you have nothing to fear from me. I just want to know what a man with your long experience in the mines thinks about the events which have happened here." Bedford paused, partially to give Stancell a chance to respond, and partially to control his mounting irritation at the man's obstinate refusal to say anything. He wanted to reassure the Chief, but he also wanted some answers. "Still no opinion?"

"No . . . I mean, yes . . ." Stancell stammered, caught between a desire to talk and a duty to hold his tongue. "I mean, still no opinion, Syndic Odigal."

Let him off the hook, partner. We won't get anywhere pushing him now.

"All right," Bedford said, answering both Issy and Stancell. "But I want you to know, Chief, that I would value your thoughts about the accidents that have occurred here, and I shall be disappointed if we have to work without them."

Eeeeasy.

"However, there will be more time for us to talk later after I've had a chance to gather some facts on my own. So, if you will kindly lead the way, we can join the Manager and see what is so urgent that she had to call for me at this hour."

It's not his fault.

—I don't give a Maiser's goblet. I'm hungry.— Even his stomach growled subvocally.

I can fix that.

—Then why haven't you done it?—

There. That better?

—It'll do until we get some real food.— Bedford followed Stancell out of the compartment and down the corridor to the elevator. Issy's trick could fool his stomach, but it couldn't stop him from thinking about how good a big slab of steaming Bellistar root would taste just now.

As the elevator doors opened on level eighty-seven Stancell turned toward Bedford and said, "I will inform Manager Boristh-Major of your arrival." He walked swiftly out the door and disappeared from view around the corner of the mine shaft wall.

"Looks like it's going to be all up to us, Issy," Bedford said as he stepped out of the elevator himself.

The first thing which greeted his eyes as he entered the nine level proper was a huge pile of shattered rock and man-made rubble. It spilled from one wall of the mine shaft like a cairn he had once seen in the caves of Calydethercine. The loose rock sloped gently from the floor up to the roof of the horizontal shaft twenty meters above in a simple concave curve that gave the whole pile a very unnatural appearance.

Something wrong here.

—Yeah, your hunger fix isn't working very well.—

Here comes the lady.

Bedford watched as Kalissae left Stancell at the base of the slide and moved gracefully toward them. An involuntary flush darkened his cheeks.

—Quit it, Issy.—

It's not me, partner.

"I trust you slept well," Kalissae said, extending her hand.

"For as long as I slept." Bedford shook her hand more firmly than necessary, but even as he did so he admired her coolness and control. "Quite a mess you have here."

"Yes," she said, turning her back to Bedford to look at the slide. "When the laser bore blew up, the shock wave brought a lot of rock and debris down from the surrounding area." She pointed to the roof where large gouges in the rock left it looking very unstable. "But you can see that for yourself."

"Indeed I can. How safe is that ceiling now?"

"Oh, quite safe," she said as she turned and looked him squarely in the eyes. "You and I wouldn't be here if it wasn't. Chief Stancell wouldn't allow it."

"And just why are we here, Manager?"

"Why Syndic Odigal, I thought you would want to get started on your investigation as soon as possible. Since we were scheduled to begin heavy cleanup operations here at the beginning of this shift, it seemed appropriate to have you present so that you could do the physical part of the investigation for your report."

Get'em in and get'em out.

—Seems so.— Bedford smiled at her. "First things first, Manager Boristh-Major. Just exactly what has happened down here?" If MZ Manager-Major wanted to get him started at once, he was more than willing, but he would start at the beginning.

"What has happened is that four people have died here trying to uncover an Isoleucine-graphite deposit. All highly skilled and proficient miners. And all experienced in this type of operation." Kalissae's words were strong, spoken in an unemotional manner, but full of professional resentment about what had happened.

"And what have your people discovered down here so far?"

"Not much, really. We have taken samples of the dislodged materials around the site for chemical analysis, but I doubt if they will tell us anything."

"Why?"

Kalissae pointed a slender green finger at the base of the slide and moved it in a slow arc along the shaft floor as she spoke. "Because despite the loss of a psychominer and the crew of the laser bore, our instruments still show an Isoleucine pocket of normal configuration and—"

"Normal?" Bedford furrowed his brow. "Have your instruments been checked for calibration and possible malfunction?"

"Of course." Kalissae tried to keep her voice level, but his stupid question offended her. "That was one of the first things we did. They checked out well within the FedStandard error tolerance, *and* Helical error tolerance, which, as you probably know, is much stricter than FedStandard."

You sure know how to make her mad.

Bedford ignored Issy, and refused to take advantage of the opportunity Kalissae gave him to respond. He wasn't about to tell her that he didn't know anything about Helical mining standards.

"Well, anyway," she continued, "our instruments show an Isoleucine pocket of normal configuration and size. In fact it would match our theoretical form perfectly except for a slightly higher than normal mineral density. It should have been an easy task for an experienced psychominer."

Time to reveal your ignorance.

—*Our* ignorance, unless you've been studying up on the subject.— Bedford looked at Kalissae and asked, "Pardon my lack of knowledge, Manager, but just what exactly does a psychominer do when mining one of these Isoleucine pockets?" He hoped her answer would give him as much information about her as about the process.

A blue flush of emotion filled the hollows of Kalissae's pale green face. Was he really that stupid? Or did he know about Theeran? Kalissae tried to push back her feeling about her half-sister's death. This whole situation was offensive. What was this Federation Syndic doing here if he didn't know anything about psychomining? . . . And why was she reacting so strongly to his presence?

With a heavy sigh Kalissae forced a smile to her face, a smile that was as cold as the walls of the mine shaft. "I assume that you are familiar with the general underlying physical characteristics of Isoleucine deposits?"

"Please, MZ Boristh-Major, assume nothing except that I am totally ignorant about anything but the most rudimentary aspects of mining." Bedford wanted the whole story from her, and the suspicion was growing in him that this mess was the result of negligence, or incompetence, or both. Or there was some other factor involved that he didn't understand yet.

Kalissae knew he could not be as ignorant as he wanted her to believe. That he thought her gullible enough to accept such an idea made her dislike him even more. "Well," she said finally, "I'll try to make this as concise as possible. But let's sit in the porta-office where it's more comfortable."

Bedford followed her into the small plasteel cubicle and sat across the narrow desk from her. Without asking him if he wanted anything, she took a small cup of steaming liquid out of a lower part of the desk and set it in front of him. The aroma told him immediately that it was Frid tea, but before he could thank her, she launched into her lecture.

"Isoleucine is a basic crystalline amino acid which is essential to the nutrition of all known mammalian creatures and a good number of non-mammalians also. It occurs in mineral form covered by graphite—and I won't go into the theoretical scientific reasons why it occurs like that—it just does. It is found in highly concentrated nodules, or pockets, within almost pure graphite shells. Those shells are imbedded in amorphous rock, and have been discovered at depths from two to seven thousand meters on planets and planetoids throughout the borders of this quadrant of the galaxy." Kalissae paused for a moment and looked straight at the scarred Syndic across from her. "Are you getting this so far, Syndic Odigal?"

Is the galaxy big? Tell her yes.

"Yes, I think so, Manager. Please continue."

"The pockets of ore are generally spherical in shape, although ovoids are not uncommon. They range in size from two-hundred-fifty to three-hundred meters in diameter—"

"I hadn't realized they were so large," Bedford said. Kalissae scowled, and Bedford immediately regretted irritating her. "Excuse me. I shouldn't have broken your train of thought. Please go on, and I will try to refrain from any further interruptions." She gave him no smile of reward for his apology.

"The psychominer's job is to perform a highly disciplined form of telekinesis on the ore pocket. As simply as I can explain it to someone like you—" Kalissae heard her own sarcasm and paused. Then she decided that he deserved it and used the pause to take a sip of her tea.

"Basically a psychominer turns an Isoleucine pocket inside out," she continued. "The result is an easily accessible ore with the structural integrity of the nodule maintained, except in reverse, of course. An expert psychominer can perform an O.P.R., Ore Pocket Reversal, as many as

THE SEREN CENACLES 51

times a quadracycle. Any more than that..."

As her voice continued in a dry, emotionless tone, Bedford let Issy listen while he tried to understand what was behind her words. They were somehow too dry, like dull lectures he had sat through as a youth at Old Imperial when all the instructors knew the Federation was going to eliminate that form of teaching. For someone with as much vested interest in the mine's continued operation, Manager Boristh-Major did not seem overly interested in the information she was giving them.

I have enough, Issy said finally. *Let's get on with our work.*

"Thank you, Manager," Bedford said as he interrupted her with a slight wave of his hand. "I think we understand well enough to examine the ore pocket itself. That is, if you have no objections, of course?"

We? What did he mean? Did he expect her to accompany him? The way he interrupted her told Kalissae that he had a better grasp of the facts than he was willing to show. She could, on the pretext of safety, refuse his request to personally examine the pocket. But no, that would serve no purpose. Let the Syndic wade in over his head and then try to get out on his own. Then he'd see who had control and who didn't.

"I doubt if you'll learn anything, and I must warn you that it could be extremely dangerous," she said with a smile, "but, if you insist, you are more than welcome to make any examination you wish." Kalissae stood up and led the way out of the porta-office.

I don't think she likes you at all, partner.

—Too bad—

Indeed, indeed.

—Now what's that supposed to mean?—

Nothing. Let's start over there.

Bedford felt Issy begin his transmutation. "Pardon me, Manager, but I think we'd like to start where the rock bore was working when it exploded."

"Certainly," Kalissae said as she turned toward him. As

soon as she saw his face, she let out a muffled gasp. "What—" She couldn't finish the sentence because she didn't believe what her eyes were seeing. The scar on the Syndic's face was disappearing, melting away into his deeply tanned skin. Impossible, she thought. Impossible. Yet there it was. Or there it wasn't. The swollen gash of dark, ropy flesh was dwindling to nothingness. Malvin! He was the one who had sent this perverted agent to her mine. Damn them both!

Bedford read Kalissae's reaction in her stare of disbelief and enjoyed it. Had she been more civil with him, he would have prepared her for Issy's movement. Since she had insisted on being rude, this was her reward. "I suppose I should have warned you," he said with as much sincerity as he could muster, "or at least made the proper introductions before we did this."

"We?!"

"Yes, Manager," Bedford said with the slightest smile and bow, "we." He paused to let her flounder in ignorance a bit longer.

Get on with it. We have an agreement about this woman, remember? Besides, I want to get your hands on this ore pocket.

Issy was right, but a little more delay wouldn't have hurt her. "Manager Boristh-Major, I would like to introduce you to my symbiont, the Issykul," Bedford said matter-of-factly.

"Your what?"

"My symbiotic partner."

Kalissae stared at him. The scar was completely gone now. "Syndic Odigal," she finally said, "are you trying to tell me that, that, that thing which was on your face a moment ago is a living being?"

"That's correct, Manager." The look of incredulity on her face did not change. "I would have introduced you two in a more gentle manner, but it was necessary for Issy to change form in order for us to examine the ore pocket. I am sorry you were so shocked," he lied. Bedford held out his hand in apology.

Kalissae took his hand automatically then immediately dropped it. "What are you trying to pull on me?" she asked as she unconsciously wiped her palm on the side of her coveralls. "May I remind you that regardless of your status as a Free Syndic, I am still the highest authority on Euphrates, an authority which extends to knowing just who or what is on this planetoid at all times." Anger pumped light blue into her cheeks and sparked her eyes. She did not like being without total control. "I demand an explanation."

Will you give it to her so we can get to work? Sometimes, partner, you are a real first-class skedge-bowl-feeder. Give her the facts and let's go.

Bedford's expression sobered. "Of course, Manager, but please hear the whole story before you respond."

"I'm listening, Syndic Odigal." Kalissae could still feel the heat in her cheeks.

"Good. First, the Issykul is an ancient creature, so old that he's not even sure how long ago he came into existence. He lived in my father until Father died, and in my grandfather before him, and in my great-grandfather before him. He has been passed on from firstborn son to firstborn son as far back as the Odigal family can remember." Skepticism darkened her eyes. "I know it is hard for many people to believe, but Issy is a sentient being who shares my body. He resides in my nervous system. He . . ."

It was obvious from her continued expression of disbelief that he was not getting through to her. She was a pragmatist, maybe even a logical-empiricist for all he knew. It was time to try another approach.

"Look," he said as he pointed to his face. "You saw Issy change. He left my face and moved to my hands." He held them up for her instinctively, but without effect. When Issy was in his hands, he might as well have been invisible. "Okay, Manager, try this. Think of what Issy does as a very personal form of psychomining. He changes himself through mental effort."

The tensed muscles in Kalissae's face relaxed slightly. The blue highlights in her cheeks faded, and her eyes brightened with a look of understanding. "All right," she said slowly, "I suppose I could accept that. But just what is the purpose of this *thing* in you? What does this—"

"Issykul. Call him Issy."

"It's male, then?"

"Yes. And neither Issy nor I know anything about *purpose*. We're not much interested in teleology. He's been with me since I was a child. Father died in the Tritsen-Fennish War and Issy was almost lost to us. They flash-froze Father's body, and Issy almost died.

"But anyway, in return for being joint inhabitant of my body, he combines his mental powers with mine to produce an acute sensory awareness which neither of us could achieve on our own. That's why he moved from my face to my hands just now."

Surprisingly, Kalissae wanted to believe him. More surprisingly, she did believe him. There was something much greater involved here than she had ever imagined. "Well, Syndic Odigal, it would appear that you are eminently qualified to examine this area. Much more so than I had assumed." She felt awkward in his presence and totally unsure of herself.

All of her Pflessian training said she had made a serious social mistake with this Free Syndic and his, uh, Issy. There were caste questions involved here, and questions of social conduct and moral reverence. But she had no way of sorting them out. Her only chance was to back off and give this man and his *Ancient* as much room as they needed to do their job. The demands of her heritage forced her to do no less than that.

With a small sigh she said, "I am sorry, Syndic Odigal, but this all confuses me. Perhaps if I watched while you and your symbiont investigate down here, I will be able to understand more clearly. That is, if you don't mind?"

"Certainly not."

Took you long enough.

Bedford turned from Kalissae and walked to the face of the mine wall where bits and pieces of the rock bore still lay entangled with the debris from the blast. He bent over, and with light, dancing movements of his fingers, began touching everything.

Strange.

—These fragments?—

No. That woman.

—Damn, Issy. One minute you're pressing me to get our investigation started, and the next you want to drop all that and talk about the Manager. Can't you wait?—

Can you think and swim at the same time? I sensed a genuine acceptance of us in her. And Pflessians don't do that. Piques my interest. Maybe she's not as rigid as she pretends to be.

With a smile of intimate understanding Bedford shook his head. —You really *do* have the hots for her, don't you, Issy?—

Hots? Issykuls do not get the hots. It's purely a professional interest, which you obviously do not share with me. Proceed with the examination.

Bedford dropped the discussion—and moved his hands across the pile of rubble with the rapid deftness of a musician, pausing only briefly here and there for an extended tactile look.

Nothing here. But close.

He moved down the mine wall to a section not covered by debris and immediately picked up a resonance beneath the rocky surface. It was like feeling a hum—not a vibration, but the wave forms of a cyclic sound. Bedford pressed his hands flat against the wall.

—Issy?— No answer. The resonance grew stronger, like the rhythmic pulsing of a gigantic solar engine.

—Issy?— He asked again out of fear, a fear he recognized but did not know, a fear that raised a stinging, itching sensation in his armpits. —ISSY?—

Familiar. Power matrix. Can't remember where. Egg? No, not egg. But protective. Of what? What? Old, but still strong. Keep out. No! Keep in. The safety of us all.

The pulsing resonance threatened to overwhelm Bedford. He heard Issy like a fading voice in the distance. The fear thickened and curled itself around his head. Suddenly Bedford knew he was falling. In desperation he pressed his body flat against the mine wall.

Bedford! Stop! Pain you cannot feel! We will die! Stop! Stop! STOP!

As though hit for an instant by a million volts of electric current, Bedford's body stiffened and froze. He hung suspended in time and space, paralyzed, yet aware of everything around him. The only thing he wanted to do was scream.

An instant later his knees buckled and he fell. The swirling black quicksand of unconsciousness quickly swallowed him in its mindless embrace.

"Bedford!" someone screamed. It was a voice that level eighty-seven had heard before. It was Kalissae Boristh-Major.

FIVE

Issy felt his connective energy expand, stretch, and strain against the bonds which held him to the present. It happened quickly, without conscious effort or pain. As he burst into a world segregated into areas of pure light and perfect darkness he thought, I am dead.

Unrecognizable objects flew past him. They cast long, sooty shadows, charcoal grey lines which etched sharp furrows into the polished ebony surface of his surroundings. Nothing was static. As he watched with growing fascination, the shadows danced around him, flickering outward into infinity. Then slowly they stopped their random movements and solidified into filaments which radiated out from a single locus. When the last shadow finally ceased its movement, Issy realized that he was the center upon which the lines had formed their evenly spaced spokes. He was a newly formed point of axis in the midst of an otherwise empty darkness.

Issy tried to evaluate what was happening to him. He was relieved to find he retained the ability to see things logically even though memories seemed strangely disassociated from his concept of Self. As he arranged the sequence of events that had brought him to this point in time, something curious happened. Each new thought took concrete form.

Like fiery comets, Issy's memories spiraled out from his dark center. They flew in all directions, blinding him with their long, bright, shining tails. Then, one by one, they struck a single radiating shadow, cooled, coalesced, and hung before him like a curtain of sparkling stars.

Issy was determined to make sense of all this. As he watched each new sliver of light shoot out across the shadow, he forced himself to remember its proper position in time and space. The blazing pinpoints of energy were like pieces of a puzzle. If he could put them together in the right order, then he would have the solution to the riddle of where he was and why.

Slowly the brilliant ministars formed themselves into a logical pattern. The more Issy exerted control over his thoughts, the more distinct the pattern became. It was easy once he understood the process. A flood of memories, millions of pieces of his past poured out from some long hidden reservoir in his heart.

For the first time he realized how far back his past stretched. His connection to ten generations of the Odigal family was only a minute part of his memories.

Bedford was left far behind.

A shock of recognition halted his flow of ancient memories. *Bedford? Who? What? Where? Why?*

A litany of questions confused his thoughts. The pieces of the puzzle blurred. He could not think of Bedford now. Later he *must* think about that part of his life. But for the moment his instincts demanded that he move on.

With a fierceness of purpose that surprised him, Issy forced the sharp edge of logic back into the door of his forgotten past. A concentrated thrust of willpower pried it open, and immediately the flaming kernels of light pulled together. The renewed flood of memories flowed fast, sharp, and clear. Suddenly Issy knew he was constructing his own life-continuum, a perfectly straight series of shimmering moments in time which ran from the distant past through him, and into the future.

He slowly scanned his life-line from the pivot point upon which he stood. The panorama of galactic millennia was finally complete. It was a static, immotile eternity which was viewable both randomly and serially. And once Issy had grasped it as a whole, he thought of Bedford again.

Bedford. This time no questions accompanied the memory. Instead, a certain knowledge that Bedford was the key to total understanding caused thousands of flecks of light to flare along the part of the continuum closest to him. He put Bedford in a safe place and opened himself to the full scope of his identity. The destination he sought immediately made itself known.

Though it was impossible to measure the distance from his *now* to the object which attracted his attention, Issy knew that it was very far back in his past. It was a large, cone-shaped bulge, an upward thrusting distortion, which, though he could not explain why, he knew bore the imprint of his race.

His race. The thought pulled him toward the bulge like an intergalactic vortex pulls an unwary star cruiser. He felt fear. But, as the swollen point of knowledge loomed larger, Issy realized that it promised him understanding. He would be willing to risk death to gain that.

The five green lights of the alpha-wave monitor flashed in sequence. A medtech silently watched as the pace of the flashing quickened until the distinction between the lights blurred and they became one solid green line. "The Syndic is regaining consciousness, Manager," he said as he turned from the monitor.

Kalissae stood against the wall of the small hospital cubical flanked by Nicholas Malvin and his secretary, Arter Rosenthal. All three of them turned their heads toward the treatment foil where Bedford lay. After a moment's pause, Malvin moved to stand beside the foil. Kalissae and Rosenthal followed.

"No, Issy, no." Bedford's whisper could barely be heard above the electronic hum of the medical equipment. Even so, it scraped the edges of the nerves of the three people who stood beside him. "No, Issy, please. No." The words wailed with a grating sound like sand against cold plasteel.

"Syndic Odigal, we are here," Kalissae said as she laid a hand lightly on his shoulder. She wanted to shake him, but she did not want to violate her person any more than she already had. "Syndic Odigal, you are safe now. There is nothing to fear." Please, she thought, come back to us. Please don't—

"Who the hell is Issy?"

Malvin's question was gruff and interrupted Kalissae's thought. She struggled to finish it, ignoring Malvin's words. What had she been about to say?

"I asked you a question, Manager," Malvin said. He was growing impatient with Kalissae's lack of respect for his authority.

"Oh, unh, his symbiont," she said with a quick, swiveling glance away from Bedford then back to him. She was still preoccupied with her own thoughts and didn't see Malvin raise his eyebrows questioningly at Rosenthal.

"His *what?*"

The harsh skepticism in his tone snapped Kalissae out of her daze.

"I'm sorry," she said, realizing that Malvin was frustrated with her vague response to his question. "It's his symbiont. It lives in him. They work together as a team."

Malvin gave Rosenthal a look which told him to make a note of what they had just heard. "Very well," he said as he returned his eyes to Kalissae. She was again staring intently at the Syndic. What's so important about this man anyway? he thought, then said, "We'll drop it for now, Manager, but I want to know more about this Issy thing later." Turning toward the medtech he asked, "Is he waking up or not?"

The medtech glanced at Malvin, then Kalissae, and when he received no sign from her, back to Malvin. "He appears to be physically healthy," he finally said, staring through the Director rather than at him, "but his brain waves are still erratic. We can only hope that he's not suffered any psycho-systemic damage."

Though Kalissae had not taken her eyes away from Bedford, she heard the medtech's words. An involuntary shudder ran through her body. Don't die, she thought. Don't die before I've had a chance to tell you of my respect. My fears. My—

"Unh!" Bedford jerked awake and half raised himself from the foil as his eyes snapped open. Kalissae jumped back, startled by the Syndic's quick movement, then reached out to steady him. Bedford grabbed her arm and asked, "Where am I?" His eyes focused and he saw Malvin and Rosenthal. "Who are those people?"

"You are in the hospital section, Syndic Odigal," Kalissae said with a sound of relief in her voice. She pointed at Malvin and Rosenthal and added, "These gentlemen are from Helical headquarters."

Bedford let the faint buzzing in his ears drown out Kalissae's words. —And where are you, Issy?— he asked subvocally. The question was really only a hope. He knew Issy was gone. —Where are you, Issy?— he asked again as the buzzing cleared and he saw Malvin standing directly in front of him.

"May I introduce Sr. Nicholas Malvin, Director of Helical mining operations," Kalissae said. She used a formal tone which seemed to please her boss even though she doubted that Bedford was capable of following her lead in his present condition.

"How long have I been out?" Bedford asked, dispensing with the balance of the introductory ritual. He wanted answers, not platitudes. With Issy gone, Malvin meant no

more to him than anything else on Euphrates. They were
all expendable as long as he did not know where Issy had
gone. And he would use each of them ruthlessly if he had
to until he found out.

"Please, Syndic Odigal, allow yourself a little time to get
your bearings." Malvin smiled and placed his hand on
Bedford's shoulder.

When Malvin touched him, Bedford realized that he
was clutching Kalissae's arm. Odd, he thought, she doesn't
seem to mind. Not normal for a Pflessian. He let the
thought linger for a moment while he looked at her face
trying to discover there what had caused her to relax her
strict social code. Seeing nothing, he turned back to
Malvin and said, "I feel perfectly all right. Now, how long
have I been unconscious?"

"A little over four cycles, roughly six Standard days,"
Kalissae answered.

Bedford swung his legs out over the edge of the foil and
released his grip on Kalissae's arm. As his feet touched the
floor he said, "Get me my clothes. I'm going back there to
find out *exactly* what happened." His knees refused to
support him. As soon as he put his full weight on them,
they buckled. Clutching frantically for support he fell into
the waiting arms of Malvin and Kalissae.

"Syndic Odigal," Kalissae said firmly, "please. You must
rest and regain your strength. You've had a severe trauma
and level eighty-seven can wait until you are well."

"Listen to her, Syndic Odigal," Malvin said as he waved
to the medtech to help them with Bedford.

Bedford had no strength to resist as they put him back
on the foil. "We must not wait. We must take ad . . . vantage
of . . . way to find out . . ." His words slurred before they
got to his tongue. The room dissolved into a grey mist.
"Issy, Issy, Issy," he whispered with a hissing sound that
followed him down into the darkness.

As soon as Bedford ceased his movement, the medtech
covered him with a blanket and threw a light strap over
the foil to hold him in place. "He's out cold," he said

quietly as he secured the strap. "The shock of whatever happened to him has drained his energy. Please, if you would all kindly let him have some rest." His voice trailed off deferentially.

"When do you think the Syndic will be fit to continue his investigation?" Rosenthal's question startled everyone. It was the first thing he had said since he had entered the hospital cubical.

The medtech looked at Malvin with a puzzled expression.

"Answer him," Malvin said as he gave Rosenthal a questioning glance.

"Impossible to say at this time, sir. Maybe in a few cycles. Maybe not. For now he needs plenty of rest before he can think of doing anything else."

"All right. We'll get out of your way. But I want to know the minute the Syndic regains consciousness." Malvin turned toward the door and motioned for Kalissae and Rosenthal to follow. "Let's adjourn to your office, Manager," he said as he stepped into the corridor outside the cubical.

Kalissae nodded her assent. As she crossed the threshold, she resisted the urge to look back at Bedford. It would not be dignified, she thought. But her refusal to look back only added a new thorn to the bramble of conflicting signals she was giving herself. Why was she reacting to Bedford in such an emotional manner? Political survival was more important than her feelings for the Syndic. Or was it? Kalissae reined her emotions with a promise supported by the fierce discipline of her aristocratic training. She would deal with her relationship to Bedford later, when the other elements of her life were a little more balanced.

"I don't give a Borgercow's triple bung hole what it is we've got down there. I think we should evacuate all nonessential personnel immediately." Malvin followed his declaration with a long sip of whiskey from the plastic mug in his hands. "We can't risk any more lives. This anomaly almost killed a Free Syndic. The Fed will burn Helical down to the nubs if a Syndic dies out here, and I won't be responsible for that."

Kalissae looked at her superior with hard eyes, then softened her expression as she resigned herself to the obvious. Malvin was right. First Theeran, then the laser bore crew, and now Bedford Odigal. Too many people had been killed or injured here. "I'm willing to agree that it *is* dangerous on Euphrates, but..." She hesitated for a moment, then continued, "But, aren't we overstepping the Free Syndic's authority? Shouldn't he be the one to make this decision?"

"The Syndic!?!" Malvin threw his cup across the room. "Damn, woman, the man's unconscious, incapable of giving us any kind of opinion." He paused long enough to move his face to within centimeters of hers, then added, "*Or* of exercising his authority."

Kalissae recognized Malvin's anger. Though she didn't want to, she sympathized with him. He was experiencing the same fear she had when the Syndic had first arrived on Euphrates. He was afraid of Bedford's power, and didn't like the thought of losing control to a man he couldn't manipulate.

Malvin pulled his face back and continued. "Helical's interests are my responsibility," he said with a much cooler voice. "My *prime* responsibility. And as part of that responsibility *I* must decide what is best for the welfare of our employees. I can't wait for some Free Syndic who is half out of his head to come around and advise me."

"Sir, if I may," Rosenthal interjected with a dispassionate voice, "I have a proposal which might offer a solution to our problem."

"What is it, Rosie?" Malvin's tone was curt and patronizing.

Rosenthal showed no signs of offense. "Well, sir," he said without any emotion in his voice, "if we were to evacuate the Syndic with the other personnel, he couldn't object, could he? What can an unconscious man say about the measures taken to protect his health?"

Malvin looked at his secretary and gave an approving smile. Too bad Rosie's so cold, he thought. But better cold and smart than a friendly idiot. He shifted his gaze back to Kalissae and said, "I think Rosie has come up with a great idea. What do you think, Manager?"

Before she had a chance to respond, Malvin continued, saying in a loud, confident voice, "I'll tell you what you think. You think it's an excellent proposal."

Kalissae said nothing.

"Well?" Malvin wanted to hear her say it. "Well, Manager, don't you think it's an excellent proposal?"

"Yes," Kalissae said finally. Malvin's grunt of pleasure told her he had completed his assumption of power on Euphrates. He was now totally in command. She had lost all her authority, at least as far as he was concerned. And there was nothing she could do about it as long as she maintained her loyalty to Helical Minerals.

"Very well then. Let's get this exercise moving." Malvin rattled off instructions to Rosenthal, who quickly took them down on his ever-present dictapad. After a few minutes of rapid-fire dictation, he looked at Kalissae and said, "I don't think we will be needing you for a while, Manager. You may attend to your other duties."

She should have been angry. She should have been furious. But she wasn't. Malvin's strong tone of dismissal bounced off a numbness inside her. "As you wish," she said flatly. "I'll keep the computer posted as to my whereabouts so you can contact me if you need to."

It was a false hope and she knew it. Malvin would have no further need for her. It is over, she thought as she left the suite as gracefully as she could. An unhappy sense of resolution settled in her thoughts. It was over, and she could now try to unravel her strange weave of feelings about Bedford Odigal.

"Huffy little greenie, isn't she, Rosie? You don't suppose

she has more than a professional interest in that Syndic, do you?" Malvin let the thought of what horrible little green and pink things might spew from such a union linger in his imagination long enough to disgust him. Then he dismissed it. "Now, how many ships does this mine have available for immediate evacuation?"

Kalissae's thoughts were strangely pacific as she made her way back to the hospital section. She used the stairs so that she would not have to see anyone, hoping that the walk down the four flights to her destination would help shake out some of her conflicting feelings. For the first time in a long time, she was unsure of her next move. A dispassionate review of where she had been since Theeran had resisted her would make easier the hard choices she knew she had to make.

Clink-clank. Clink-clank. The metal heel and toe caps on her boots beat out a bi-tonal rhythm as she descended the stairs. "That's exactly how I feel," she said aloud: Bi-tonal, torn between two loyalties."

On the one hand there was Helical, her company. She should give her full allegiance to Malvin. He *was* the Director and his decisions in this matter should be respected. But there was something in the way he had shown up on Euphrates unannounced after she had sent headquarters the news about the Syndic's condition. He did not trust her. And she needed no greater proof of that than the way she had been curtly dismissed from playing any further part in the evacuation of the mine. Maybe it was his obvious bigotry. Maybe he had motives that were more complex than that. She did not know for sure. But without Malvin's trust she could not keep faith with his decisions no matter how much he professed to have Helical's best interests at heart.

On the other hand, there was Free Syndic Bedford Odigal. He too had arrived on Euphrates unannounced. However, it was apparent from the gruff way he had spoken to Malvin that his connection with the company was nothing like what she had first believed it was. As a Federation Syndic he had a broad-based authority over what happened in the Margin District. And that meant Euphrates. If nothing else, law required her to respect his right to have a say in what happened here. But it was more than a need to adhere to the law which nagged at Kalissae. Bedford had shown a great deal of courage when he examined the ore pocket, much more, she speculated, than Malvin would have shown under similar circumstances. It was to Bedford's credit that his actions made her feel an instinctive desire to align herself with him rather than her Helical superiors.

Kalissae was so wrapped up in her thoughts that she almost missed the landing for the hospital section. She realized her mistake and turned back. Then she paused for a moment and looked at her hazy image reflected in the shiny plasteel of the door. I feel *much* better, she thought as she smiled at herself for the first time since level eighty-seven had exploded in her face. With a confident shove she pushed the door open and headed directly to Bedford's cubical.

Kalissae entered the hospital cubical quietly and saw that Bedford still lay unconscious upon the treatment foil. "How is he doing?" she asked the medtech as she slowly walked toward the Syndic.

"Better, Manager, I think. All his patterns are normal now. I used the Syndic's implant I.D. disk to code the brainwave monitor's mimic function. He responded quickly, and his readout matched the disk pattern within a few minutes. I think we can safely say that the Syndic is well on his way to complete recovery."

"Good." Kalissae stood over Bedford and stared at his face. The muscles were relaxed, and she thought it was not all that ugly without Issy's scarlike manifestation. Or was it just that she now looked at Bedford differently? She started to reach out and touch the cheek where Issy had been, but stopped herself short. Turning to the medtech she said, "Why don't you go get yourself some Frid tea or something. I'll stay and watch the Syndic for a while."

The medtech gave her a curt nod of his head and a slightly disapproving look. "Buzz me if his wave patterns change significantly," he said as he left the cubical.

Kalissae stood silently for a few minutes after the medtech had gone. She listened to the low hum of the medical equipment and watched the unlabored rhythm of Bedford's chest as it rose and fell with the tides of his breathing. As she watched and listened, mesmerized by the regularity of sight and sound, she thought she saw the Syndic's lips move. A quick glance at the instruments indicated no change, but when she looked back at him she was sure she saw his lips move again. Bending her head close to his mouth, she strained to hear what he was saying.

"Issssssy." The word was a soft hiss in her ear. "Isssssy."

Bedford opened his eyes and lay perfectly still. It took his brain a few moments to assimilate what he was seeing. "Kalissae?" he finally asked.

She instinctively jerked back at his word. He had used her first name without her permission. And? And somehow the strict requirements of Pflessian interpersonal etiquette seemed unimportant now. "Yes, Bedford," she said as she brought her head close to his again.

Bedford gave her a weak smile. As groggy as he was he still recognized the break in protocol. "I'm . . . sorry I used your first name."

Kalissae smiled back at him. "No harm done, Syndic Odigal. It's about time we started being less formal. After all, we aren't on Pflessius, are we?"

"Please," he said, "call me Bedford. After all, we aren't on a Fed adjudication planet either." The low, gentle laughter he got in response to his riposte pleased Bedford. Its range fell a full octave lower than that of the usual Homo sapien, and he found it immensely attractive.

"As they would say in Alt-Frac, *tooque*, Syn—Bedford."

"Now, as I recall, before my failing body interrupted

me, I was about to ask your superior, what's-his-name,
just—"

"Malvin. Nicholas Malvin."

"Yes, Malvin," Bedford said as he raised himself slowly
into a sitting position. "I was about to ask Sr. Malvin what
measures he had taken concerning the ore pocket." He
held out his hand to her to steady himself. She took it,
bracing herself against the foil's support rods as he put his
feet on the floor.

"Should you—"

"We'll know in a moment. I feel much better than I did
earlier. It was earlier, wasn't it? Not cycles ago?"

"Just a few hours, Bedford."

"Good." He released his grip on her hand and checked
his balance. "See," he said, "good as new." He stretched
the muscles in his legs by bending his knees several times.
Then, assured that he would not fall, he said, "Tell me
what Sr. Malvin has planned."

Kalissae hesitated. She was afraid that Bedford might
pass out again, especially when he heard what Malvin
intended to do. She let him make several circuits around
the cubical and not until some color had returned to his
face did she decide that she could tell him. "Sr. Malvin
has decided to evacuate all nonessential personnel from
the mine as soon as possible. He suspended all activity on
level eighty-seven shortly after he arrived." As soon as she
finished she held her breath in anticipation of Bedford's
reaction.

"What were his reasons?" Bedford asked as he stopped
walking and thrust his hands into the pockets on his baggy
hospital coveralls.

Kalissae looked at him in surprise. He was taking the
news much more calmly than she had expected. And
without any hesitation he so casually questioned the motives of Helical's top operational man. Incredible, she
thought as she realized how easily he wielded the power of
his office. "I'm afraid he did not say. And frankly, I did not

ask. After all, he is my superior. It would have been presumptuous of me to question him."

"Fortunately I'm not bound by any such restrictions. Where is Sr. Malvin now? And when can I see him?" He moved around the room again, stretching and bending as he tried to loosen his tight muscles.

"About that—"

"About what?" Bedford broke in sharply. The more he limbered up, the more clear his mind became. And the more clear his mind became, the more worried and angry he got. Issy was missing and some hard decisions had to be made. The thought of having to deal with the problems on Euphrates without the help of his friend and partner frightened him. It had been a long time since Bedford had felt that kind of naked fear.

"About Sr. Malvin," Kalissae said, wishing she didn't have to tell him about Malvin's other decision.

"What about Sr. Malvin?" Bedford shot her a suspicious look.

"He has decided to evacuate you along with the nonessential personnel." Kalissae knew she had blurted it out crudely, and was surprised at the anger she felt when she said it.

"He what? Who in the name of Brett's Constant does Malvin think he is? I decide where I go, not Malvin."
—Dammit, Issy, where are you?—

Kalissae stood silent, her back against the cubical wall.

Bedford glared at her until she lowered her head. He knew he shouldn't vent his anger against an innocent party, but he did not like this turn of events. Besides, how did he know that she didn't play a role in the decision making. "And how did you vote on my evacuation, Manager?" he questioned angrily.

Kalissae flinched. She felt cut off from all sides, isolated by events over which she had no control. With a slow, deep breath she raised her head and looked directly into Bedford's eyes. She would be honest with him. "I agreed that you would be evacuated."

"I see." Bedford was startled by his sense of disappointment. He had hoped for more from her. "Very well," he said with a tone of finality. "But you listen to this, and you listen well. I will not leave Euphrates until I've completed my investigation. I did not ask to be sent to this mine, but since I'm here, I will do everything within my authority as a Free Syndic to root out what has happened here and why—regardless of any decisions you or Sr. Malvin make." He walked closer to her. "And another thing. I will expect, no, I will demand full and complete cooperation from all of you. That means no interference with my movements or actions. Is that understood?"

"Oh, I understand, Syndic Odi—"

"Good. As soon as you get someone in here with my clothes, you can deliver that message to your boss."

"Immediately, *Syndic Odigal*." Kalissae spat the words at him. "I see that you're good at ordering people around." She wanted to scream in frustration. "You'll get your clothes, and Sr. Malvin will get your message. Then the two of you can butt heads until they crack and let in the fresh air of decency."

Before he could respond she was out the door and headed down the corridor.

Kalissae had wanted to defend herself. Instead she had let anger get the best of her. She had wanted to tell Bedford that she had stood up for his right to make his own decisions, but she knew that her defense had been halfhearted. She had wanted to tell him that she would do whatever she could to help him. But pride had gotten in her way. A tear straggled down her cheek and added further anger and confusion to the thoughts which tore at the center of her mind. Damn him anyway, she thought as she roughly wiped the moisture from her face. Damn them both.

Bedford zipped the closure on his jumpsuit with a quick, hard yank and winced with pain when several of the curly hairs on his chest were pulled out. "Damn," he said as a brief flash of anguish watered his eyes. His carelessness only added to his growing despair and anger. He had lost Issy. Without his symbiont the delicate balance between actions and thoughts was lost. They had been partners too long. The virulent "thing" inside the ore pocket had robbed him of the one relationship upon which he could depend and—

Bedford, I still exist. Issy's voice echoed off the sides of old memories, and Bedford knew it was not real. Issy was gone.

He finished dressing quickly and tried not to think about his lost companion. It was impossible. He kept going over the moments which led up to the separation only to have them fade into a fuzzy darkness. He had to get back down to level eighty-seven. It offered hope that some new memory might be triggered by the sight of the ore pocket. There was only one thing he knew for sure: He would not mourn his loss until he had positive proof that Issy was dead. To mourn would be to accept that his friend was gone forever. Bedford could not accept that.

Neither could he escape the constant awareness of Issy's absence. He had relied on Issy for too many things over the years, too many little things that he now had to do alone. Even fastening his soft boots seemed different and somehow wrong without Issy.

Whew! You sure have smelly feet, partner.

That's what Issy would have said. A sarcastic retort which would have added immeasurably to the simple task precisely because it was both chiding and correct. Maybe that was the answer, he thought. Maybe he should just try to operate as though Issy were still there. A little delusion would help a whole lot with what lay before him. "Done," he said aloud as he stepped to the small hospital cubical sink.

As Bedford splashed his face with warm water and scrubbed away the grime which had accumulated during his period of unconsciousness, a small panel on the ceiling slowly, soundlessly opened. An inverted, cone-shaped nozzle projected from the opening and spewed a colorless, odorless gas into the cubical. Seconds later Bedford lay sprawled on the floor, unconscious.

Within thirty seconds after Bedford fell the cubical was cleared of gas and two men rolled him onto a stretcher. They carried him swiftly and quietly from the room. Though the two men were as efficient as any of the medtechs on Euphrates, Bedford would have instantly recognized that they were not part of the regular hospital staff. The distinctive uniforms of the Helical Minerals Security Force would have been a dead giveaway.

The dark figure stood alone inside the main entrance of the Euphrates communications office. After a brief pause he made his way across the empty room. Stopping in front of the transmitting equipment, the figure reached out and flipped three switches marked POWER, NEAR-SPACE, and SEND. He did so with the effortless ease of someone very familiar with the controls. Just as effortlessly he grasped a small microphone from its receptacle on the front of the transmitter.

"S-Commander Byosin, execute Neutral Red. Authority, Port Captain. Repeat. Execute Neutral Red. Authority, Port Captain."

SIX

MZ Jones's red security lamp blinked at Kalissae through the transparent plastic panels of her inner office door. The silent, fifteen cycles-per-second flash threw bright splinters of light across the darkened room. It drew her attention away from the introspective thoughts that had nagged her since she had left Bedford.

"Damn, what now?" she finally asked, unable to ignore her electronic secretary any longer.

"I-dent, please."

Kalissae sighed as she flopped into the chair beside her desk and snapped on the security-link intercom which connected her to MZ Jones. "Boristh-dash-Major, K.," she said in a carefully modulated voice for the benefit of the secretary's speech recognition circuits.

"Code sentence, please," MZ Jones responded almost immediately.

Must be a major breach of rules, Kalissae thought as she pulled the intercom around so that it faced her and rapidly typed on its attached keyboard, THE DETRYAL MANA-CLES HAVE BEEN BROKEN.

74

MZ Jones hummed for a moment while its analytical devices matched both the sentence and Kalissae's typing style to preprogrammed security locks. "I-dent positive," it finally said in its usual cheerful tones.

Sometimes Kalissae wished she had a newer model secretary, one which could be programmed to report in a variety of tones. The sickeningly sweet responses seemed out of place at times. It got on her nerves. "All right, MZ Jones, let's have it."

"Central processing informs me that an uncorrelated transmission has been monitored on our near-space communications channel."

"Saint Gunson," Kalissae said with a half laugh. "That's all I need, some unauthorized shoptalk between miners while Malvin is here." Hardly a cycle went by when she did not have to handle that problem, but for the umpteenth time she wished the loneliness and boredom of mining did not make it so chronic. She sighed. "Read the transmission to me, please."

"*START.* S-Commander Byosin, execute Neutral Red. Authority, Port Captain. Repeat. Execute Neutral Red. Authority, Port Captain. *STOP.*"

Kalissae sat silently for a few moments wondering what the message could mean. The first thoughts which came to her were not pleasant. "Read it again, please."

As MZ Jones repeated the message, the muscles around Kalissae's aortic membranes tightened. The military tone of the transmission meant something. . . . "Neutral Red," she said under her breath. "Any voice I-dent?" she asked.

"No, Manager. The message was sent using a masking device. However, we followed standing orders and made a subset-positive on the tonal type. As you know, there are fifteen major subsets of tonal classification within the Hassoubah audio I-dent system. Those types—"

"Cut all the ROM flotsam and get to the point, MZ Jones," Kalissae interrupted. The damn computer wanted to reinvent the tarter-latch every time it gave a technical report.

"It was Ceminal c-dash-four, Manager."

"Thank you," Kalissae said sarcastically. Damn machine won't even appreciate the sarcasm, she thought with a smile. Then she realized she had been rubbing the tense muscles around her aortic membranes without being conscious of it. And damn the Gods that created Pflessian physiology too, she thought. "Run me a list of personnel on this mine who match the Ceminal c-dash-four tonal type."

While she waited, Kalissae vigorously massaged her muscles and tried to relax. The tension eased up a bit, then came back even stronger. She didn't need this. She didn't need any of it. Ever since her argument with Theeran . . . She let that thought trail off.

A short, high-pitched sound notified her that MZ Jones was finished. Kalissae turned to the printer and ripped out a short piece of paper. Four names were listed: Colgart-Mintazzi, Stancell, Odigal, and Silet.

Theeran Silet. Kalissae's muscles tensed again with a sharp twist of pain. Theeran Silet had been scratched from the list by the unknown which had started all this. What was it Theeran had faced down there? What was it that had killed her? Kalissae shivered. Theeran?

With a shake of her head she looked at the names again. Colgart-Mintazzi could also be eliminated. He was on a somnambular sabbatical, working the mine in a hypnotic trance while he mentally prepared his doctoral dissertation. He was, in effect, not mentally present. And like all Snambues, his only motivation was the attainment of his professional credentials. No, Colgart-Mintazzi was too detached from the real world to have sent a message.

That left Stancell and Odigal plus anyone whose voice might not have been imprinted. Kalissae ruled Bedford out immediately. Why? She didn't know. It was an intuitive judgment. She sensed that even though he might have some private reason for sending such a message, he was not the one. Besides, being unconscious for such a long time made him an even more unlikely candidate.

Stancell was the logical choice. He had a lot to lose if Malvin discovered how much he had cooperated with Kalissae's attempt to downplay the accidents on Euphrates. Yet, even if Stancell had sent the message, what did it mean?

Kalissae laid the list of names on her desk and asked MZ Jones to repeat the message again. As she sat listening, trying to dig out some meaning she might have missed, she doodled on a small pad of paper using a split fingernail on her index finger for a pen and droplets of her pale green perspiration as ink. It was an old habit and helped her to concentrate. "Of course," she finally said as she scrawled a broad line across the paper. With a quick flick of her wrist, she activated a switch on a control console marked INTERAC. "Make administrative correlation number zed-alpha-twelve," she said excitedly to MZ Jones.

"Affirmative," the computer answered sweetly.

Kalissae impatiently tapped her fingers on her desk top as she waited for the results from her inquiry. The time it was taking MZ Jones to execute her request seemed to drag by. Finally, as she was about to get up and make herself a cup of Frid tea, her wait was terminated by the sound of the JOB COMPLETED signal. She bent over and quickly read what had come out on the printer. Now for some proof, she thought as she tore the paper from the machine. With her shoulders back and a growing anger fed by the computer's latest information, Kalissae marched toward a confrontation.

"Enter," Nicholas Malvin said harshly. He looked across the small table at Rosenthal and in a lower tone added, "What does she want now?"

The entrance iris flared open and Kalissae walked confidently into the VIP suite. "Sr. Malvin," she said, "I have a few questions to ask you." She took an empty chair beside the table and sat down before Malvin had a chance to offer it. Giving Rosenthal a hard, penetrating look, she added, "*Alone* please."

Malvin raised one eyebrow at his secretary and sighed. "Rosie, we can finish this later." He pointed to some papers scattered on the table top.

"As you wish, sir." Rosenthal carefully slid the papers into a large portfolio case and silently left the suite.

"Yes?" Malvin tersely asked as soon as Rosenthal had gone. He was tired of this woman who didn't know when she was beaten.

Kalissae shoved a small sheet of paper across the table to him. "Read this first."

Malvin read the message, laid it on the table, and asked, "What don't you understand?" He hoped she wouldn't see by his expression that he had some questions about the message himself.

What in Saint Gunson's name was he talking about, Kalissae thought. Does he really think I know what the message means? "I don't *understand* any of it," she said.

Malvin smiled. At least he would be able to concoct an explanation which she could not refute with any concrete information. "I'm sorry we didn't give you any warning," he said with an accommodating tone. "But here it is straight out. I have ordered the Helical Security Force to take up positions around Euphrates and seal it off from any outside contact until we have had a chance to evaluate the situation here and take appropriate actions." Pretty good, Nicky, he thought as he smiled at Kalissae again.

Kalissae didn't like his smile. It was thin and nervous and all but screamed deception at her. "Why? What purpose will be served by that?"

His smile faded. "There is a serious problem here which may affect all our mines in this sector," he lied. "It seemed only prudent to quarantine this area until we've found out just what we've got down there." Malvin spoke with hesitation. He realized that the message was an operational order to the security force, but he was not sure of its purpose. The more meat Kalissae forced him to add to his story, the less confident he felt that it would satisfy her.

Something was missing. She knew that. "You'll have to excuse my ignorance, sir, but what actions do you anticipate taking in the mine that will require the security force?"

Damned greenie, he thought. And it was all Rosenthal's fault. He saw the unmistakable mark of his secretary in this. Best terminate this discussion with the Manager until he had a chance to question Rosie. With a sigh he put on his best bureaucratic face. "I wouldn't worry too much about that if I were you, Manager. We have made no decisions in respect to any use of the security force other than what I've told you. We just want to take adequate precautions, that's all."

How could you think I'm so stupid, Kalissae wanted to ask. But she knew that Malvin wouldn't give her anything further except more synth-talk. "I suppose it *is* my loyal duty to accept your explanation," she said more bitterly than she meant to.

"Exactly," he replied. She was buying it for now, he thought with relief. "You will do as you are told like any other Helical employee. When you have a need to know, we will tell you."

Kalissae stood up slowly. Dismissed again, she thought as she tried to hold the flush of anger back from her cheeks. "That is frank enough, sir. I hope you appreciate my need to know when any other major decisions have been made?"

"Of course, Manager. After all, it is your mine." Malvin's empty smile returned as he too rose from the table and escorted her to the door.

"Thank you for your time," she said as she took his extended hand. "It's always good to know the situation as exactly as possible." There was no conviction in her voice. With a brief shake she dropped his hand, turned, and stalked through the door convinced more than ever that Malvin would tell her anything as long as it kept her in the dark as to his real purposes.

Malvin closed the door to his suite as soon as Kalissae stepped through. He hit the service-com with his fist. Hard. "Sr. Rosenthal, report to Sr. Malvin *immediately.*" He flipped the service-com off with almost as much force as he had used to turn it on. "Damn all the fools in the universe," he yelled. The rolls of skin on his neck had turned a brilliant red. Anger knew no color barriers.

"What's the story, MZ Jones?" Kalissae asked, eager to hear what the computer had come up with.

"Malvin, Nicholas. Primal b-dash-five."

"Damn!" Her theory wasn't worth a broken Petararm. Kalissae almost let her disappointment get the best of her. But there was something that didn't make sense. If Malvin's voice didn't match, then what was his story all about?

"Rosenthal, Arter. Ceminal c-dash-four," MZ Jones said.

"What?!? Repeat that." Kalissae almost jumped out of her chair when MZ Jones repeated the last statement. "Wait a minute. Why didn't you have his name on the list you gave me earlier?"

"Delayed record update. Disk inputs two-seventy-seven gamma through zeta were down for regular maintenance. Current files now show Ceminal c-dash-four matches on Colgart-Mintazzi, Stancell, Odigal, and Rosenthal. Silet has been deleted."

"Thanks MZ Jones," Kalissae said heavily as she sank into her chair. Silet certainly has been deleted. And so have I, in a way, she thought. Deleted from any position of power around here. At least that's what Malvin would like to think. Correction. Malvin *and* Rosenthal. Can't forget Rosenthal. After all, he's the one who sent the message.

*   *   *

"Sit down, Rosie," Malvin said as he tried to control the emotion which threatened to explode inside him. He took a long sip of whiskey, straight from the bottle. It was time to dispense with the superfluous. "What the hell is this?" he asked as he tossed across the table the message Kalissae had given him.

Rosenthal picked up the message and glanced at it briefly before throwing it back on the table. He didn't need to read it. "Now *you'd* better sit down, Nicholas," he said softly.

Malvin was startled by Rosenthal's tone. "What the—"

"*Sit down*, Nicholas."

Not since his days in the Federation Off-World Forces had Malvin heard that command voice. He sat down almost without thinking about it.

"Make yourself comfortable, Nicholas. Sip on your precious alcohol. And listen. Listen closely. It is about time you understood what is going on around here."

SEVEN

Biendal Tariik looked down the rows of pylons which
dotted the floor of extension unit seventeen and cursed.
"Damn brass don't understand what a hard-rocker has to
go through just to satisfy their whims." He finished his
quick visual inspection and turned to the construction
supervisor who stood next to him. "So what's the problem
now?"

"Down on the end, Sr. Tariik. We've bent three driver
shafts trying to pound the last pylons into place. Some
kind of obstruction. I need your permission to use
explosives." The supervisor pointed to a knot of men and
equipment a hundred meters away on the other side of the
construction site. "They're about as far as they can go until
we set those pylons."

This hitch on Tigris is getting to be too much, Tariik
thought. It isn't worth all the aggravation, especially with
the rush put on by the sudden transfer of most of the staff
from Euphrates.

"I hate rushing," he said with a pained expression, "but

82

let's do what we have to do. Just start off easy. I don't want any cave-in, understand?"

"Got it, Sr. Tariik. We'll use six-kilo charges to start off with."

"Sounds all right to me, Selkit, but if that isn't enough, don't increase them by more than a kilo at a time. You know how hot upside is to get this finished, and I don't want to disappoint them. *But*, I don't want to bury us all either. So get busy . . . and be careful."

"Will do."

The two men separated. Tariik went back to a small shed that served as his office. Selkit went directly to the equipment bay to fill out an order for the explosives he needed.

Selkit liked explosives. They were quick and easy. And now that Tariik had managed to get the Old Man to sign blank requisition forms, getting to use the explosives was going to be much easier. Better start with eight-kilo charges just to be on the safe side, he thought. That wouldn't be too much, and it might save them some time. Besides, Tariik would never know.

Within half an hour the crew had planted the charges in the series of holes which had been pounded into the rock floors before the drivers broke down. Standing at the point he had chosen for blast control Selkit smiled as the crew efficiently played out the fine cable from each charge to the detonator at his feet. They're good men, he thought, the best crew I've ever supervised.

As soon as the last cable was played out to the detonator, he sent his men to the safety of the designated shelter area. No sense in taking any chances, he thought as he watched the last man disappear behind the protective wall. Then he knelt to synchronize the charges. One by one he clipped the bare leads from each cable into a terminal box mounted just below the detonator's oscilloscopelike screen. As soon as all the cables were connected, he ran a quick test to make sure each charge matched the preset frequency. Satisfied that all was as it should be, he yelled, "Clear!"

Each member of the crew responded by sounding off with his or her name. Once all twenty-three were accounted for, Selkit adjusted the timer on the detonator and activated it. This is going to be a good blast, he thought as he moved quickly to the shelter area. He could feel it in his bones.

The charges went off with a muffled *whump* five minutes later, exactly as planned. As the sound slowly died away, Selkit signaled everyone to stay in place. It was his job, and only his job, to make sure the blast area was safe before anyone left the shelter.

Suddenly a second sound, a much louder sound, a totally foreign sound, rolled heavily through extension level seventeen.

Like the agonizing moan of plasteel pylons yielding under the strain of excess weight, the sound vibrated everything with a steady, dull rumble. Then with agonizing slowness it changed.

The pitch increased. The rumble became a roar. The roar became a high-pitched squeal as the floor erupted in a shower of white-hot sparks and chunks of flying rock.

Biendal Tariik bolted through the door of his office thinking the explosives had ignited a hidden gas pocket. This is what too much rushing will get you, he thought as the floor trembled violently. It was the last thought he ever had.

Crackling with billions of kilowatts of naked electrical energy, a huge sphere broke through the rock floor. It rose effortlessly through stone, plasteel, and the briefly squirming bodies of the construction crew with a sizzling that consumed everything in its path. Slowly, but without hesitation, it ascended through the levels of the Tigris mine.

High in the darkness of his journey toward the past, Issy had to swerve to avoid a seething ball of radiation. It boiled past him, popping with incandescent fires, and swirling with blue light. Then with a mindless purpose of its own, it expanded and changed direction, and hurtled back toward him.

Issy did not know how to stop, or how to hide, or where he could go to escape. He had been so intent on reaching the oddly familiar bulge in his past that he had not seen the fireball until it was almost upon him.

The heat blasted his senses. The light seared his mind's eye. The raging furnace pressed in on him until he could do no more than curl himself into a dark, desperate ball.

Suddenly with a final, snarling hiss it was gone.

Issy waited. He was unsure of what would happen next, and fear made him hesitate. Maybe Bedford could have told him what this was all about.

Bedford? There it was again, that name which implied a connection he could not put into its proper place. Bedford?

Welcome home, my Lord. A voice interrupted his thoughts.

Issy uncurled himself very delicately. The voice had startled him, and he was still afraid. But he knew he could not stay where he was indefinitely. There was a past to be rediscovered.

As he opened his mind's eye, what he saw staggered him. A short distance away stood a short bipedal creature with its sensory pad extended in an obvious gesture of welcome.

For whom? Had he been expected? The questions seemed to stretch as far as the flat, limitless plain on which they stood. Issy looked around and saw that the dusty, yellow ground had no structures, no hills, no vegetation, nothing to break its endless monotony. *What an odd place to call home*, he thought as he turned back to the creature.

Patience, my Lord. All will be explained in time. Then this will not seem so odd to you. Welcome home.

A telepath? Issy's mental question was quickly followed by another. *Is it Bedford?* An avalanche of memories roared through his consciousness. It was not Bedford. Bedford was of another time and place, one which came much later than this. Bedford belonged to a place . . .

Older, deeper memories fell on Issy and soothed him like a gentle rain that released his natural soul from drought-parched soil. He held up his mind like an empty cup and let himself be filled. The memories soaked through him, leaching out the centuries of impurities which blocked his self-understanding. With a quiet, almost gentle suddenness Issy knew who he was.

I am Thysorn.

The sphod who had greeted him said, *Yes.*

I am Thysorn returned from exile. Tell me the history as you have been instructed so that my report to the Council can be put into proper perspective.

As you command, my Lord. The sphod sank into the dusty plain, pulling in its extremities as it vibrated with a soft hum. Moments later Issy/Thysorn sensed a process of change in the air around him.

Behold the history, exile, the sphod said.

As Issy/Thysorn watched, the yellow, talcum-like dust billowed up in a rolling cloud that left the ground scoured clean behind it. A panorama teeming with life sprang up in its place.

Issy/Thysorn no longer questioned what he saw, no longer felt lost. Past had become present, and present had become past. He turned slowly and drank it all in. For as far as he could see and as far as he could feel he was surrounded by a thriving, dynamic civilization: His civilization.

From horizon to horizon *his* people moved about their great business. *His* people worked their wonders in the universe and on the universe. *His* people held up the light of understanding for him, and allowed him to bathe contentedly in the luxuriant glow of his past.

"What do you mean, he's gone?" Kalissae snapped at the medtech.

The man refused to be cowed by her anger. "He was sent to Tigris in his ship, Manager."

Hmph, Kalissae thought, *sent* indeed. Given the mood the Syndic was in when they talked last, he was not about to be *sent* anywhere by anyone. "By whose orders?"

"Sr. Malvin's. He said the Syndic was to be moved off-mine as soon as possible because of—"

"Moved off?" Had Bedford had a relapse? Or worse?

The medtech straightened his shoulders and continued. "Because of his ill health and the possible dangers here," he said with the conviction of a man who knows how to follow orders.

Kalissae looked past him to the empty treatment foil. A faint sense of apprehension and concern moved quickly through her thoughts. She turned from the medtech without a word and slapped the door button. As soon as the iris flared open she strode out of the hospital cubicle with her shoulders squared back and anger in her eyes. Nicholas Malvin had some questions to answer for her.

She walked straight to Malvin's suite and opened his door without hesitation or permission. He looked up with a startled expression on his face as she planted herself in the center of the room. "Why and how was the Syndic sent off-mine?"

Malvin's expression shifted from surprise to resignation. There was a tiredness in his eyes and a heaviness in his posture that he could not totally shake off. But as he rose from his foil, his anger at Kalissae's blunt intrusion helped him stand straighter. "Syndic Odigal was sent off-mine because he was totally incapable of performing any function here. He left on his back. Now what do you mean bursting in here like this?"

She ignored his question to ask her own. "Was he unconscious?"

"Yes, but—"

"Before or after he came to see you?" Underneath her concern for Bedford Odigal she felt a renewed sense of

authority. Kalissae liked that. It partially made up for the
fact that she had let Malvin come in so easily and take over
her mine.

"Just a moment, Manager. I want to know why you
think you can—"

"Syndic Odigal was not unconscious when I saw him."
She sensed a weakness in Malviń and pressed her point
home. "He was coming to see you. Therefore, he either
had a relapse or . . ." She let her sentence trail off.

"Or what? He was carried to his ship on a stretcher,
unconscious, totally incapacitated. So what. His condition
was marginal at best. You knew that." Malvin relaxed a
little and tried not to think about how hollow his words
probably sounded. Kalissae's concern for the Free Syndic
only increased his sense of helplessness.

"Who piloted his ship?"

"Chief Stancell. He was the only one qualified to operate that old tub."

And knowledgeable enough about mine operations to
know when you are exceeding your authority, she added to
herself. "Who went with them?"

"No one. Look, Manager—"

"No, you look, sir. The last time I saw Syndic Odigal he
was fine. Now you tell me he had to be carried onto his
ship and taken to Tigris because of his health. But you
didn't send anyone to take care of him. I don't understand
that. I don't understand that at all."

"It's not your job to understand, Manager." His ability
to cope with the situation on Euphrates was rapidly slipping away and Malvin knew it. He didn't understand what
had happened to the Syndic either. He didn't understand
any of it. But if he was going to sort it out, he had to get
this useless woman away from him. "Why do you care so
much about the Syndic anyway? Do you *need* him for
something?"

The sneering barb in his question had a sexual implica-
tion which shocked her. Kalissae wanted to strike him. But
in that instant of disgust she realized that despite her

self-denial, her concern for Bedford ran much deeper than she had acknowledged. A faint blue blush spread into her cheeks.

"Yes," she finally said with double conviction, "I need him to finish his investigation. Or don't you care anymore about what happened down on level eighty-seven?"

"The investigation will have to wait. Will there be anything else?"

His tone was all wrong, but the subtle waves of thoughts about Bedford kept her from paying close enough attention. Yet she was still detached enough to realize that something essential was missing from Malvin's reaction. "Where is Sr. Rosenthal?" she asked suddenly.

Malvin tensed, and Kalissae put another piece of the puzzle together. When he answered her, his voice was filled with a heavy mix of resignation and defensive sarcasm.

"Sr. Rosenthal is up at the surface reception locks."

"Why?"

"Because, my dear Manager," he said with a weariness he had tried to hold back, "he has to welcome Helical's illustrious Security Guard to your precious Euphrates."

For a long instant Kalissae held her breath as though her body was trying to freeze time and negate what Malvin had said. Then the air seeped out of her lungs. If the Security Guard had entered the mine, she had totally lost control. It was no longer her mine to run, or Malvin's— it was theirs. And there was no one to whom she could appeal or turn for help. "The Security Guard," she said quietly. "Well, Director, that doesn't leave us much to talk about, does it?"

Malvin looked relieved. "No, it doesn't."

"I suppose I should prepare to evacuate." Behind the flatness of her voice she heard the creeping sound of despair.

"That would probably be a good idea."

"Shall I report to you when I am ready to leave?" Kalissae was not going to give up that easily, but he didn't have to know that.

"Please report to Sr. Rosenthal," Malvin said barely covering the anger in his voice. "He is directing this part of the operation."

The bitterness in his words startled her. It also told her that Malvin was no longer in charge. She did not know if he had voluntarily turned over the reins of power, or if Rosenthal had taken them from him. It did not matter. The structure of authority on Euphrates had shifted drastically.

"Better leave now, Manager," Malvin said after staring at her for what seemed like an endless minute.

"Certainly." Suddenly she felt sorry for him. "I apologize for barging in on you . . ." Her voice trailed off. She did not know what else to say.

"No matter, Manager. No matter." He turned away from her.

Kalissae left the suite almost reluctantly. For a long moment after the door closed behind her she stood in the corridor unsure of what to do or where to go. What would Syndic Odigal do now, she wondered? Or Issy?

Issy? It seemed odd to think of the symbiont now. That brought a slight smile to her face. Free Syndic Odigal and his unreliable friend had certainly affected her life in strange ways. But Bedford was gone. So was Issy. Even Stancell, the one person who understood the situation on Euphrates as well as she did, was thousands of kilometers away unaware of the recent turn of events.

As she started toward her quarters the full weight of her conversation pressed down on her. The Helical Security Guard was arriving to take responsibility for her mine. What would she do now? Where would her future lie?

And what would Theeran say if she could see her half-sister now?

EIGHT

Bedford stared for a full five minutes at the display of ancient Terran artifacts which hung on the bulkhead of his cabin aboard the *Lady Victoria*. It took him that long to clear his head enough so that he could recognize what he was looking at.

Dull pain pounded his temples. When he tried to move, every muscle in his body protested. He could not put two sequential thoughts together without feeling lightheaded.

–Issy?–

Silence. The lack of response numbed him even further. Yet the question still echoed in the back of his mind. –Issy?– he asked again subvocally. And again. And again, until he remembered the moment of their separation. –Why, Issy? Why?–

Distraction, he thought, I need distraction. He tried to pull himself out of the depths of despair by focusing on one of the artifacts in his collection. It was his favorite, and he had paid a premium price for the object even though no one had been able to tell him exactly what it was used for.

The whole device was thirty-six centimeters long. Most of its length was made up of two pieces of heavy, chrome-plated wire twisted around each other and around five, evenly spaced fins with sharp, serrated edges. At one end was a gold-plated handle that looked like some form of crude pistol grip. But it was too small to be used comfortably by an adult hand. The handle was deeply engraved with a beautiful floral pattern that depicted long extinct plants. Yet strangely, in the center of this design and completely encircling the base of the handle was an uninspired repetition of the letters *NM*. In smaller letters on the pommel of the grip were three words. The first two were meaningless. The last one was, "Stick."

Bedford took a perverse pleasure in the Stick. No one could find any meaning for the two unknown words, nor could they give him any explanation of the Stick's probable use. For Bedford, owning the Stick was like owning a key which would open the lock to some imaginary door. Not knowing what his Stick really was made it very special to him because he could make it anything he wanted it to be.

As he flexed his sore muscles with brief isometric exercises he held his gaze on the Stick. He was finally coming around. He realized that he would have to get up soon, take something for his headache, and attend to the demands of his ship. But for the moment he was content to admire, flex, and let the hum of *Lady*'s engines carry him into a reasonably civilized state of mind.

"Engines?" Bedford sat straight up.

Pain from the sudden movement darkened his vision. With stoic patience he waited for the darkness to clear. "If the engines are running, then we are under way. And if we are under way, who is running the ship?" It helped to hear the sound of his own voice.

He wanted to jump up and run to the bridge, but he knew any rapid movement was going to cause him problems. Still, he had to find out who was handling *Lady*'s controls, and why.

The last thing he remembered was . . . He took a deep breath and blew it out slowly. The last thing he remembered was . . . was getting ready to go see Malvin. Yes, that was it. Or was it? Was there something else there?

As gently as he could, Bedford eased himself off the bunk and walked over to the small, cracked, Fetbour tub which served as his gravity washbasin. He stared at the runes which covered the inside of the tub and wished that it really could work the curative magic the Fetbourvolk claimed it could. But as he stared at the runes, he only felt worse. The dull thumping in his head continued its monotonous beat. His stomach started turning slowly upward and threatened him with nausea at any moment. Maybe the curative powers only worked if one was as small as the Fetbourvolk and could totally immerse oneself in the tub. All it did for Bedford was hold a few liters of cold water which he apathetically splashed on his face.

The splashing motion hurt his arms and the water hurt his face. "Guess I'll have to give in and trust modern medicine," he said sourly. He reached into a small, recessed cabinet beside the tub and pulled out a clear tube of a red, jellylike substance. After taking several deep breaths, he held the last one, squeezed a dab of the red gel onto his fingertips, and quickly rubbed it into his temples.

When he finally released his breath and sucked in a lungful of air, the stench from the gel almost triggered the nausea he was fighting. But as fast as the odor dissipated, the gel eased the throbbing in his temples and the soreness in his muscles. In less than ninety seconds all but the last hints of his pain had been masked.

"Thank the FedMeds I don't have to use that very often," he said quietly. Meticulously he emptied the water from the Fetbour tub into the recycling drain, then clipped the tub back into its holder. An idle string of memories went with those motions, memories linked to Issy.

Not now, he thought. Now it's time to see who is on the bridge. He started to step out of his cabin, then hesitated. A weapon? He didn't even carry a knife. Yet at this moment a weapon might be a nice thing to have. Looking quickly around his cabin, his eyes settled on the artifact display. A small grin turned the corners of his mouth. "This ought to keep our pilot friendly," he whispered as he unlatched the chrome and gold Stick from the display. If not friendly, at least it will keep him guessing . . . I hope, he thought.

Bedford walked quietly through *Lady Victoria*'s humming companionway, keeping a sharp lookout for any other uninvited crew members who might be aboard. Just before he reached the final hatch to the bridge, he decided to backtrack and enter *Lady*'s control center through the service tunnel. So far he had seen no one, but he did not want to take any chances.

The service tunnel led directly to the command module and was safer than the main corridor. Entering there would put him in a good position to discourage any violence on the part of the person or persons who were operating his ship.

He entered the tunnel amidship and crawled through the tangle of cables, feeling like an intruder. He didn't like having to skulk about on his own vessel. Whoever was at the controls had violated more than his property right. They had also somehow dirtied his relationship with *Lady Victoria*. That angered him as much as anything else.

Just before he reached the command module's inspection plate, *Lady* lurched sharply. Good, he thought, a course change shift. Whoever is in there should be standing by the warpulsar's SIC with his back to me.

Slowly and silently he released the six latches which held the inspection plate against the bulkhead. As soon as all six were free, he slid the square piece of plasteel on the edge of one of its soft seals to one side of the opening. He could just see a man standing with his back to the service tunnel.

Bedford eased himself through the opening and crawled toward the figure. He held the Stick up and away from the floor to keep it from making any noise. He felt a little foolish with it in his hand, but there was no way to put it down, and with its serrated fins he couldn't put it into his jumpsuit without cutting the fabric, himself, or both. He would just have to make the best of his decision to bring it.

When he came within a meter of the pilot, he held his breath and stood up quickly and as quietly as he could. Why the man hadn't heard him Bedford didn't know. But it was too late for the pilot now.

In one long step Bedford threw one arm around the pilot's neck and jammed the end of the Stick into his ear. "Hold still or I will—"

"Syndic Odigal! It's me, Stancell," the Chief said as he went limp in Bedford's grasp and offered no resistance to the attack.

Bedford was surprised, but still wary. Just because it was Stancell didn't mean anything. With a quick step into the Chief and a jerk of his arm he flung Stancell around and away from him.

Stancell's eyes were wide with fear when they finally met Bedford's. "Please, sir, take it easy with that thing." He rubbed his sore ear as his gaze shifted to the Stick which Bedford held leveled steadily at his stomach. "Please, I'll do anything you say."

"What are you doing here?"

Stancell's knees buckled slightly, and he started to sit down, but caught himself and looked at Bedford for permission.

"Sit," Bedford said with a flick of his Stick.

The Chief sat heavily in the warpulsar chair and tried to regain his composure. The weapon that the Syndic was pointing at him looked as lethal as it did foreign. He couldn't tell what it was, but he certainly didn't want a demonstration of how it worked. What he wanted was to calm the pounding in his chest.

"Last chance, Chief," Bedford said impatiently. "Now what are you doing here?"

Stancell found his voice as Bedford raised the muzzle of

his weapon. "I'm ferrying you to Tigris under Sr. Malvin's orders."

"How did I get here?"

"You were brought aboard unconscious. They said you would be all right, but that it was best for you to be transferred to Tigris with the other nonessential personnel."

"They?"

"Sr. Rosenthal and the two security men who carried you aboard."

Suddenly a glimpse of memory flashed before Bedford's inner eye. It was something that had happened just before he passed out. The image was blurred, and he couldn't quite make it out, but he was almost positive that he had been gassed. All the symptoms he had felt when he came to in his cabin pointed to some form of nerve gas. But why? It didn't make sense unless someone was trying to hide something on Euphrates, something they didn't want him to know.

He stared at the Chief and wondered if the man was just doing his job, or—"Tell you what, Chief," he said, interrupting his own thought, "let's get *Lady Victoria* headed back to Euphrates. Tigris can do without an unscheduled visit from a Free Syndic."

Stancell hesitated for a moment and frowned. "I'm sorry, sir, but I can't do that."

"Don't make it hard on yourself, Chief. I can do it myself."

"Yes, sir, I know you can. But it would be my duty to try to stop you. My orders were clear: get *you* to Tigris as soon as possible." Stancell sat up straighter when he said that. He was aware of the conflict between Bedford's authority and Rosenthal's, but he had been a company man too long to resist company orders.

"I could use force to restrain you," Bedford said as he raised the Stick and leveled it at Stancell's chest. It was a stupid bluff, but it was all he had at the moment. "But I don't think force will be necessary . . . do you, Chief?"

It was hard for Stancell to take his eyes off the weapon. He glanced up to the Syndic's eyes, saw no hesitation there, then felt his gaze drawn back to the strange device that might send him into oblivion. Or could it? Somehow it looked familiar. "What is that thing? I don't think I've ever seen anything like it before."

Bedford put as much conviction into his voice as he could. "That's because most people who see this weapon from your viewpoint don't live to tell about it." As he spoke he saw Stancell tense in the chair. Maybe I'm relying too heavily on this bluff, he thought.

"Relax, Chief, and listen to reason. And if reason won't convince you, then maybe my authority as a Free Syndic will. I have to get back to Euphrates. I don't know what the hell is going on there, but it should be pretty obvious to you that—"

A sharp, hollow boom filled the command module.

Lady Victoria shuddered.

The sudden shock threw Bedford against the bulkhead. Stancell was popped out of the chair and thrown to the deck. "Sounded like a tri-p hit," Stancell said as he pushed himself up to his hands and knees. "But who?"

"And why?" Bedford asked. He braced himself against the main support joist and looked down at Stancell. "Are you with me, Chief? Someone's going to kill us both if you're not."

"You bet your last FedCredit I am. What do you want me to do?" He stood up carefully and brushed at his jumpsuit.

"How much do you know about Yendos?"

"Enough to pilot one. But this . . . it's been a long time. I didn't realize how long—"

"Too long," Bedford interrupted as he stepped over to the SIC. "You turned off the collision detection alarm." He flicked it on and watched the SIC come to life. A bright pinpoint of red light moved away from the *Lady*'s position in what was clearly an elliptical path. After a quick check

of the distance scale Bedford said, "Looks like our adver
sary is about four hundred kilometers away and abou
ready to begin turning back on us."

"What do we do?" Stancell asked.

"First you get over to the commgear and try to find ou
who they are."

"Right." Stancell sat in front of the main communica
tions panel and set the transceiver for the Standard open
band channels. Once the needles and dials matched hi
chosen settings, he snatched the microphone from it
cradle and said, "This is the Free Syndic vessel *Lady
Victoria*. Repeat. This is the Free Syndic vessel *Lady
Victoria*. Identify yourself immediately and break off a
offensive action against this ship."

He did not really expect a reply and looked at Bedfor
with a cocked eyebrow. They were both startled when th
overhead speaker blared at them.

"This is the Helical Security cruiser *Deeden*. Prepare t
be boarded or face destruction."

Bedford narrowed his eyes. A grim smile tightened hi
lips. What kind of galactic nonsense was this? Fatal nonsense
he thought in answer to his own question. "Think we ca
trust them, Chief?"

"Not with my life."

"Not mine either. Let's prepare for action and sho
them how tough these old Yendo trawlers can be." In th
brief minutes since the explosion Bedford and Stancell ha
been joined together like millions of men before them by
common threat to their lives. Whatever questions Bedfor
had about Stancell's motives were pushed aside by th
needs of the moment.

"Shall I answer them?"

"Of course, Chief. Tell the lousy Fed-tit suckers to com
and get us."

It was common knowledge that security forces for th
big corporations like Helical were supported in part b
secret funding from the Federation. But Stancell ha
never heard anyone in power say it aloud.

With a grin he turned back to the mike. "Okay, *Deeden*. If you can get your mouths away from the Fed-tit long enough to do something on your own, come and get us." He flipped the mike off and turned to Bedford. "Now," he said, the grin still on his face, "what kind of weapons do we have?"

"None." Bedford watched Stancell's grin turn into a frown as he slumped in his chair. "But," he added with a smile, "we do have some nonstandard modifications to the Yendo's normal complement of equipment."

Stancell brightened a little. "Well, I hope they work, because after the way I invited the *Deeden* to come and get us, we don't have much time." His voice was edged with nervousness. "So what do we do?"

–Yeah, Issy, what do we do?– There was no answer, but Bedford had a good idea of what Issy would have suggested. Many of the major modifications had been his symbiont's idea. "First we turn on the mag-tows."

"Pardon?" Stancell looked puzzled.

"The mag-tows, Chief. The mag-tows. I thought you knew something about Yendos."

"I do. Mag-tows are used for towing barges. How are they going to help us now?"

"Better than any signal scrambler, Chief, if you have a set like *Lady*'s."

"You're going to use them to confuse *Deeden*'s sensors? But they'll only protect half the ship. Even if we keep our stern to them they'll pick up enough image to blast us."

"Not if we turn on the bow and stern tows at once."

Stancell's puzzled look deepened. "Excuse my rusty brain, Syndic," he said as he watched Bedford turn on the mag-tow monitors, "but as I recall you can only have one of the tows on at a time. If both were on, we'd be as blind as the security cruiser trying to pinpoint us."

"Normally that's right, Chief. In fact, it's still right. But as I told you, there have been modifications." Bedford activated the master control, and the mag-tows beeped to life. "See?"

With a low whistle Stancell shook his head. "That's pretty slick." The red lights which indicated when a tow was on were flickering back and forth. Stancell didn't know how short the pause was between each on-off cycle, but he knew enough about ship sensors to realize that for anyone trying to locate them both tows might as well be on simultaneously. He wondered what his old fleet commander would have thought about this setup. Any ship scanning the *Lady* would probably only pick up a series of pulsating dots. "How do we navigate?"

"During the switching pause. It's an accurized warpulsar, the kind used in heavy traffic areas. The combination ought to drive the *Deeden*'s navigation officer crazy."

"I'll bet," Stancell said as he stared in amazement at the flickering lights. He had served on five different kinds of ships during his nine years in the fleet, but he had never seen anything like this.

"Commander Byosin, we have a problem with target acquisition," T.A.C. Operator Jehnks said as he pointed to the large, rectangular screen. A series of pale yellow dots pulsed just to the left of center on the display.

Commander Hygeld Byosin turned from the forward optical viewer and stared at the target acquisition screen. "Abort!" he commanded as soon as he saw the multiple dots. "All ahead slow. Secure from attack and come about to heading . . ." He looked closely at the screen. "Heading four-four-niner: delta seven-six-one-five."

Deeden's bridge crew reacted swiftly to the orders. Within seconds the ship had executed a snap-maneuver and slowed to the proper speed and heading.

"Damn. What is that, Jehnks?" Byosin asked as he moved to stand closer to the screen. No matter how much he peered at the strange lights they made no sense to him.

"I don't know, sir. Just as we started to match the target triad, it started to wobble all over the screen. The grid points indicate an instantaneous movement over two de-

THE SEREN CENACLES 101

grees of arc. At this distance . . . well, sir, it's impossible."

Byosin squinted at the screen. What kind of jamming equipment could the Syndic have on that old tub? He didn't care. If he had known about this possibility, he would have approached the mission much differently. Now they would have to change the tactics to meet the situation. That didn't matter either. Situational tactics were Byosin's specialty.

"Prepare for an optical approach," he ordered. "Reroute the weapons status to the main screen and await my order to close." There was no way he would let the *Lady Victoria* get away from him. It would be like the old days with the fleet before he moved up to all the fancy automatic fire-control equipment. He had been known as the best optical weapons man in the business. Now he would have a rare chance to prove that he still was.

"Worked like a Votis Goat," Stancell said as he watched the *Deeden* veer off its attack course. "Now I wonder what the bastards will do?"

"I hope they make another attack run," Bedford said with a knowing smile.

"What happens then?" Stancell's opinion of the Syndic had shifted rapidly up the positive scale. He had no idea what Bedford planned to do next, but after what he had seen so far, he had confidence that they had more than an even chance of getting out of this encounter in reasonable condition.

"Thought you'd never ask," Bedford said as he pulled a small key from his pocket. "Do you remember from your training the one thing that made Yendos such superb exploration vessels?"

"Well," Stancell said with a puzzled look, "they had a six-to-one power-to-weight-hauled ratio, and they could land just about anywhere."

"Right. And *how* could they land anywhere?"

A look of understanding crossed the Chief's face. "The

rough-landing blasters," he said. Stancell would never forget the first time he had seen them work. Four pairs of saturated, ultra-high-density, photon lasers coupled with a broad-beam microwave pulse maser had vaporized a granite outcropping seventy meters high in less than a minute. Stancell had been a nineteen-year-old apprentice engineer, and he had been more than impressed. He had been awed.

"I suppose I shouldn't ask, but what about their five-hundred-meter range limitation? Or the fact that they won't operate at speeds over point-two-five Mach?"

"Don't worry about the range limitation. If my guess is correct, *Deeden*'s commander will take care of that for us. As for the speed problem, this," he said, holding up the key, "will give us an override on that."

Bedford inserted the key into a black box on the control console, twisted it, and lifted off the box to reveal a large plunger switch. "If you would kindly push that switch, Chief, we will be almost ready to meet our antagonists."

Stancell leaned forward and pushed the switch. He found it remarkable that the Syndic had discovered a way to circumvent the maze of safeguards designed into the blasters. Only a genius could have done it, he thought as he returned his gaze to Bedford. "Okay, now that we have done that, we'd better hope the *Deeden*'s commander follows the plan, whatever it is."

"We'll know pretty soon. Look at that, Chief." Bedford pointed to the enhanced image on the main screen.

Stancell stared at the tiny light he knew was the *Deeden*. It was slowly growing bigger and brighter, closing the gap between itself and the *Lady Victoria*. "I hope you are right about this, Syndic Odigal. Otherwise we may end up as so much space dust."

"Tri-p carillon activated," *Deeden*'s weapons officer called out in a voice that made everyone on the bridge tense a little.

Good tactics so far, Commander Byosin thought as he watched the *Lady Victoria* grow slightly larger on his optical view screen, but noninstrument attack runs can be tricky right up until the fire sequence. He checked the small speaker plugged into his ear, then ran a standard test pattern to ensure that the tones of the carillon could be clearly heard. Since he was manually operating the fire-control system, clear tones were essential. He would have to anticipate when to strike a new note on the carillon's keyboard and bring the tri-p cannons up one notch in readiness.

His timing had to be perfect. One note too soon and he would fire before his target was fully in range. One note too late and he would fire past the target altogether. For a brief instant he wished he had the electronic controls backing him up. But as quickly as the uncertainty came, it passed. *The best optical weapons man in the business.* The thought gave him the reinforcement he needed.

Around the bridge crew members cast surreptitious glances of uncertainty to one another. Even those who didn't like Commander Byosin usually respected his judgment. But this decision to attack with manual fire-control made almost all of them wonder if he was making the right choice.

"All hands prepare to engage," Byosin said as he tapped a white key. The carillon's tone went up an eighth of an octave.

—Sorry you had to miss all this fun, Issy,— Bedford said subvocally. There was a brief, emotional catch in his heartbeat when he said it, but he quickly calmed himself. This was no time to worry about Issy. The mystery behind that pain would have to wait. He unlatched the main thrust levers and said, "Prepare to execute a ninety-degree roll with a forty-five degree pitch at my mark, Chief."

Stancell tightened the clasp on the webbed harness

which held him firmly in front of the console. He didn't want to be thrown back by a sudden maneuver when it came time to fire the landing blasters. "Yes, sir," he said. He wanted to take a look at the main screen and see how close the *Deeden* had come, but he knew he didn't dare.

"Ready..." Bedford said, "and, MARK!"

Lady Victoria shuddered slightly as she made the half snap-roll. The old trawler was not built for quick battle movements, but the turn was fast enough to make Bedford smile.

"When we take the hit, let them have it, Chief." There was an excitement in his voice that surprised them both.

The shrill sound of the carillon's final readiness tone vibrated in Byosin's ear. The commitment sequence was complete, and there was no turning back now.

Suddenly he couldn't believe his luck. The *Lady Victoria* had turned in an attempt to escape and had exposed its entire underside to his guns. Fools, he thought.

Byosin ignored the closing-distance readout and relied entirely on his own skill and depth perception to tell him when he was close enough to fire the one shot which would be fatal.

Then he sensed it. Tendons tightened. In an instant he mashed down the carillon's one red key. "Firing all tubes!" he screamed excitedly.

Deeden lurched heavily from the recoil of the tri-p cannons. It took six thousandths of a second before her control mechanisms recovered, and she was able to execute the first step in the process that would turn her away from the *Lady Victoria*.

Six thousandths of a second. The last tones of the carillon were still ringing in Commander Byosin's ear. But a harsh, crackling noise filled the *Deeden*. Byosin flinched.

*   *   *

The roar of the landing blasters rattled every loose thing aboard *Lady*.

Stancell felt like he was firing an automatic shoulder weapon. He had placed his fingertips gently on the blasters' actuator button and had slowly let his breath out. Then the tri-p hit the mag-tow field. The shock had knocked the rest of the wind from his lungs and forced his fingers down on the actuator.

When he recovered from the double shock he turned and stared at the view screen. Out of the corner of his eye he realized that Bedford stared with him. *Deeden* was disintegrating before their eyes. *Lady*'s landing blasters had done their work.

Small chunks of metal and a luminous cloud of radioactive gas were all that was left of *Deeden*. It was a horrible sight, yet neither of them could take their eyes away from the screen until the last remnants of their attacker had been left behind in the void.

"Well," Bedford said finally, "let's go back and see how much damage we sustained." Neither spoke as they made their way to *Lady*'s stern.

"It's not as bad as it could have been," Bedford said as he threw a twisted piece of heat-scarred metal to the deck. *Lady* had sustained only minor damage because the tri-p blast had struck at an acute angle, and most of the force had glanced off her heavily plated underbelly. The shock inside the ship had caused most of the damage. "At least the hull wasn't breached," he said quietly. Even minor damage to *Lady Victoria* brought with it a feeling that he himself had somehow been hurt.

"Sir?" Stancell interrupted after a quick survey of the stern bulkheads.

"What is it, Chief?" He was surprised how easily his initial feelings about Stancell had been pushed aside by the camaraderie of battle. He smiled to himself. Those positive feelings would have to be tested, but he was already beginning to think of Stancell as an ally.

"Well, it looks to me like we need to seal that split in the seam joints over there and reinforce both of those long suspension ribs, otherwise—"

"You're right, Chief. I'll get the tools we'll need. You get this debris out of the way. Then check those flat lockers over there and see if you can find some quick-closure strips in sizes we can use. If we—"

Ding-ding-ding! Ding-ding-ding!

"What the—"

"Incoming distress signal," Bedford said, wondering what they were in for next. "Look, you get started here. I'll go see what that signal's all about."

"Right. But watch out for those Helical Security creeps. This could be some kind of a trick."

"If it is, I'll give you a long, steady buzz back here and you come running. Okay?"

"Okay."

As Stancell worked to clear away the debris, he thought about what had happened. A small shudder made him pause. Saint Gunson only knew how many people had died aboard *Deeden*. And for what reason? It didn't make any sense. The answer would have to wait, he decided. By the time Bedford returned Stancell was laying out the quick-closure strips he thought they could use.

"Better make it quick, Chief," Bedford said as he handed him the thermal-rivet gun. "That distress message was from Tigris. Looks like we'll be going there after all."

"What's their problem?" Stancell looked worried, but he did not stop working.

"Don't know. . . . This one here?" Bedford held up the first strip against the seam joint as Stancell tested the rivet gun. "It was an automatic signal. I couldn't get them to respond to my confirmation call."

Stancell wiped the sweat from his face and lined up the gun with the first hot-hole on the closure strip. "What about Euphrates?" The gun hissed loudly.

"They'll have to wait. We may be the closest ship which can render aid . . . by the short hairs on our chest, I might add."

The thermal-rivet gun hissed again and again before Stancell said anything else. "I have friends on Tigris," he said as they changed positions and he began to rivet the other side of the strip.

"I know, Chief. So the sooner we get this finished, the sooner we can get to Tigris and find out what's wrong."

For the next hour they worked at a steady pace, and their conversation stayed centered on the repairs. Only after they had sealed both sides of the seam joint and reinforced the cracked ribs did either of them pause for rest. Then it was only for a moment to wipe the sweat from their faces and sip some water.

"There's a question I'd like to ask before we leave for Tigris, Syndic Odigal."

"What's that?"

"Well, I'd really like to know what that strange weapon was that you used on me. It looked familiar, but—"

"It's my Stick. Or to be more precise, my Texas Swizzle Stick."

"What?"

"Texas Swizzle Stick. That's what it says on the handle. And don't ask me what it means, Chief, because I don't know. As for it looking familiar, you probably saw it hanging on the bulkhead of my cabin."

Stancell shook his head with a wry grin. "You mean it wasn't a weapon?"

"I mean I don't know." Bedford started loading the debris into a small, wheeled bin. "It sure worked as a weapon, didn't it?" He smiled in a conspiratorial way.

"Scared the hell out of me. But what does Texas Swizzle Stick mean? You said you didn't know, but—"

Bedford laughed. "Believe me, Chief, I wish someone could tell me. It might translate to mean, deadly weapon. It might not. That's half the fun of it."

Stancell had a hard time believing Texas Swizzle Stick

meant anything serious. But he had found out one thing, anyway. The Syndic must trust him more now to have told him that he didn't know if the thing was a weapon or not. That made him feel good. But his concern about what might be happening on Tigris quickly pushed that good feeling out of the way.

NINE

Arter Rosenthal strode down the central corridor of the administrative level on Euphrates followed closely by a fully armed Helical Security Team.

A bit thrusty, Kalissae thought as she approached them from the opposite direction. When her eyes met Rosenthal's, he halted his men with a hand signal and waited for her to come to him. The arrogance of that act further inflamed her anger.

"Why are these people here?" she asked as she stepped up to him. She was not about to mince words with Malvin's private assistant. She outranked him, and besides, she was tired of all the subterfuge. Kalissae had decided it was time to reestablish her authority on her home ground. Whatever resignation she had felt with Malvin had boiled away in the heat of her anger.

"We must insure adequate containment of . . . this mine, MZ Boristh-Major." Rosenthal's words were filled with lightly veiled arrogance.

"We, we, we!" Kalissae exploded. "That's all I've heard since you and Malvin arrived! This is my mine. Period. I cannot make it any more simple for you. And Euphrates is quite secure, thank you. So you can just turn these people around immediately." Her face twisted into a grimace of determination which displayed her sharp canines.

Neither the aggressive exhibit of her teeth nor her verbal outburst had any apparent effect on Rosenthal. He simply smiled.

"I am sorry," he said in a tone one might use with a small child, "but I cannot do that. I have other instructions."

Kalissae refused to move. She braced her legs and glared at Rosenthal, trying to think of some way to stop this violation of her domain. If he wanted to go any further, Rosenthal would have to physically push her out of the way. He wouldn't dare, she thought.

"I'm glad I caught both of you together."

Malvin's urgent tone shifted Kalissae's attention. She turned sideways so she could see him and still not have her back to Rosenthal.

"We've just received a distress signal from Tigris," Malvin continued. "It didn't say what the problem was, but it's a priority message and I want an emergency rescue team sent over there as soon as possible." He paused to gulp some air, then asked Kalissae, "Can you get a team off right away?"

"Of course. I'll order out the *Spandau* tug and they can leave within the hour." So now Malvin needs my help, she thought, then added, "The nearest com-link is just down—"

"Just one moment, Manager," Rosenthal said quietly. He put his arm out to stop her. She shoved it away, but stayed where she was. After a brief, cold glance at her, he turned to Malvin. "I'm afraid that time has run out on this little . . . uh, shall we say, power game?"

Kalissae looked at Malvin, then back to Rosenthal. "What's that supposed to mean?" she asked. "If Tigris needs help, the last thing we need to be doing is—"

"That's quite enough, Manager," Rosenthal said without taking his eyes off Malvin. "The Tigris situation will be taken care of in due course. By me. Now, unfortunately, it is time for me to do something I had hoped wouldn't be necessary."

"Listen here, Arter—"

"Be quiet, Nicholas!"

Rosenthal's voice carried a viciousness Kalissae hadn't heard before. The man's crazy, she thought as he turned his gaze toward her.

"MZ Boristh-Major, there is something you should see before I . . . well, see for yourself." Rosenthal unzipped a small pocket flap on the left breast of his tunic. When he pulled the flap up it revealed a six-centimeter square of bare flesh on which there was a red and blue circular tattoo.

Kalissae took a half step forward and leaned toward Rosenthal with morbid fascination. She took a hard look at the tattoo, then stood upright with a shocked expression on her face.

It was a symbol legendary in the galaxy, a symbol which millions of mothers had used to put fear in the hearts of their misbehaving children, the symbol of the QuietSuns.

But they're all dead, Kalissae thought as she glanced at the tattoo again. She couldn't tell if it was an original or a genetic mutation. "I, uh . . ." she said with a puzzled look.

"I know. You thought we had all disappeared with the Old Empire. So naive, MZ Boristh-Major. *All* governments have a need for people like us who can accomplish certain tasks out of the public eye." Rosenthal smiled as he spoke, then set his jaw in a way that made his face look like a solid block of cold, pockmarked flesh. "As we served the Empire, so do we serve the Federation." His smile returned.

Kalissae shivered. The QuietSuns had been accused of countless atrocities committed in the name of political purity, and countless more committed for reasons all their own. She swallowed the thickness in her throat and asked, "Do you expect me to believe that what you are doing here is in some way authorized by the Federation?"

Rosenthal's smile widened. "You have the Pflessian's

excellent ability to get to the point. My compliments to your mother." He signaled the Security team to go around them, then zipped his tunic flap shut. "Yes. I am authorized by the highest officials of the central government, though I doubt they would admit that to anyone."

As the armed team pushed past her, Kalissae felt lost and angry. A QuietSun. What did it mean?

"Now," Rosenthal said after whispering some final instructions to the Security Team leader, "shall we retire to the communications center so I can get on with my work?" He pointed the way to the elevators and added, "Please, after you." The small piezo-electric stun pistol in his hand made any further discussion pointless.

Issy/Thysorn felt as though he had been stationary for eons when the images of his past flickered and finally went out. The flat, yellow plain reappeared. The sphod reassumed its original form. And though the vast emptiness around him had returned, Issy was full.

I understand. There was no need to elaborate. The images had explained it all, including most of the reasons for the events in his recent past. Those that were left unexplained were too new to fit clearly into place.

It should have been easy, now, to submit to the historical tangent that had led him to this place. It should have been simple to combine new facts with old ones and structure his report for the Council. But the pull of something deeply rooted in him, something more powerful than the knowledge of his true identity kept him from doing what was easy and simple.

I must return, he said. *I am no longer Thysorn-the-Seren. I am Issy. I must return to who I am now.*

The sphod sat still, unresponsive to Issy's statements.

Issy shut off the picture of the sphod and concentrated on Bedford. It was hard. The perspective of their relationship had changed. No matter how much either of them might want it to be the same, the bond between them had been irrevocably altered. For the first time since the disconnection, Issy was truly afraid. But the fear was not for himself.

The way back, he thought. *That is the way back*.

A thin sliver of light shot down the shadow of Issy's past and pointed toward the center of his time continuum. He turned away from the sphod, and the yellow plain, and the fresh memories of his ancient history. The future awaited him—his future and Bedford's.

Behind him the sphod cried, *The Council must hear your report. You cannot leave until you have given your findings. The Council must hear . . .*

Issy let the sphod's monotone complaint fade from his concern. He did not care about the Council, or the fact that denying them meant denying a responsibility to his race. He cared only about that single person in the galaxy who meant more to him than anything his rediscovered race could offer. He had to reach that person and warn him about the death trap which lay in wait on Euphrates before it was too late.

Bedford, his mind cried out as he moved off toward an uncertain future.

Kalissae sat in the observer's chair opposite the main view screen and read the telltales which told her that Euphrates was surrounded by Helical Security Guard ships. Rosenthal had been giving instructions for almost thirty minutes, and for most of that time she had listened with fascination and horror. Across the room a guard stood with a stunner slung casually over his shoulder. It looked big enough to control a mob. Every time she looked up the guard had his eyes on her. Malvin stood beside her chair with his back against the bulkhead. His eyes were glazed with the look of a man who had lost everything.

"Affirmative, Commander Lanse," she heard Rosenthal say, "detail Spec-Team Delta to the surface as soon as they are ready and prepare for demolition maneuvers." Rosenthal apparently had no difficulty extending his authority into the heart of Helical's Security Guard. Then she realized how naive her thinking was. That extension of authority had probably taken place long before Rosenthal arrived on Euphrates. She watched him as he gave a few more brief commands, then shut off the transceiver and turned to them.

"Don't look so glum, Nicholas," he said with the same smile he had used in the corridor. "You're still the Director of Helical Mining Operations. And you are going to keep that job . . . but under slightly altered arrangements, of course." He walked toward Malvin and Kalissae. "It won't be like old times, but I'm sure we can find a way to continue working together." When he reached Malvin he patted him on the shoulder.

For a brief instant Kalissae thought she saw a sign of affection in Rosenthal's gesture.

Malvin jerked away from Rosenthal's touch. "Leave me alone, you traitor," he said weakly. It was clear he had taken his assistant's betrayal very hard and very personally.

Rosenthal gave a small shrug of his shoulders and turned to Kalissae. "I really don't know how he got to where he is in Helical. Do you, Manager?" There was no sympathy or affection in his voice or expression now. "It probably wouldn't have worked out anyway. So, he will just have to join you during the last hours of this doomed mining enterprise."

"Why?" Kalissae asked as she shook her head slightly. "Why are you doing this?"

"I really shouldn't have to explain this to a Pflessian," he said after a moment's thought, "especially since your ancestors were among the most violent food-gatherers this galaxy has ever seen. But I suppose you deserve some form of explanation before you die."

Kalissae flinched at his last word. Die, she thought as she glanced quickly at Malvin. He showed no reaction. Suddenly she realized that she was totally alone against this insane man.

"Surely you don't intend to kill us, do you?" she asked with more hope in her voice than she thought proper. Her heart sank as she saw the answer in his face.

"Regrettably, yes," Rosenthal answered flatly. "We can't have any survivors who might be inclined to tell about the mysterious ore pocket you have here on Euphrates, especially a survivor with as much credibility as the mine manager."

He gave her another of those smiles she had learned to hate and continued. "The reasons are simple. My superiors cannot risk getting the Federation's industrial safety people involved here. It could mean the closure of all Isoleucine mining operations until they conducted a full, time-consuming investigation."

"Shavas-Korp," Kalissae said, suddenly remembering how one of Helical's minor competitors had gone out of business after a series of unexplained accidents several years before.

"Exactly," Rosenthal said with a small smile. "To accept such a risk here is more than we can afford. Helical's operations are far too extensive. We can't gamble with the stability of the Federation's social and political structure. The central government must have this protein source." He paused and looked straight at her. "You know what life was like before Isoleucine was discovered, don't you?"

Kalissae knew. Part of her history was the tragedy of those times and what they had done to her race. "All right," she said quietly, "I'll grant you that we don't want to see a return to the pre-Isoleucine days. But then it makes even less sense to destroy a producing mine." And a skilled manager, a hopeful voice inside her added.

"Not at all, Manager. Not at all. Not at all."

There are places for mentally deranged people like this, Kalissae thought as Rosenthal's words echoed in her ears, and Euphrates isn't one of them. Why would the accidents cause an end to the Isoleucine food supply? How would destroying the mine help protect it? By his own admission it wouldn't.

She had to keep him talking if she could. It would buy her time to find a way out of this mess. "Isn't that a bit drastic? I mean, what can be gained by your actions?"

"I haven't the slightest idea, nor do I care." Rosenthal looked amused. "My orders are to help maintain the status-quo, and to that end I am given a free hand." He stepped in close to her and added, "And the fact that you have to die means no more to me than the reasons for which this mine must be destroyed."

His breath blew across Kalissae's face with a heavy, rotten smell that made her stomach turn. "What about the Free Syndic?" she asked, desperately trying to turn his attention away from herself. Maybe he would reconsider if he thought Bedford would ruin his plan.

Rosenthal laughed softly.

"You can't just blow Euphrates to kingdom come and expect him to ignore it. He knows what has been happening here, maybe even more than we do." She certainly hoped so.

"Yes, Syndic Odigal might have caused us problems."

"Might have?" Tension gripped her spine. "What have you done to him?" The cold look in Rosenthal's eyes frightened her.

Rosenthal lowered his eyelids in a perverse gesture that looked like he was thoroughly enjoying the mental anguish he was causing her. "The Syndic is dead," he said finally, "the unfortunate victim of an accident while on his way to Tigris."

"Neutral Red," Kalissae blurted out.

"Neutral Red," Rosenthal affirmed. "You must admit it was a stroke of genius on my part to eliminate the Syndic before I had to take action here."

Kalissae was shocked into silence. Bedford dead? Bedford dead before . . . before she had a chance to give him her respect? The shock doubled. Bedford dead? No! It was unfair. How could he die after stirring all this turmoil inside her?

She thought of his face, his eyes at once stern and sparkling. She remembered the look he had given her when she had failed . . .

It didn't matter. Nothing mattered now. She was about to die at the hands of a madman. Whatever relationship she might have developed with Bedford was lost forever. Dark tears rolled down her pale green cheeks.

BEDFORD! her mind screamed.

Issy twitched as he fought to keep his course. A prick of pain touched his mind. *Bedford?* Yes. No. He was still too far away to be sure, but it pricked him again. *Bedford.* Issy struggled against the growing fatigue which weighted him down, and forced himself to go faster.

"By the gods of Veel, be careful with that thing!" Demolitions Specialist Malotte yelled to the young man who was pushing a large grey box roughly across the floor of level eighty-seven. He knew everyone was spooked by rumors they had heard about this mine, but that was no excuse for carelessness. His team would get the job done quickly *and* professionally, or he would have their hides.

"Sorry, sir," the young man said. "I'll try to be more careful."

"Just relax, son, and we'll do it right. I just don't want to be here when those things go off. The canisters in that box will blow out fifteen cubic kilometers of solid rock." Malotte signaled for someone to help the boy move the box. Once they placed it in the proper position, he let himself relax a little.

"Where's the first one go, Molly?" a large burly man asked as he unlocked the lid on the grey metal container.

"Just a second," Malotte answered. He scanned a few pages in a small book he had taken from his pocket. "We're going to put these two on that wall over there, one on either side of the ore pocket. Get the chain team to drill us two implant channels about a meter up the wall. We can arm the charges while they work."

It took the chain team less than ten minutes to put two four-meter-deep channels into level eighty-seven's most dangerous wall. They did it without incident. As soon as they cleared their equipment away from the implant areas, they informed Malotte that the site was ready.

"All right, Willie, you stay with me," he said to the burly man who had opened the canister case. "The rest of you get the equipment up to level fifty. We'll be right behind you as soon as we've set the charges."

They left as quickly as they could lug the equipment into the elevators. They were glad to leave the arming of the canisters to someone else, and more than happy to leave level eighty-seven. None of them had felt comfortable working there.

When the elevator closed on the last team member, Malotte turned and came back down the tunnel to Willie. Then he rolled his eyes toward the ore pocket. Without speaking they each took a canister from the case and headed for the wall where the freshly drilled channels lay waiting for their deadly implants.

A total proscription against conversation during the setting of charges was standard procedure for all good demolition teams. It was also a widely held superstition that speaking while the charges were being set would invite the wrath of the spirits which protected the teams from the evils of their highly lethal work. But then, demolitions men had lots of superstitions.

Everything went swiftly and quietly until Malotte let out a pain-soaked scream.

When Willie reached Malotte's side a few moments later, Malotte was groaning through clenched teeth and trying desperately to hold his arm steady against his canister. His hand was caught between the large, outer snap-ring on the charge and the detonator spikes of the electronically fired striker mechanism. He had made a mistake and in a moment of panic thrust his hand under the spikes to prevent them from driving home and starting the ten minute delay fuse.

"Dammit, Willie," he said as the tension in his arm caused his whole body to shake, "do something."

Willie snapped out of his daze and quickly realigned the spikes and removed Malotte's pierced and bloody hand without speaking. He would not break the taboo against talking even under these circumstances.

Malotte had and did so again. "Thanks," he said hoarsely. "As soon as I bandage this hand, let's finish this and get the hell out of here."

It took a few minutes to get Malotte's hand bandaged properly, and ten more to finish setting the charges. After checking the site for forgotten equipment, they made their way to the elevator.

On the way up to level fifty, Willie spoke for the first time. "You know, Molly, I can see why the Old Man wants to tear this place down. It gives me the creeps." He paused for a moment then added softly, "I only hope that what happened to you is the last bad luck we see before this one blows."

The vac-seal security lock hissed as its small pump sucked air from between the two rubberized gaskets which encircled the door to Kalissae's quarters.

"Your secretary seems to have kept up on his classified reading material, Malvin," she said with a hint of bitterness. "He even knows how to manually activate the decompression mechanism." She paused, listening for the telltale smack of the rubber lips as they snapped together to form a vacuum-tight seal. She didn't have long to wait.

"Well, that should do it. If the explosives they're setting don't kill us, I figure we have roughly half a cycle before the air runs out in here . . . assuming, of course, that we don't panic and use it up before then."

Malvin sat on the floor with his back to the wall and his

knees pulled up against his chest. He gave no indication of having heard her. The look in his eyes was what someone had once called "the light-year gaze," a hollow, unfocused stare that saw nothing.

He's lost, Kalissae thought as she took a chair and pulled it around in front of him. "Nicholas?"

This man had struck fear into her heart before he arrived on Euphrates. Now he sat almost catatonic in front of her, totally crippled by his loss of power. Or was it because he now knew he had never really had any power to begin with? It didn't matter. Never again would she let herself be blinded by someone's position and authority... or lack of it.

"Nicholas? We have to try to escape from here." Kalissae knew it was probably hopeless, but she needed help, so she continued. "We have to stop Rosenthal. Do you hear me? We have to save the mine." Nothing.

"Listen to me, dammit. He betrayed you. He took advantage of your confidence. He worked under your protection as a double agent. He *used you*. Doesn't that make you mad? Doesn't that make you want to strike back? *Nicholas*, we have to try to stop him. He's a madman."

Malvin turned his blank stare in her direction. All she saw was the expressionless pain of deep shock. It would be useless to expect any help from him now. Her former boss was too far gone.

Kalissae let him sit.

Getting out of her quarters would be the first problem. She quickly relegated all other concerns to the back of her mind until she could concentrate solely on a way to open the space-tight door.

The vac-seal was purposely designed to prevent forceful opening. Its functional objective was to seal off the entryway if the outer skin of the mine suffered a major breach in its environmental skin. The double, overlapping gaskets around the door were sucked together so tightly that

Kalissae doubted if anything short of a laser could pry them apart.

A laser or . . . Kalissae thought as an odd tingling sensation ran down her scalp and tightened the skin of her cheeks. "A laser or O.P.R.," she said softly.

The idea of doing an Ore Pocket Reversal had jumped into her mind from nowhere, and she immediately tried to push it away. It was impossible. She hadn't performed an O.P.R. in far too long a time. It would probably kill her if she tried to force those mental skills to work now.

"I can't do it. Even if it is the only way to open that door, I can't do it," she said loudly in an attempt to drive the crazy idea from her head. "I can't. I can't. There's—"

Yes you can, a strange voice whispered in the center of her mind.

"No! I can't!" She pressed the heels of her hands hard against her temples. "I can't! This is crazy!"

Yes you can, the voice repeated.

It was like swimming. Issy understood swimming because Bedford had enjoyed that strange immersion in water.

As he approached the center of his personal time continuum, Issy realized that events had moved on without him. He would have to overshoot his intended target, reaching past the time-point where he had separated from Bedford, if he hoped to get back to the proper location.

When he entered what was for him the future, the atmosphere around him thickened. His movement slowed appreciably. *Swim. Swim and you will make it through.*

He struggled against the fatigue, and against the current of time as he searched the black, inky depths of his future shadow for the familiar glow he knew he would recognize.

Then he saw it, the bright point of light he was looking for. The color was wrong somehow, but he didn't have the reserve energy to worry about that. He had to move toward it immediately. Issy recalled how Bedford had taken a deep breath before diving. Mentally he did the same thing, and like those free dives they had made together, he plunged toward the light through the thickening haze of time.

The closer he got, the more he slowed, but his momentum carried him to the target. He touched the physical present and clung to the ore pocket in relief. He was back on Euphrates, back on level eighty-seven, back where he had lost Bedford.

The air was still and cold. Issy sensed no connection between this place and Bedford's mind. Bedford was gone from here. But Issy knew where he was and what he had to do.

What about me? a voice asked.

Issy had expected the voice. *Soon*, he answered. *Soon.* Then he turned to the task he had come here to do.

There was no way for Issy to warn his host that he was coming, no way to apologize first for what he was about to do to her. He was too exhausted, too drained by all that had happened. But she needed him as much as he needed her. And in some way he didn't yet understand, she was connected to Bedford.

Hurry, the voice pleaded. *I am in need.*

I know, he reassured her. *I know. Be still so I can do what I must do.*

Issy concentrated his energy. He wished once more that he had an alternative. But there was none. Bedford was gone and he had no choice.

With all the gentleness he could muster, and all the open affection he knew how to express, Issy entered Kalissae's mind.

TEN

"So far it doesn't look like we'll be needing any disembarking passes down there," Stancell said. "I've made three detection scans, and all I get is a bunch of garbage." He tried to keep his voice light, but his concern seeped out between his words. He only hoped that the Tigris mine had sealed itself and saved the personnel.

"Visuals look normal. What about the radio?" Bedford asked. He made no attempt to hide the concern he felt.

"Nothing. Even the distress signal has stopped."

"How long until apex?" Bedford was anxious to get down to the surface with whatever help they could offer.

Stancell glanced at the instruments. "About ten Standard, Syndic," he answered. The Chief wondered what could have so heavily damaged the mine. He tried another detection scan and received a negative reading. He realized that only an on-site inspection would reveal what had happened on Tigris. They would have to go down to the surface to find the reasons for the disaster.

"All right, Chief. As soon as we establish a stable orbit I want to suit-out and descend to the surface."

"Request permission to come along, sir."

"Of course, Chief. Permission granted." Bedford was more than happy to have Stancell come with him. He would have felt stupid leaving the Chief behind. Not only did he need Stancell's knowledge of the mine layout, but it would also be nice to have someone to guard his back. Bedford smiled to himself. After what had happened to them so far, he obviously felt he could trust Stancell... but not enough to leave him alone aboard the ship.

Lady Victoria achieved orbital stability within minutes after arrival at the threshold point. Bedford could have brought them in closer, but he wanted to keep *Lady* at the standard entry distance in case something new went awry. Theoretically, at that distance even a major mine blowout would not disturb *Lady*'s geosynchronous orbit. And the old Yendo might be the only escape from Tigris for anyone.

"That should do it," Bedford said. He had locked the automatic controls and run a landing-program disk for the cargo lighter they would use to descend to the surface. "Let's get going."

Stancell responded by following Bedford up the shiny, plasteel ladder into the exo-bay. A slight quiver of nervous anticipation passed through him as he popped his head up through the hatch into the brightly lit compartment. We will find out soon enough, he thought.

"Grab a suit, Chief," Bedford said after they had both entered the bay. "Any color you want as long as it's white." He reached out and took down an X-Ninety Hostile Environment suit from the clamp-rack where they were stored. All the suits were white. As soon as he unclipped the suit he began the laborious process of putting it on.

"You'd think after all these years someone would come up with an X-suit that was easy to get into," Stancell said as he took a suit for himself. He knowingly twisted open the myriad number of toggles and valve controls which covered its exterior.

"Probably won't happen in our lifetime. You know how they test new suits these days. Forever. At least this model has the new bio-clasp sealers."

It took the better part of thirty minutes for each of them to put on and adjust their suits. After checking each other's environmental packs, and their cables and tubing, they each took one of the nutrient flasks from the small locker beside the suit rack and attached it to their suits.

Stancell got his in place first. He closed the suit's semirigid hood, then gave the nutrient flask's stopper cord a sharp yank. "Grow, little buggies," he said. "Grow."

Almost immediately after the release of the nutrient fluid into the capillary tubes which crisscrossed the suit, it began to inflate. Convinced that it was working properly, Stancell opened the faceplate of his hood. "Scary, isn't it?"

"It always amazes me how fast the bacteria grow," Bedford said as he pulled the cord on his own flask.

In less than a minute the specially engineered bacteria in the capillary tubes had multiplied sufficiently to do their job. The minute silicone channels which formed the exterior network of the suits acted like tiny, hollow O-rings. As the bacteria grew they forced the suit closures together until they were space-tight. Only the faceplates were sealed by conventional means.

The X-Nineties were not the most comfortable suits in the galaxy, but with their bio-clasp improvement, they had a huge appeal over almost every other type. They were self-repairing. A tear or puncture could quickly be countered by the introduction of additional nutrient fluid, which would accelerate the bacterial growth and force the edges of the damaged material together. The bacteria which died when forced out of the capillaries quickly formed a tough, rubbery scab that would effectively patch all but the largest rips with a strength almost equal to the trilon suit material. So, comfortable or not, the X-Nineties were extremely reassuring garments to wear in a hostile environment.

"Pressurized," Stancell said, indicating that his suit was fully operational.

"I've got P-one here also," Bedford said a moment later. "This way, Chief." He grabbed two universal tool belts from their lockers and led the way through an airlock to the shuttle bay. As he waited to secure the lock, he wondered what Issy would be saying if he were here now.

A deep hollow opened inside Bedford. Issy. Where was Issy? What had happened to him? The hollow threatened to expand and engulf his thoughts. Bedford closed it off with a muted grunt of dismissal. Issy was gone.

"You all right, Syndic?"

"Fine, Chief. Just thinking about something. We'll use the small lighter." He pointed to the smallest of three cargo lighters which sat on the docking rails in the bay. "It actually has a better power-to-weight ratio than the other two and also handles a little better."

The lighter was little more than a smooth-bellied space sled with a pressurized cabin and an enclosed cargo deck. It was designed to shuttle small quantities of material and equipment between ships in space, but could do double duty as a planetary lander, where necessary or more convenient.

Bedford had kept the three lighters which came with his purchase of the *Lady Victoria* because he liked the idea of having three backup vehicles in case of emergency. At least that was the rational reason he gave. The lighters were also a great deal of fun to fly, and more than one old, unusable Yendo trawler had been purchased by people who only wanted to salvage the cargo lighters which came with them. In Bedford's case, the small, swift vehicles were just a bonus, an extra he had easily learned to enjoy. After flying all three he had given them names. The two larger ones became *Albert* and *Edward* respectively, and the smallest one he had named *Vicki*. He knew *Lady* would have approved of his choices had she been able to.

Even in their bulky suits it was fairly easy for the two

men to climb into *Vicki*'s cabin. She was designed for work. Bedford took the pilot's seat, and Stancell sat directly behind him. Bedford fed in the course disk he had made, powered *Vicki* up, and said, "Here we go, Chief." He pushed the launch control button with an irrational feeling of satisfaction.

Vicki shuddered briefly with acceleration as it shot down the docking rail. Simultaneously, a small slit opened in the flexible exit hatch. Seconds later the little lighter was well clear of *Lady Victorta* and following its preprogrammed course toward the surface of Tigris.

"You all right, Chief?" Bedford asked.

"I guess so," Stancell answered a little weakly. "I just never have gotten used to quick acceleration launches."

"Me neither. But I've learned to like them." Bedford fought an urge to chuckle. The seriousness of what they were about to do loomed larger and larger as Tigris filled the lighter's view screen.

It was easy to spot the mining complex even without the landing and caution beacons which should have encircled it with a ring of protective incandescence. But when Bedford took over *Vicki*'s controls to make a manual approach to the docking area, his heart froze at what he saw. Where the service bays should have been, a long, ragged split gaped up at them like the mouth of some hideous monster captured in its last agonized scream by rigor mortis.

"Bad," he said with a shudder.

Stancell stared mutely down at the ruptured mine.

Bedford set *Vicki* down on the inner apron of dock three. If the breach in Tigris's outer skin had been explosive, it could very well have killed everyone in the miningplex.

"Poor bastards," Stancell said echoing Bedford's thoughts. He pulled down the faceplate on his suit and prepared to disembark.

As soon as *Vicki*'s engine whined to a stop, Bedford turned in his seat and said, "I think we need some ground rules, Chief. There's no telling what kind of damage we're going to find in there, but from the hole in the super-structure, my guess is that it's going to be pretty grim."

Stancell shook his head in agreement.

"I want us to stay within eyesight of each other at all times. Absolutely no separation unless we discuss it in detail first. Our main concern has to be our own safety. We can't help any survivors or assess the extent of the damage if we let ourselves get into trouble because of carelessness."

"Understood. I'm ready when you are."

Bedford unbelted himself and moved past Stancell to the exit lock. "One more thing, Chief. I'm depending on you to let me know when I'm getting us into trouble. You're the mine expert, not me. If you have any doubts at all, just tell me to stop. I'll respect your decision on any technical matter."

Stancell's snort fogged his faceplate momentarily. "Thanks, Syndic, I'll try my best. You keep us headed in the right direction, and I'll try to keep us alive."

"Good luck to both of us then," Bedford answered. What he really wanted was to have Issy with him. The three of them would have made a much stronger team. But—"Okay," he said, interrupting his own thought, "let's check our suits and get out of here."

Both X-Ninety suits were functioning flawlessly. Bedford turned to the exit controls and immediately depressurized Vicki. When the twin gauges over the hatch read zero-zero, he released the locking lever, and the oval door popped out and up on its integral hinges. "Watch your step," he said as he moved out of the hatch and stepped down into the darkness of dock three's landing apron.

Once they were both outside, they walked slowly to the edges of the ragged hole on the complex side of the apron. Vicki's landing lights cast stark shadows into the upper level of the gaping pit. The damage was so severe that very little of the surrounding superstructure was recog-nizable. For a long moment they stood side by side.

staring into the blackness and wondering what had happened. And why.

Finally Bedford broke the gloomy spell cast by the pit. "Let's try that door over there," he said, pointing to a large, white building on their side of the apron. It had a broad door in its center across which was stenciled PARTS in bold, black letters. "That's the storage depot, if my memory serves me correctly. Should give us access to the freight elevators, and I believe they have self-contained emergency power, don't they, Chief?"

"Sure do." Stancell turned from staring into the hole and followed Bedford to the PARTS door. "Decompression," he said. "Look at the gauges." The dual set of pressure and security gauges beside the door all read zero. "I think we can pry it open." As he took a small prybar from his tool belt, he speculated on what they would find inside. It wouldn't be nice. The storage depot had the best pressure security of any of the structures on the mine. Zero here surely meant dead miners, he thought as he thrust his arm with a deft twist of his wrist and extended the prybar's telescoping handle to its full one meter length and locked it into place.

"You want help?" Bedford asked quietly.

"No, thanks. If I can catch the inside bolt with the hook end of the bar, it ought to just pop open."

Bedford watched as Stancell worked the end of the prybar between the seals at the edge of the door. He was surprised by the sound of Stancell's regular breathing echoing in his helmet, and pleased when the door popped open as predicted. Stepping past Stancell, he flicked on his helmet light and stood in the doorway. Just inside he found the main lighting switch. It was in the ON position, but the interior of the depot remained dark.

"Nothing," Stancell said. "No power here." He quickly checked his Geiger counter, then continued. "Radiation levels are normal. In fact, they're a little below normal. Must have been a massive failure in the transmission lines." He turned his head and looked around the depot's receiving room. His helmet lamp cast eerie shadows over the twisted shapes which rose oddly from the floor. "Bad," he whispered.

They stood side by side and turned their lamps up to maximum dispersion so that they could get a better overall look at the room. The depot looked like it had been picked up by some giant hand and shaken vigorously. Equipment was scattered everywhere. Split packing crates stood at odd angles on the edges of piles of parts. Pieces of fragile machinery leaned haphazardly against their holding racks. Nowhere did they see any bodies.

Bedford's light revealed a crack in the wall to their left. He traced the crack up to a large, S-shaped perforation just below the roof line. "Looks like it happened pretty fast," he said as he pointed to the ceiling.

"Yeah," Stancell said quietly. He directed his beam away from the crack and across the wreckage to the opposite wall which was barely visible in the dim light. "The elevators will be over there. The question is, how do we climb over this mess and get there?"

"It looks clearest along the walls. First thing I think we should do is break our ground rules. You follow the right wall, and I'll follow the left. If you run into trouble, or find any bodies, stand still and yell."

It took them thirty minutes to make their way around the walls to the elevators. They talked to each other constantly, but neither ran into any serious problems. They still saw no bodies.

"Strange," Bedford said as he walked to where Stancell was standing by the elevator doors. "I'm surprised no one was caught in here when this happened. They must have had some warning."

"I don't think so." Stancell directed his light to the rip in the wall. "From the looks of that it happened too quickly. And I noticed coming around the wall that none of the expensive instruments had been taken to Z-grav storage like they should have been in an emergency. No, I don't think they had any warning at all."

"You're probably right, Chief, but . . ."

"Yeah, I know. Where are they?"

"We'd better get down to the interior and see what we can find."

"We'll have to take the service shaft," Stancell said as he popped the elevator doors open with his prybar. What was left of the elevator was jambed sideways in the shaft.

"Right. Which way?"

"Over here. The service shaft has much stronger shoring than the main shaft, and if you don't mind ladders, it ought to be a fairly easy climb."

"Let's rope ourselves together, then I'll lead the way."

"That's all right with me, Syndic. Climbing is something I've always tried to avoid. But stick close, and remember, I know the shafts and you don't."

Bedford laughed lightly, but there was no humor in it. "Climbing is a hobby of mine. Maybe we can balance each other out." They tied themselves together with a five-meter section of light rope, then Bedford leaned through the doorway of the service shaft and shined his light down into the darkness. Beyond his beam he saw the dull red glow of battery-powered emergency lamps pointing the way down to the heart of Tigris. "How far down will this take us?"

"All the way to the bottom."

"Good. We'll take our time and rest as much as we need to." Without another word, he extended his hand to Stancell. They shook hands clumsily, then Bedford stepped onto the platform in the shaft and climbed down the ladder. Stancell played out a few meters of rope and followed Bedford down.

The climb into the bowels of Tigris was long and arduous. The explosion had shifted the shaft in several places and required them to make two lateral detours through passageways constricted by debris from floor to ceiling. Whatever had exploded in the mine had caused extreme damage. Both men were quickly convinced they would find no survivors, but neither of them made that thought known to the other.

On the second detour, as Stancell tried to squeeze the bulk of his X-Ninety between a twisted plasteel beam and the shaft door frame, Bedford slipped on a broken rung further down the ladder. He fell free until the rope caught short, and it was only by luck that Stancell at that moment had both hands on the beam.

When the rope jerked him, Stancell automatically clutched the beam. That saved them both from a lethal fall to the bottom of the shaft, but a jagged spur on the beam tore a ten-centimeter rip in Stancell's suit.

"Sisters of Shame!" he yelled as the air hissed out of his suit. He tightened his grip on the beam with his right hand, and with his left gave the cord on the nutrient flask a hard yank. The bacteria responded immediately to the nutrient solution. Within five seconds the rip was filled with bubbling, dying microorganisms. Within ten seconds the rip was sealed, and in another ten Stancell's suit was back up to normal operating pressure.

"You okay?" Bedford asked.

"I think so. You?"

"Just hold on to that rope and I will be." Bedford dangled at the end of his line like some strange, puffy insect. He slowly pulled himself upright and climbed the rope hand over hand. It was narrow and slippery, but he only had to go up a few meters to where the section of ladder had broken off.

Stancell felt the pull on his belt from Bedford's weight and thought it was going to cut him in half. Despite a reinforced grip, he felt his hands slipping on the beam. "Hurry if you can. I'm not in the best possible position."

Bedford gave two more long pulls and swung himself to the narrow ledge just below the broken end of the ladder. "Take a break," he said with a sigh as he secured himself to the lowest rung and let his body sag slightly against the shoring.

"You sure you're all right?"

"A few Jansul-years older, but otherwise okay. You, Chief?"

"The same times ten. I'll never bitch about how much testing goes into these suits again. You can count on that."

"Chief?"

"Yes?"

"Thanks."

The rest of their descent went without further serious incident until they reached the point where the service shaft ended in a broad ledge around a smaller hole that dropped another twenty meters to the lowest level of the mine.

"They must have been building in an awful hurry," Stancell said as they looked down the hole. "Not supposed to leave things like this. Goes against all the regs."

"I want to take a look. If there's nothing down there, then we can begin working our way back up."

They anchored a long piece of their rope to the ladder stanchions, and Bedford slowly rappelled down the hole to the rough floor below. As his feet touched the rock, he said, "Can't see anything here, Chief. I'm going to hook a trail line to the end of the rope and take a fast look around. Call me every two minutes."

"Got it. Be careful."

"I will."

Before the first two-minute check was due, Bedford's voice barked from the earphones in Stancell's helmet. "It's incredible! There's a hole in the roof that's a hundred, no, two hundred meters in diameter. It looks like something a wide-spread laser beam might have done. But I've never seen one that could cut a hole that big."

"You okay?"

"Yeah, fine, but I'm coming back up."

Bedford and Stancell made their way up through eight levels before they found a passageway clear enough of debris for them to cross over to the chimney Bedford had discovered. When they finally reached it, all they could see was a rough, grey, circular shaft which disappeared somewhere above them.

"Ready to do some *real* climbing?" Bedford asked.

"Do I have a *real* choice?" Stancell looked up the long cavery which stretched at a forty-five degree angle up toward the surface, and shook his head. His light danced in crazy circles over the debris on the slope. "I hope it's not too far. I'm more than a little tired."

But he wasn't as tired as he was concerned. He didn't doubt that the right kind of explosion could have killed everyone on Tigris, but this thing was totally different. The personnel here might have escaped if there had been enough ships, and if the complex hadn't been hosting additional miners from Euphrates. They might have escaped, but Stancell felt sure they hadn't. That thought brought him back to the basic, nagging question: Why had they seen no bodies?

"Anything you need to tell me, Chief?" Bedford detected a note of hesitancy in Stancell's actions.

"Still no bodies," he answered simply.

"I know. It's been bothering me, too. A lot. But I don't think we are going to find any."

"And no survivors," Stancell added bitterly.

"We don't know that for sure, Chief. I know it looks bad, but—"

"No survivors."

"We'll see." Bedford hated to admit it, but after all they *had* seen, he agreed with Stancell's evaluation. There probably were no survivors. "We've got to get moving, Chief. We have to find out as much as we can before we get back to the ship." He checked the gauges on his life-support system. "I figure I have about three hours left before I go on reserve. What about you?"

"Same here."

"Then let's start climbing."

The ascent was a brief one and much easier than they had thought it would be. The upper side of the chimney looked like the rock had melted and glazed over, but the bottom side upon which they climbed was strewn with loose debris. In some ways it reminded Bedford of the pipe of a volcano, though the fact that they climbed up through it so soon after it had been active ruled that natural phenomenon out as the cause of Tigris's destruction.

Five levels above where they had started, Bedford stopped and stared. "Do you see that?"

Stancell looked up and saw nothing at first, then..."What in the name..." He almost lost his grip on the rock he was pulling himself around.

Above them, wedged tightly between the walls of the shaft, was what appeared to be a gigantic, grey, oval-shaped object that looked like a monstrously oversized egg.

"Ever see anything like that, Chief?"

"Never." Stancell wanted to get closer to the thing, but he knew that no matter how close he got it still would not look like anything he had ever seen. Except maybe—

"Let's climb up there."

Stancell shook his head. It couldn't be what he was thinking. He clambered up the slope after Bedford, catching up with him just two meters away from the egg's grey surface. As they stood side by side and stared, a sudden chill rolled down Stancell's spine. He thought of what would happen to them if the thing broke loose and rolled back down the shaft.

"Get a sample," Bedford said quietly.

With a small pick-hammer from his tool belt Stancell chipped off a hand-sized piece of the grey material. As he tried to grip it, it broke into flakes and powder. "Graphite! If I've ever seen graphite, then this is some of the purest I've ever come across."

"Can't be," Bedford said automatically. "How could a big ball of graphite cause all this?"

"Look for yourself." Stancell held out the sample.

Bedford took the small piece from Stancell's hand and looked at it closely in the bright light of his helmet. "Well, you may be right, but I don't see how..." He looked back at the giant sphere and swept his light across its dull surface. A darker shadow caught his eye. "Over here,

Chief." Without waiting for Stancell he moved toward the
shadow.

A section of the egg had fractured and caved in forming
a narrow gap like an inverted V in its dark shell. Bedford
shined his light cautiously through the opening, then
stepped over the slippery rubble and pulled himself into
the graphite ball.

The soft forms of brown and black shadows looked like
nothing he had ever seen before. –Issy?–

The request was perfectly natural for Bedford. The
silence was as cold and forbidding as the place where he
stood.

"What in the name of all the Gods is this place?"
Stancell asked as he added the light from his helmet to
Bedford's.

In the few moments longer that he had been there,
Bedford already knew the answer. "Some kind of graveyard.
Look."

The mushy organic material they were standing on, and
which stretched out to the limits of their lights, was
interrupted by the stark forms of bones. The egg was a
charnel house filled with rotting piles of grey-green flesh
and blackened skeletons.

Stancell fought the urge to retch when he realized what
he was seeing. "What? Why?" Coherent questions refused
to form. Nausea grabbed his stomach and twisted it. He
doubled over and swallowed hard. *What* and *why* stabbed
at his brain.

"Easy, Chief. Just take it easy," Bedford said as he
grabbed one of the Chief's arms to steady him.

Sour bile crept into Stancell's throat, but he knocked
the nausea back. Then, less than a meter in front of him,
he saw a hand and vomited violently in his suit.

Bedford reacted immediately. He popped the flood valve
on Stancell's air supply and opened his faceplate. Most of
the vomit was swept out by the rushing air. Then in a
grotesque game of opening and closing Stancell's faceplate

while regulating the valve, Bedford let him empty his stomach.

"Get control of yourself," he barked in a commanding voice. "I can't keep doing this."

Stancell nodded weakly inside his helmet. After a minute or two he felt strong enough to stand up straight. "Okay," he said thickly. "But look at that."

Bedford's eyes followed Stancell's light to the toe of his boot, where a hand protruded from the muck. Suddenly he too felt like vomiting. Using all the control that Issy had taught him, he stopped the spasms of nausea before they became unmanageable. That same control allowed him to reach down to the hand and pull a large golidium ring free from the decaying fingers. After wiping it with a utility rag, he wordlessly handed it to Stancell.

"Friesh."

"Positive?"

Stancell stared at the ring and wished desperately that he had the air to vomit again. The sour smell in his helmet and the unique ring in his fingers made his stomach churn and grind. "Positive."

"Euphrates, Chief. Friesh was on Euphrates."

"Until they shipped him here."

Suddenly Bedford had an intuitive feeling about what had happened. He was almost sure what this monstrosity was and what it meant. "Come on, Chief. We've got to get some samples of this stuff and get back to Euphrates. It may be too late to warn them already."

"But—"

"Now, Chief!" In his heart a silent cry went out for Issy.

ELEVEN

Kalissae gasped violently and clutched her head.

Peace, a soft voice whispered soothingly in her brain. *Peace*. Then in the two major languages of Pflessius it said, *Meechla . . . Simk*.

"Nooooo," she moaned as she sank to the floor. "Nooooo."

The foreign voice whispered, *Yes*.

Even as she fought the invasion of her mind, Kalissae sensed an affection in the alien presence, a tenderness toward her that was more than she could bear. Her resistance broke. With a desperate, nonverbal scream of defiance she slipped mercifully into unconsciousness.

The great Assembly was in session on Pflessius, and Kalissae's father had generously provided rooms for the Sagation Prefect. During the last Quatrile, just before the seasonal recess, the Prefect caught Kalissae spying on him from a small alcove across the hallway from his quarters. Then, not realizing that she was paralyzed with fear, he crossed the hall and confronted her with his tri-lipped, toothless grin.

She remained pinned against the rear wall of the alcove by an invisible force as the Prefect reached out and placed a single, twelve-fingered hand on her head.

"Ah, such a pretty child," he said in his peculiarly lilting form of Galactic Standard. He tipped her head back and looked straight into her eyes.

Kalissae wanted to scream. She wanted to run away from him and seek refuge within the familiar walls of her own room. But she did nothing. Fear bolted her to the floor. Shame riveted her in place. Despair froze her muscles.

"Do not be afraid, child. I will not harm you. It is just that the sight of you peeking at me has almost made me regret not fathering children of my own. Ah, but the government, my government, requires celibacy and—hmph. What can you care about that? Just stay as delightful as you are now, Daughter." With a quick, sentimental pat on Kalissae's head he turned and went back to his rooms.

As soon as the Prefect's door snapped shut, the invisible tension holding her in place gave way. She ran to her quarters, and bathed in a frenzy, desperately trying to scrub away the imaginary soil left by the Prefect's touch.

He had touched her! He had dared to place his hands...to violate her body...to, to...There were no words in her childhood to describe what had happened. Later she would learn terms like *clogh*, and *rape*, and *ulinkaeda*, but none of these words would ever fully encompass the sense of violation she had felt.

For months after the encounter her scalp itched as though the Prefect's fingers had left unhealed wounds on her head. She scrubbed her head and hair two or three times a day in an effort to rid herself of the imagined impurity, but only succeeded in irritating her skin and producing real sores which plagued her long after the irrational fear had gone.

He had touched her!

Kalissae had suffered her trauma in silence. The Sagation Prefect could not have realized that touching a Pflessian Major child without permission was an offense punishable by death. She knew that. But even though his ignorance of the law was no defense for the misery he had caused her, she also knew there had been genuine affection in his actions.

It took Kalissae a long time to overcome the sense of self-degradation the Prefect had aroused in her. Yet all during that time she told no one. Somehow the Prefect's uninhibited expression of affection acted like a buffer, a silent lock on her feelings that prevented her from demanding a Major's right to justice. Even after the intervening years blurred her memory of the incident Kalissae never fully understood her reaction.

Bedford, the affectionate voice whispered. *Think of Bedford.*

Kalissae stirred and opened her eyes. From her position on the floor of her quarters she could see Malvin staring sightlessly into the pit of his despair.

Bedford, the voice repeated.

Strange emotions whelmed her. "Bedford's dead," she said harshly. "Leave me alone." Desperation frayed the edges of her voice. She was losing her mind. She knew it.

Bedford lives. We must help him. Issy quickly evaluated his strength and decided to take a chance. He let Kalissae see him in her mind's eye.

Issy? That thing? No! The image blurred as a wave of nausea rolled through her stomach. *Go away! Go away!* "Go away!" she screamed.

Bedford lives. Help me save him. Please. Please.

Issy's cry reinforced Kalissae's vision of him. *Bedford? Issy?* She opened her mouth to shout again, but nothing came out. *How?* she wondered. Her eyes widened with further shock as she realized she was actually talking to Issy.

"How? What?" She did not know how to ask the right questions.

I am back, but Bedford is gone, Issy responded.

Dead, she thought.

No. Gone. He will return. You must help.

How? "How?" she repeated out loud.

Level eighty-seven.

Fear followed Issy's answer through her mind. "Damn you! Go away!" Kalissae ground her fists into the fine red hair that curled at her temples, as she rolled onto her back. She squeezed her eyes shut and screamed half-heartedly, "Go away!"

No. I cannot. You must come to me. Issy's patience faded with his declining energy. Kalissae's mind was as alien to him as his presence was to her. But she was his only hope. Her emotional ties to Bedford were very strong. Yet she barely knew they existed. Issy fought his growing weakness by concentrating on her hidden attachment to his partner. *Bedford lives. Believe me. Bedford lives.*

She sat up slowly like an awkward child, with her legs splayed and her hands moving gracelessly in an attempt to keep her balance. Could he really be alive? Had Rosenthal lied to her? She shook her head violently and almost fell over. With forced deliberation she pulled in her legs and crossed them. Then, elbows on knees, she rested her head in her open hands. "Don't torture me," she whispered. "Go away."

Please listen to me and trust me. I feel your revulsion. I know what I am doing to you. I am sorry, but there is no other way. You must come to me. You must come to me now before it is too late.

"Can't you see I'm locked in here?" There was sharp anger in her voice: anger at Issy for violating her, anger at Rosenthal for locking her in, and anger at Bedford for not being there. With her anger came energy.

Good, Issy said. He needed her energy almost more than she did. *Anger is good. Use it.*

"How? How?" She still did not want to acknowledge to herself that Issy could read her thoughts.

Your Ore Pocket Reversal, will it work on the door?

Kalissae took a deep breath and exhaled slowly. "If I could do it," she answered bitterly. "But it's been too long. I've lost my skills, my powers of concentration."

I can help.

Issy's offer made her skin twitch. Her scalp tingled under the pressure of her fingers. She ground her teeth in frustration. But from somewhere deep inside, her anger fueled her desire to fight and live. That desire pushed its way through the tangle of confusing emotions which stymied her.

"All right," she said finally. Then in an attempt to justify her compromised ideals she added, "But if you are lying to me, Issy, I will destroy myself to prevent you from violating anyone else. You have already sullied me beyond—"

SILENCE. Issy still had a reserve of energy, but his patience with Kalissae was gone. Her threat to kill herself over a rule of social etiquette was more than he could tolerate. Far more important things were at stake. *Just do the O.P.R.,* he commanded, then added in a softer tone, *I will reinforce you.*

Kalissae's new sense of resolve to fight for her life, and Issy's stern order combined to subdue her emotional turmoil. She would do it because it was the logical thing to do.

As she stood up and faced the door she glanced briefly at Malvin. If he still had any connection with reality, it didn't show on his face. Reality? She almost laughed. What did reality mean when a strange creature settled into your brain?

The question had an hysterical edge which she quickly shook off. It was time to go to work on the door. That much she knew was real.

Issy had helped her push away the question of reality without her knowing it. The mind-imprint technique he was using on her was nibbling away at his energy reserves faster than he had expected. But if a physical union could be achieved soon enough, he would be all right. The key was to get her down to level eighty-seven, fast.

Issykul!

Kalissae stopped her inspection of the door and tilted her head slightly. "Is that you, Issy?" There was no response.

Issykul!

The voice had an odd timbre, something like Issy's, but resonating at a higher frequency. A small shiver of panic rippled through Kalissae. What was that voice?

It is nothing to fear. Please, hurry. Issy's tone was insistent, but calm.

"All right," Kalissae said as she turned back to the door. But it was not all right. Was Issy not alone? The strange new voice added to her apprehension. Two violators? That thought made her doubt if she could go through with the O.P.R.

You can do it, Kalissae. I will support you just as I supported Bedford. But you must do it quickly. Issy could not let her dwell on what she had heard. Explanations had to wait. Now he needed her skills and her body. *Begin,* he said quietly. *Please?*

Kalissae thought of Bedford in a warm flush of emotion. Her memory of him was stronger than it should have been. Was Issy doing something to . . . The question faded as images of Bedford brought not only warmth, but also hope.

She concentrated. Compared to an ore pocket, the door would be simple to reverse—at least in theory. The practical application of her long-unused O.P.R. skills was another thing altogether. But she believed she could do it. She believed in herself.

The old ritual came back with surprising ease. The steps were as fresh as they had been for her years ago. Issy again? It didn't matter. She was the one who had to complete the process. She was the one who had to make it work. But . . . now, now . . .

The door shrank as Kalissae wrapped her mind around it. Power surged through her thoughts. Self joined to self. With a mental twist she turned the door seals inside out. Her mind released its grip. The iris popped open. The door was in ruins. A sigh slowly escaped her lungs.

Very nice. I knew you could do it. Now you must hurry.

Kalissae looked at the wreckage of the door. She had done it. A slight smile spread her lips. Then it broadened and brightened. She had done it. She had really done it. "Damn the first person who gets in my way now," she said defiantly.

Now, Issy commanded.

His voice wavered like a scratchy intersystem broadcast, but she caught the urgency in it. She took a long look at Malvin and shrugged her shoulders. The former director was beyond her help for the moment, and Issy needed her.

Cautiously she peered up and down the corridor. There was no one in sight. Apparently Rosenthal had not thought it necessary to post a guard once he locked them in. Or, she thought suddenly, maybe they were all gone. She shuddered at what that might mean.

Without further speculation she left her quarters and swiftly made her way down the corridor to the elevators. She waited with nervous impatience until one responded to her call. Then she stood to one side as the doors opened. It was empty. With a heavy sigh of relief she stepped in and punched the controls for level eighty-seven.

"Thanks, Issy," she said softly. Her tension eased as the elevator began its long descent.

Issy did not respond. He needed all his strength if he was going to successfully merge with Kalissae. Given her antagonistic reaction when he had entered her mind, he hoped he had enough energy to stay alive until he was physically united with her.

*   *   *

The stars above Tigris seemed dimmer, and the thick mat of darkness between them seemed more oppressive when Bedford and Stancell finally came up out of the mine. They had been able to retrace their steps back up to the surface, and the going had been easier. But the climb had still been difficult enough to keep them from dwelling on what they had seen.

Bedford stepped out of the ruins first. As he walked onto the margin of the freight dock, seeing the stars again brought back the vision of the grisly tomb. Tomb? Not really. The monumental aspects of that structure and its decomposed contents were adequately described by the word, tomb. But somehow the thing they had visited was much more than just an elaborate grave.

"The samples are secure," Stancell said interrupting Bedford's thoughts.

Stancell came out of the parts depot carrying a small, square case slung over his shoulder on a wide strap. "I found this instrument box in there..." He paused and noticed that Bedford wasn't reacting to what he was saying. "Syndic Odigal?"

Bedford held his eyes on the dark sky for a few moments longer before turning to Stancell. "I heard you. I was lost in thought about... well, anyway, let's get *Vicki* going and head back to the *Lady Victoria*. I want to run some tests on those." He pointed to the case.

"I'm for that." Stancell fell in behind Bedford as they walked back to the cargo lighter. The Syndic is brooding, he thought, and doesn't want any more surprises. There have been enough of those already on this trip. "What do you think you'll find?"

"Find?"

"In the samples. You said you wanted to run some tests."

Bedford stopped walking and turned to face Chief Stancell. "I'm not sure. Let's just say there may be a connection between what happened here and the ore pocket on Euphrates." With that he turned and started walking again.

"Oh," Stancell said softly to Bedford's back. If the samples were the key to what had happened, then Stancell wanted to know exactly what they were up against. "What do you suspect?"

"Don't worry, Chief," Bedford said with irritation in his voice. "I'll let you know if it's anything you need to be aware of." He increased his pace and effectively ended the discussion by adding, "Now let's get a move on."

Stancell raised his eyebrows, but remained silent. It really isn't my business anyway, he thought. If the Syndic wants to keep quiet, that's fine with me. But . . . He reached *Vicki*'s cargo bay and quickly strapped the sample box inside. As soon as it was secure, he climbed into the cabin where Bedford was already in the pilot's seat checking out the instruments.

But as Stancell strapped himself in, his thoughts were still rolling. I'll be damned if I'll risk my career anymore. Helical is where my loyalties . . . An image of the Helical Security cruiser making its attack run on the *Lady Victoria* froze that thought. Suddenly his perspective changed. Loyalty no longer meant what it used to.

The *Lady Victoria* was well on its way back to Euphrates when Bedford finally emerged from the tiny laboratory adjacent to his cabin. His face was expressionless as he made his way to the bridge. There was nothing in his manner or stride to betray his thoughts. The only indicator of what had consumed his time and interest since they had set their course was a small, stoppered beaker filled with striated chemicals that he carried very carefully as he walked down the corridor.

"Chief," he said as he entered the command module, "I think I've pinned it down."

As soon as he heard Bedford's voice, Stancell rose from

the pilot's seat and turned. He looked down at the beaker in Bedford's hand, then up into the Syndic's eyes. "How bad is it?" he asked as a worried look deepened the creases on his face.

Bedford smiled slightly in response. Stancell was no one's fool. He probably had his own suspicions about what they had found, and that was a good sign. It showed the Chief was thinking, something Bedford needed to know about Stancell if he was going to take him further into his confidence.

"Bad enough," he said as he set the beaker down on the small plotting table. "But see for yourself."

Stancell bent his head closer to the beaker.

"Do you recognize that?"

"It's an Isoleucine test," Stancell said as he cut his eyes up to Bedford then back to the beaker. "And, it's positive."

"Correct."

"From the samples?"

"Right."

"Does that mean . . ." Stancell paused. Better to let the Syndic give his own conclusions before jumping in with opinions which may not be valid, he thought. "Let me rephrase that. What exactly does this mean?"

Bedford hesitated. It was obvious that the Chief already knew enough to realize what the egg on Tigris held. But Stancell was a company man, a longtime member of an organization that had tried to kill him. How would he react to measures against Helical Minerals? What were his allegiances now?

"Chief, before we continue, there is something we have to get straight . . . something I have to know." Bedford watched Stancell's eyes narrow and his face harden into a scowl. But before he could continue, Stancell held up a hand.

"Believe me, Syndic, I've been giving that a lot of thought. It's not easy turning my back on a twenty-year career. But"—Stancell's expression melted into a broad, toothy grin—"but as far as I'm concerned Helical can go to the seven hells of Andar. The bastards tried to kill us. Like my first Exo instructor used to say, 'A partner who tries to kill you is a partner to no one.' I don't intend to be in their camp when Helical's shaft caves in."

Bedford returned Stancell's smile, but he had to be positive. "Are you sure, Chief? We may not succeed."

"I don't even know what we're going to do. But that doesn't matter. Look, Syndic, you don't crawl around a ruined mine with someone without learning something about them. We may have been thrown together in an alliance of necessity, but that's over now. I'm sticking with you because I want to, not because I have to."

"Good. But are you willing to obey my orders, whatever they are? It's probably going to get rough from here on out, and I've got to know you're one hundred percent behind me, regardless of what you think we should do."

"You know what made up my mind?" Stancell asked after a pause. "It wasn't the attack, or the wreckage we found on Tigris. It wasn't even the way you handled the emergencies on this crazy trip." He leaned toward Bedford. "It's the fact that for the first time in my life I've had to make decisions on my own, without specific orders or rules to guide me.

"It's scary, and I'm not totally sure I'm doing the right thing. But you can count on me to carry my weight no matter what happens . . . for myself, not for you, or against Helical. Just for my own, slow, stupid self." Stancell straightened his shoulders as he spoke. "Syndic, you are the first person to ever let me make up my own mind. For that alone you have my loyalty."

Bedford hesitated a moment. He wasn't exactly sure what Stancell was talking about. But Stancell seemed to be, and he would make a good partner, a man who could be trusted because he was guided by the finest discipline in the universe: Self-discipline. "How would you like to be a Deptenens?"

"A what?"

"Deptenens. My official assistant. Well, not assistant so

much as my second in command. I have the authority to appoint someone to carry out the duties of my office in my stead. But I never really needed one before. I had Issy." The thought of his lost companion tightened Bedford's chest. He took a deep breath and pushed the memory aside. "Well? Will you be my Deptenens?"

The offer was startling. It was more than an honor, it was an expression of confidence in him as a person. "Sounds okay to me," Stancell said as casually as he could, but the pride he felt made his voice quaver slightly.

"Good. Consider it done. I'll need some information from you. Then I'll send a message notifying my head-quarters. But as of this minute, you are my Deptenens." He held out his hand and Stancell shook it firmly.

"Thanks, Syndic Odigal."

"Thank *you*, Chief." A slow wave of relief swept through Bedford. He felt more confident now about what he might have to face on Euphrates knowing that Stancell would be there to back him up.

"Now that we're a team," Stancell said, "let's get back to the Isoleucine test." It feels good to be alive, he thought, good to be my own man. But he could not dwell on that pleasantness. There was work to be done. "What does the test mean?"

They both sat down at the plotting table. "It's impossible to know for sure, Chief, but it appears to me that the thing we found on Tigris was able to convert decaying animal matter into its separate components. Then it either converted all those components, or eliminated all of them except Isoleucine. The samples we took from the bottom layers of the egg only show traces of other biochemical compounds—"

"Wait a minute," Stancell interrupted. "Do you think that thing is still doing it?" That thought stirred an uneasy feeling in his gut.

"No. I think the thing on Tigris is dead. It probably destroyed itself when it came up through the mine." Bedford saw a look of fear flash briefly across Stancell's face. "It may sound crazy, Chief, but I'm almost certain that the egg-thing we found was an Isoleucine-graphite ore pocket, the same as the pockets Helical specializes in mining." The new look on Stancell's face was colder than fear.

"But . . ." Stancell could not talk. Was Bedford trying to tell him that an ore pocket could have done that much damage, and be . . . eating people? It didn't make sense. It couldn't be true. The idea was too grotesque. Finally he found his tongue and asked in a stunned voice, "How is that possible?" He wanted to ask more, but his thoughts were still whirling through his mind.

Bedford looked at him steadily. "I wish I knew." Seeing the confusion on the Chief's face, he waited a few moments. Bedford did not want to rush him. It had taken a while to assimilate the facts himself.

Like sand in a swirling glass of water, Stancell's thoughts settled themselves quickly. He still could not accept the idea of an ore pocket with powers of its own, but something even larger than that disturbed him.

"Don't try to figure it all out at once, Chief. There are a lot of unanswered questions about this thing. All we know is that the Tigris mine was destroyed and that the ore pocket appears to be responsible."

Stancell flinched and looked hard at Bedford. An image of Theeran's head and the burned bodies of the drilling crew flashed through his mind. "Then," he said slowly as he fought to control the sudden wildness he felt inside, "that means Euphrates could have a live one. We've got to warn them!" He got quickly out of his chair and headed for the commgear.

"No, Chief," Bedford said quietly. "We can't risk calling them. Whoever is running Euphrates has to think we're dead. If we call them now, how do we know they won't send another cruiser out to do the job right this time? We'll have to go there and tell them in person."

"That's a big risk, in more ways than one."

"I know it. And it gets worse. It's not just a mine that's

at stake here. There's..." Bedford's voice trailed off. There's Kalissae Boristh-Major, he thought.

That startled him. Why would he think of her? The stakes he meant were those of Federation political survival. Once the news about the ore pockets got out, that would be the problem. Kalissae did not even count in that situation. Yet her safety was of more than casual concern to him. Why?

"All right," Stancell said, breaking Bedford's thought, "but if you're wrong, we will have killed everyone who is left on Euphrates."

"Believe me, Chief, if I thought we could trust Malvin, it would be different. But we can't." He glanced at *Lady's* forward view screen and noted their plotted position superimposed on it. He pointed to the screen and said, "Anyway, it looks like we'll be there in a few more hours."

Stancell looked up at the screen, then turned his eyes back to Bedford. "It frightens me."

"Me too, Chief. Me too. But we can't worry about that now. It's time to start planning." Like how do we deal with an unknown this strong? he thought. And what are we going to find when we get back to Euphrates and back to level eighty-seven?

TWELVE

Kalissae stepped warily out of the elevator. Level eighty-seven held an uneven stillness. As she walked into the main tunnel her footfalls echoed strangely back at her.

"Issy?" she asked with apprehension.

I am here.

Kalissae felt relieved. She had come as he had told her to, but she needed the comfort of knowing he was still with her. That odd thought was quickly superseded by a question. "Why does this tunnel feel so different?"

Because of me, Issy lied. His energy faded with every passing moment. *We must hurry. Come to the ore pocket, now.*

As she walked quickly through the hollow stillness she pushed her apprehensive thoughts aside. "What do I do now?" she asked as she stepped up to the wall. A chill passed through her. Whatever Issy wanted her to do, she was ready to get it over with.

Press yourself against the wall, and empty your mind. I must leave you for a while.

"No."

152

Do not be afraid. You will be safe. But you must not pull away from the wall. Just clear your mind and let what happens flow through you.

"Yes."

Do not pull away from the wall. If you do, I will die. I trust you, Kalissae. I trust you with my life.

He had used her first name. Kalissae smiled to herself as she remembered how she would have reacted to that before. Now Issy's improper address was inconsequential. He was inside her mind. "I understand," she said quietly. She closed her eyes and pressed her body against the cool, damp mine wall. "Is this all right?"

Excellent. Now clear your mind of every thought.

Kalissae called up her renewed O.P.R. skills and emptied her mind as easily as she would have emptied a vial of votive oil at her annual reconsecration to the tenets of Saint Gunson. It was a pure, unreserved act of faith, which left a hollow nothingness in the center of her mind. *I can do it,* she thought from the fringes. Then even that faint stirring was gone. Within seconds she was as still as the rock against which she was pressed.

Issy gave no warning of his departure. He just silently severed the last connection with Kalissae's mind and concentrated himself in the ore pocket. During the brief instant it took for him to leave, he touched a dark crease in her brain that left her open and defenseless. It was the easiest way for him to prepare a place for himself. But as the last tendrils of mental contact with her fell away, he knew that if his efforts failed she would lose her sanity.

Once inside the ore pocket Issy dredged up his last remaining stores of energy. With a powerful pulse of naked will he shattered the tough, rigid edge of his time continuum.

It was the future he was after, but he would have to wait before he could reenter and physically merge with Kalissae. The laws of time, like those of physics, required that there be a reaction for every action. Kalissae would have to view and know all that was in him before they could be joined as a symbiotic pair. It was this part of the process Issy feared most.

He had entered Bedford when Bedford was still a child, and the child had accepted Issy's knowledge with a naive sense of inevitability. Kalissae did not have that innocent acceptance. She might not be able to survive the shock of seeing all that Issy's history implied. If she did not, they would both die—he quickly, she far more slowly. But it was too late to hesitate now. Issy let himself go.

A thin, milky wave of dynamic energy spread effortlessly through the plasteel, rock, and synthfiber of the Euphrates mining complex. It slid unnoticed between the atoms and molecules of every person and thing. As it moved, it carried a silent, deadly message, a story so full of implied horror that even Arter Rosenthal would have cringed had he been able to see it. But the message was meant for only one person in the mine. It was coded for one soul. Kalissae would have to absorb its contents and try to understand.

Her body was splayed across the face of the ore pocket. The pores of the rock and the pores of her skin seemed part of one system. Her heart beat with slow rhythm. Her mind was hollow, an empty sponge which waited unawares for the pulse of energy to fill it up.

"Theeran!" an unfamiliar voice cried out.

Kalissae turned to see who had called to her. She knew the call was for her, but she could not understand why.

"Theeran!"

Now Kalissae saw who called. A small, green woman with red hair was pointing at her. The woman mouthed words that were lost between them.

"Theeran!"

The voice was harder now, and Kalissae realized it—

"You killed Theeran!"

Kalissae squeezed her eyes shut, and the image disappeared.

"We must be kind to your sister, Kalissae."

Mother. A face wedged itself into her mind.

"She may be half-low-caste, but we must always remember that she is also a Boristh."

Yes, Mother. Yes, Mother. Yes, Mother. The echoing words pushed open a bright door in front of her.

B-E-H-O-L-D.

A long, spiraling rope flung itself out along her line of sight. Every few centimeters its fibers held small circular mirrors, thousands of them. Each caught the light in such a way that all the mirrors focused on one spot: Kalissae's empty mind.

With each breath she took, the rope vibrated, and a different image burned itself into the fabric of her soul. Somehow she knew that everything she saw had happened long ago, in a past that was not her own.

She breathed faster.

Millions of strange beings and even stranger objects moved out of the mirrored rope and into Kalissae's brain. Each new image weighed her down. Her sense of revulsion twisted the rope and increased the flow into her crowded mind.

She could not turn away. She would not let the truth frighten her. Her Pflessian principles offered no refuge. The time had come to see, and know, and understand.

The flood of images was oppressive. The weight of their messages, and their relentless intrusion quickly filled her to overflowing. Kalissae opened her mouth to scream. Her vocal cords strained to make the sound which would release her.

Suddenly everything around her flickered and went dark. The rope was gone. The visions in the mirrors had disappeared. Her mind returned to stillness.

Only the memories remained, the newly acquired history of Issy's long forgotten race. Kalissae now knew the path Issy's forebears had taken. That knowledge brought shock, pain, and disbelief. An intense melancholia drove her to the floor of level eighty-seven.

The naked, living ore pocket boiled with blue-white energy. It sparked, and crackled, and threw long tongues of ghostly flames in all directions. On its shimmering surface danced the ghosts of centuries, animated skeletal shadows which loomed up from within the pocket for brief, spasmodic moments before returning to its interior.

Kalissae looked up at the towering cauldron of glistening nightmares. Her mind was her own again. But it was no longer her own mind.

Though what she saw was frightening, she understood what it was and climbed fearlessly to her feet. Just as she stood upright, the ore pocket lost its blazing fire and took on the slippery texture of molten wax. At its center one image stood out in a halo of blue light: Theeran.

Kalissae stared as the waxen image of her half-sister began to melt. The hair and skin fell down across Theeran's slippery bones in large, tearlike globs. Kalissae moaned in horror when Theeran's eyeballs left their sockets and rolled down the exposed cheekbones.

It was too much to bear. As the final shreds of Theeran's flesh ran and puddled on the floor, Kalissae screamed.

Theeran's skeleton jerked up and down. Then it raised one glistening, bony arm and pointed a stark, white finger at her. It held its accusatory gesture for one long moment. Then it melted into the background of the ore pocket. But Kalissae saw nothing. The dark safety of unconsciousness had taken her into its arms.

"How did she get out of here?" Rosenthal asked as he inspected the ruptured seals on the door to Kalissae's quarters.

"I don't know, sir." The young security lieutenant was nervous. He had been informed of the breakout after a guard had discovered the shattered door. When he arrived, he had found the seals inexplicably reversed. No weapon or tool he knew of could have done that. But even stranger than the ruined door was the fact that Sr. Malvin was still inside the manager's quarters.

Rosenthal looked across the room to Malvin. "I want

this mine turned upside down, Lieutenant. Find her." He stepped into the room and walked slowly over to Malvin. "Now, Nicholas, I want you to tell me what happened here, and where your greenie has gone."

Malvin sat unmoving, staring into space.

"I'm waiting, Nicholas," Rosenthal said quietly. As the last of the security team left the room to continue their search, Rosenthal looked at them with disdain. Then he pulled a chair up in front of Malvin, sat down, and smiled. "I am still waiting, Nicholas."

I'm a good man, Malvin thought, a reasonable man, a man who is hardworking and loyal, a man who knows how to handle himself under many conditions. I am a good man, a good man, but him? He's not, not at all. Malvin looked up at Rosenthal and spat into his face.

"Damn you," Rosenthal said without anger. "You're a fool. But have it your way. I'll get the answers to my questions one way or another."

He wiped his face on the sleeve of his tunic, then reached into a small pouch on his belt and pulled out a neatly folded piece of material. With a flick of his wrist he snapped it open like a table napkin.

Malvin stared at the cloth as Rosenthal dangled it in his face, and realized it wasn't a solid piece of fabric. It was a one-meter-square net with a long length of tubing that trailed off from the edge Rosenthal held in his hand. I'm a good man, a good man, Malvin repeated to himself.

"Make it easy on yourself. Just tell me where she went." Rosenthal anticipated Malvin and dodged a second glob of spittle aimed at his face. "As you wish."

The net went easily over Malvin's head. He refused to resist when Rosenthal pulled it tight around his neck so that the thin net touched almost every part of his face. Not him, Malvin thought. He's not a good man.

As soon as the net was secure, Rosenthal leaned back in his chair with a faint smile. "Where is she, Nicholas?"

Silence.

Rosenthal squeezed the bulb on the end of the tubing,

and a column of colorless liquid ran up into the webbing of the net.

Malvin screamed and clutched his face. Then he screamed again. At one centimeter spacings throughout the net the liquid dripped through small holes and burned him.

"It's the best quality sulfuric acid, Nicholas. Comes from our own labs. Would you like some more?"

Malvin wanted to fight, but his mind was numb, and his legs refused to budge when he tried to move them. He forced himself to ignore the burning pain and wiggled his toes. Rosenthal could not destroy him. He refused to let him.

"Tell me where she went."

Ansole, ansal, anselim. Malvin conjugated the Erterian verb with precision and fluency. The pain ate at the edges of his resolve. Yet he felt a new, tingling pain as he moved his feet slightly in his boots. Bartier, bartore, barte—

Another, louder scream interrupted the past tense of a word which in Galactic Standard meant, to love.

"End your suffering. Tell me." Rosenthal squeezed the bulb again.

Acid dribbled down Malvin's cheeks and into the open collar of his tunic. Fiery, red marks made his face look like it was covered with twisting lava flows. Burning pain fired his nerves. Connections sizzled and broke.

Somewhere deep inside, the pain drifted away from him. He was a good man. He would not speak. He did not know where Kalissae had gone. But he would not tell Rosenthal that. He was a good man. Rosenthal was not. Malvin flexed one foot.

Rosenthal pulled a small bottle from the same pouch he had taken the net from, and refilled the bulb. "You know, Nicholas, there's only one thing about using acid. It dulls the senses after a short while." He smiled.

"Fortunately, long experience and my vocational needs have led me to a perfect complementary chemical." He stared at Malvin for a moment, surprised that the man had not lost consciousness. Maybe Malvin had more in him than he let show, he thought. "You know what deuterial sulfate is, don't you?" He smiled again. "Of course you do. You invented it."

The look on Malvin's face turned slowly from pain to something darker. Deuterial sulfate was a strong, stable compound made from sulfuric acid and deuterial hydroxide. His discovery that an organic hydrocarbon could be used as a catalyst to combine the two had been the high point of his scientific career and had brought him to the attention of Helical management.

With a broad grin Rosenthal noted the change in Malvin's expression. "I see you understand. But in case you have any doubts, I'll give you a little sample." With a dropper he drew off some of the liquid he had used to refill the bulb.

Malvin tried to resist, tried to force his legs to work, tried to push Rosenthal away, but all the energy seemed gone from him.

"I'm really sorry, Nicholas," Rosenthal said as he let one drop of the liquid fall onto Malvin's forehead.

There was a loud popping sound and a small flash of flame as the deuterial hydroxide made contact with Malvin's skin. The pain was so intense he couldn't even scream. Almost instantly the liquid had eaten a hole completely through his flesh and part of the way into his skull.

"Now you will tell me."

Malvin's rational brain ceased to react. Only animal functions remained. He had to survive. Kill! Kill!

With a powerful surge of fury he lunged at Rosenthal and grasped him by the neck. Kill! the remnant of his mind screamed. Kill! Kill! Kill!

Reeling backward under Malvin's unexpected attack, Rosenthal fell to the floor. His chair spun out from under him. Malvin clung to his throat. Fingers tore at the muscles in his neck.

In the midst of the struggle Rosenthal lost his grip on the bulb. Frantically he tried to reach it with one hand as he pushed against Malvin with the other. He twisted and turned on the floor, desperate for breath, furious at his carelessness.

Just as Malvin's choke hold was having its effect, Rosenthal grabbed the bulb. With a hoarse scream he pushed Malvin away and squeezed the bulb at the same time.

No scream of agony came from Malvin's mouth. Nothing registered in his brain. The flashes of light and kinetic popping sounds marked forever the end to his consciousness.

When the acrid cloud of grey smoke cleared from around where Malvin's head should have been, there was nothing left except a half-empty shell of bone that hissed and smoked in one final denial of victory.

Rosenthal rolled away with an effort as the smell burned his nostrils. Then he forced himself to relax and breathe slowly and deeply. "You might have made a good QuietSun, Nicholas," he said finally as he massaged the aching muscles in his neck. "But you were too weak to ever have passed the training."

"Saint Gunson, would you look at the bastards," Stancell said as he pointed to the view screen.

Bedford turned and looked. Security Guard ships were pulling out of orbit from around Euphrates at random intervals and heading into deep space. "Why would they do that?"

Stancell pulled his eyes away from the screen and stared at Bedford. "Don't know . . . unless they're through with whatever they came to do."

"You know Malvin better than I do, Chief. What is he capable of?"

Stancell grimaced. "Anything."

"At the rate they're leaving," Bedford said as he looked back at the fleeing ships, "we should be able to land unhindered in a little while. Let's wait them out. I'd just as soon not have to fight our way back into the mine."

Helical Security doesn't spook easily, Stancell thought as he nodded in agreement with Bedford's suggestion. He didn't mind not having to fight, but he was worried about what they would find once they got down on Euphrates.

"I tried to stop them, sir, but they just pushed me aside."

"Don't you know how to use your weapon, Lieutenant?" Rosenthal asked angrily. The junior officer stared back at him with a fearful, sullen expression. Rosenthal sighed internally. The idiot had let over half the Security Guard abandon their posts without putting up a fight. Probably no one had ever taught him how to handle a mutiny. "All right, Lieutenant, how many are left?"

"I'd say thirty or forty men, sir."

"I want an exact accounting."

"Yessir."

The wounds on Rosenthal's neck ached, and he pressed his hand softly against the bandages. "As soon as you count butts, you tell those who are left that they will either wait here until I give the order to leave, or"—he paused and stared hard— "or they will die here. Is that understood?"

"Understood, sir."

"Excellent. And if you can't hold them, Lieutenant, then you use that weapon. Is that understood?"

"Yessir."

"Fine. Now just one more thing, and I'll let you get on with your duty. What caused your men to panic?"

"Level eighty-seven, sir." His voice quavered slightly.

"What about level eighty-seven?"

"It's a terrible sight, sir. The ore pocket down there has been exposed. When I saw it the thing was shooting out awful flashes of blue light, like nothing I've ever seen, sir. Frightful it was. And no shadows either, like the light was coming from all around us."

He heard the hint of hysteria in his voice, but the scene was all too vivid for him. "Some of the men thought it was a sign . . . a bad luck warning. Then someone screamed something about devil lights, and, well, after that, sir, it all got a bit confusing." His eyes were downcast as his voice trailed off. He took a deep breath, looked up at Sr. Rosenthal, and said what he had to say. "But there are no excuses for what happened, sir. I accept full responsibility."

"Of course you do, Lieutenant." Rosenthal held his immediate reaction in check. He was tired, and no ore pocket could act the way the lieutenant had described it. But something had panicked the Guard. "Thank you, Lieutenant," he said finally. "You're dismissed."

"Yes, sir." The officer saluted and left the room.

Just as he decided to go down to level eighty-seven and take a look at the ore pocket himself, the sounds of weapons fire came through the door.

Instinctively he jumped behind the nearest desk. Then he peered around its side and watched the doorway. In his hand was the small piezoelectric stun pistol set for a full charge. An unconscious smile spread thinly across his lips as he waited for someone to enter the room.

After a few minutes the firing stopped. It was followed by an eerie silence. Rosenthal waited. A shadow fell across the doorway. Then the young lieutenant fell into the room, his left leg soaked in blood, a bloody burned spot marring the side of his chest.

"What the hell is going on?" Rosenthal called from behind the desk.

"Fire fight. They . . . they won't stay. All my men . . . dead. All dead." He choked out a few unintelligible syllables and fell silent.

Rosenthal moved slowly around the desk, and as he did so he glanced at the main view screen. It showed two Helical cruisers leaving the ground, and a third preparing to. Sudden anger jerked him to his feet. Hatred twisted his face as he watched the ships lift one by one. Somewhere deep inside his mind part of his self-control snapped like an overstretched wire.

"You can't leave me!" he screamed as the last ship fired its main thrusters and cleared the flight apron. "You can't leave me here! I'll get you all! Have you on charges! You can't—"

An object on the secondary screen stopped Rosenthal's raving. At first he thought it was one of the cruisers returning to pick him up. As it came closer he realized it was not a Helical ship at all.

He couldn't believe it. Three quick strides took him to the screen's controls and he turned up the magnification. Impossible, he thought. Impossible. Yet there it was, the Free Syndic's ship. What did he call it? The *Lady Victoria*. There was the *Lady Victoria* coming in for a landing on the surface of Euphrates.

For the first time in Arter Rosenthal's life he was glad that one of his orders had not been successfully carried out. He was almost happy that the Free Syndic was alive, not because of the man—because of his ship. *Lady Victoria* was Rosenthal's passage to safety. In appreciation for that he would kill Bedford Odigal quickly and cleanly.

Kalissae sat on the wide bench with her knees tucked up under her chin and watched the dials and gauges on the opposite wall fluctuate with the pulse of Euphrates. The auxiliary life-support monitoring station was her special place to get away and think. More than once it had offered her sanctuary from the pressures of running the mine. But always before she had sat in this dim cubical alone. Now that was impossible. Issy was a part of her.

"Issy?" she asked as she rocked almost imperceptibly back and forth.

Yes. Issy had remained quiet since she had brought them here, answering her questions, but saying no more than was necessary. There were things they would have to do soon, but he knew Kalissae needed time to assimilate what had happened to her.

He had to be patient. Given the time it was taking him to adjust to her annoying biochemistry, and given how that slowed his process of borrowing selected samples of her body cells for his own use, patience was easy. The change-over from generations of male Odigal biology to female Boristh-Major biology demanded the largest part of his attention.

"It's my memories of Theeran. They still hurt. I think I understand now why she died, but I cannot understand why I continue to believe it was my fault." She felt swollen with Issy's presence, yet comfortable at the same time. It was a paradox she accepted with a complacency that was new to her.

Such things are impossible to understand. We exist in a galaxy which does not recognize Fate as a valid cause for the things which happen to us. Issy paused and allowed Kalissae time to form a rebuttal. When she remained silent, he continued. *You did what you thought was right. So did Theeran. She sensed something was wrong, but without hard corroborating evidence from the mine's detection instruments she decided to go against her instincts.*

"But I ordered her, threatened her, forced her to do it."

So? The fact remains that she did it against her instincts. If there is fault to be found, it lies in the error of not trusting intuition over machines. You were both equally guilty of that.

"But she is dead." Kalissae stopped rocking and curled up tighter. Dead, and I killed her, she thought as tears slowly filled her eyes.

You did not kill her. My race, Seren fanaticism against any form of belligerence killed her.

Kalissae's thoughts were too muddled. She wanted to change the subject. "Issy, do you think we will ever find Bedford?"

She was too close to a breakthrough for Issy to let her go. *Kalissae, you must settle your mind over what happened to your sister.* He instantly formed a vivid image of Theeran in Kalissae's mind. Then he formed an equally vivid image of Kalissae herself. *Watch,* he said as the images started to move.

The images spoke to·each other. Their words and actions were the same as Theeran and Kalissae's last meeting. But Kalissae found she could shift viewpoints and see the scene through her own eyes, or through Theeran's.

The reenactment of what they had said and felt during that fatal conversation did not take long. When it was over, the images faded and Kalissae sat silently for a few moments. A transformation had taken place. For the first time in her life she truly understood her sisterhood. That understanding cleansed her of guilt and eased her sorrow. She wondered how Issy had known what she needed.

Because of your perfect Pflessian dignity, Issy answered her thoughts, *you felt it was beneath your rank to express emotion for a low-caste. But the emotion was there. The conflict turned Theeran into a symbol of everything you found disquieting about your society.*

Kalissae stood up with a hesitant smile, and stretched. "I suppose you're right. I never realized how rigid my life had been until you let me see through Theeran's eyes. You did do it, didn't you?"

Yes, with your help. You had to be the one to see yourself as you really are. I could not do that for you.

"I see." Kalissae stepped over to the wall of instruments and blindly looked at their readings. "Then . . . then I was ready, wasn't I?"

To abandon your Pflessian social conventions? Yes.

"I think I . . ." Kalissae paused and smiled, then, wanting to for the first time, continued subvocally. —I think I can leave all the worst of those rules behind me now.—

If Issy could have grinned, he would have. *I think so too.* Kalissae stared at the dials and gauges for a few more minutes. Thanks to Issy's help she was free now, free to build her future relationships on a new basis, free to enjoy the diversity of her emotions, and free to . . . to what? To let herself love.

An image of Bedford passed lazily through her mind. She let her senses savor it like some rare and delicious fruit. To fall in love, she thought as the image faded away.

Look at the instruments.

It took Kalissae a moment to clear her head. Then she focused sharply and saw what Issy meant. The high-side pressure relief gauge registered zero. That meant some-one was entering the mine through an unauthorized surface-access hatch. Most of those entrances were permanently sealed, and only a few people knew which ones still worked—herself, three or four of the engineers who had been sent to Tigris, and . . . Stancell!

Quick. We must reach them before the Security Guard.

Issy had barely completed his sentence before Kalissae was through the door and on her way to the surface locks. If Stancell, then Bedford . . .

THIRTEEN

When Arter Rosenthal came out of the communications center, he looked with disinterest at the loyal corpses which littered the corridor floor. Then he stooped down and picked up a rubylyte laser pistol. It still held most of its charge, so he stripped a holster off one of the bodies, put it on, and holstered the laser.

The mining complex was empty except for him and Kalissae Boristh-Major. He no longer cared about her or her whereabouts, but he would not pass up the opportunity to shoot her if he saw her. The laser gave him far greater range to do that than the piezoelectric stunner still in his pocket.

As he made his way to the surface air locks there was only one thing on Rosenthal's mind. He had to take the *Lady Victoria* and escape. He had a score to settle with the cowards who had left him in this predicament. He would have his revenge on them. But he would kill the Free Syndic first.

He dimmed the lights and looked cautiously out the view port beside the main air lock. Two figures were just moving away from the ship. Of course, Rosenthal thought. Stancell. I'll kill him too. However, instead of heading toward him, the pair veered off and headed toward the superstructure of one of the ventilator shafts. Rosenthal was almost disappointed. He would have enjoyed putting an end to both men's lives. But now self-preservation was far more important.

As soon as he was sure they were far enough away that they could not prevent him from reaching the ship, Rosenthal tightened the helmet seals on his X-Ninety and cycled the air lock. It had barely opened before he was out and running as fast as the suit would allow.

"Fools," he said aloud when *Lady*'s hatch opened at his command. He looked in the direction they had disappeared and laughed. Moments later he was waiting for the internal hatch to open with the smile still on his face. The ship was now locked from the inside. Even if they did come back, they couldn't stop him. In ten minutes he would have *Lady Victoria* ready to take off. Within a few hours Euphrates would be a smoldering grave.

"Damn you, Syndic! Damn you! I should have guessed you would have some lockup system." Rosenthal talked to himself in harsh, self-effacing tones as he went through the takeoff procedures one more time. All the instruments responded until he tried to fire the engines. Then everything went dead. There were no abort lights, no malfunction indicators, nothing.

Nothing, nothing, nothing. Rosenthal kicked the side of the control console and cursed again, but there was no spirit in it. He knew there was nothing he could do. It might take him days to trace the circuits which controlled the lock-out. And Rosenthal didn't have days.

He would have to go back to the mine and drag Bedford out. It was his only hope of escape. But it was no simple task he set for himself. First he had to find the Syndic.

Then he had to force him to help without using so much force that he wouldn't be any help at all.

The vision of what he would do with Odigal once he was through with him played in Rosenthal's head as he retraced his steps back into the mine. And the horror of that vision would have made any sane creature cringe in fear and disgust. Arter Rosenthal smiled.

"You're a pretty handy man to have around," Bedford said as he ducked his helmeted head and followed Stancell through the hatch. "What are these hatches used for?"

"Emergencies mostly, but sometimes for an oddball bit of maintenance. Most of them were sealed up after each section of the complex was completed." Stancell let Bedford get past him in the small circular room, then turned and started resecuring the hatch bolts. "This'll take a minute."

Bedford looked down the narrow access tunnel that led out of the room. It was obviously a tunnel designed for suits far less bulky than their X-Nineties.

"That should do it," Stancell said as he tightened the last bolt. "We'll have to wait a few minutes until the pressure gets back up to normal. Then we can take these suits off."

"I was wondering how we were going to get through that tunnel. Where does it lead?"

"All the way down to life-support. But we won't be going that far. We'll exit down on mess level twelve. That should put us in a pretty good position to reach the main admin areas without being noticed."

"A kitchen, Chief? Won't there by people there? I want to get as close as we can to the communications center, but I'd feel a little better if we didn't have to risk upsetting someone's meal." He checked his external gauges. "Can we take off our suits now?"

"Yes," Stancell said after checking his own gauge. He pulled back the safety cover at the waist of his suit and yanked hard on a small D-ring. The bacteria in his suit were infused with a mixture of oxygen and nitrogen cyanide and immediately started going dormant. After thirty seconds the pressure subsided enough to begin taking the suit off. Bedford followed his example.

"There won't be anyone on mess level twelve. That's the auxiliary mess, and it was shut down as soon as we started transferring people to Tigris." He paused for a moment when he thought of Tigris and wondered what they would find here on Euphrates. Then he continued. "We shouldn't be bothered by anyone there."

"You think of everything, don't you, Chief?" Bedford smiled as he said that.

"Try to, sir. I definitely try to."

As soon as they were both out of their suits, Stancell stepped up to the narrow tunnel. "Just keep your head low and follow me," he said as he crawled into the opening.

Bedford followed as soon as there was room. He inched his way behind Stancell on the roughened plasteel surface, grateful that the Chief had thought for them to bring the small headlamps. He would not have liked to have been in this tunnel in the dark.

After a few minutes of steady movement they came to a fork in the tunnel. Stancell stopped and looked down both paths. Then he turned to Bedford as much as he could and said, "I think we take the one on the right."

"You're not sure?"

"It's been a long time since I was up here."

"What happens if we take the wrong path?"

"Well," Stancell said with a hint of amusement, "if I've guessed wrong, we'll end up in the ventilation system for the waste aeration sump. You know what skedge frost is?"

"No."

"Take my word for it that you don't want to. Condensation from the sewage system cools pretty fast up here. Coats the tunnels after a while—"

"And smells pretty bad too, I'll bet."

"You guessed it. That'll be our clue we've taken the wrong turn." He gave Bedford a weak smile. "Sorry my memory isn't as good as it should be."

"I'll take my chances on it, Chief."

Stancell's face brightened. He appreciated the vote of confidence. "Well, my gut feeling is the tunnel to the right. One of the design criteria for these mines is SAFETY LIES TO THE RIGHT. It was done that way because most people favor their right side when they're lost."

"Then let's take the right." Bedford was feeling a trifle impatient and ready to get moving again.

"Right you are," Stancell said as he crawled down the right side of the fork.

"Hope the designers for Euphrates weren't left-handed," Bedford said as he followed him. Stancell's chuckle became slightly quieter as his feet disappeared down the right fork.

Twenty minutes later they stopped again. "I think this is the place," Stancell said softly. He took a rag from his coveralls and wiped a small section of the tunnel wall. "Yeah, this is it. I can tell by the section marks stamped on this plate."

Bedford was grateful that the tunnel was a little roomier at this point and asked, "What next?"

"We take off this plate and climb the rungs down to level twelve." Using the same wrench he had sealed the access hatch with, Stancell started unbolting the plate from the tunnel wall. In two minutes he had it off and stuck his head through the opening. "Lights are working. You ready?"

"As ready as I'm going to get."

"Then down we go."

When Bedford followed Stancell into the shaft, he was surprised and relieved by how large it was. He grabbed the rungs on the shaft wall and pulled himself out of the tunnel. He looked up and saw a sealed hatch twenty meters above. Then he looked down and saw Stancell waiting by one of the red emergency lamps a man's-length below him. Before Bedford could say anything Stancell started climbing down.

The descent was easy at first, but gradually a weakness in his knees forced Bedford to slow down. He checked on Stancell's steady progress below him and was about to suggest that they take a break when Stancell stopped.

"This is mess level twelve," he said when Bedford stopped several rungs above his head. He reached between the rungs and pulled out a large lever. A round hatch a meter in diameter opened with a protesting squeal and flooded Stancell in bright light.

"See anything?"

"Just a moment." Stancell shaded his eyes with his free hand and waited for them to adjust. As soon as they did he could see that the back area of the mess where the hatch opened was deserted. "All clear," he said in a whisper. With one step up he pushed himself through the opening and crawled out onto the plasteel floor. Bedford followed moments later.

"Damn, I'm glad we didn't have to stay in there any longer."

Stancell stood up and a sharp pain stabbed at his lower back. He rubbed it vigorously. "I'm getting too old for this sort of thing. I hope being your Deptenens won't always be so strenuous."

"I'll second that," Bedford said as he rose and looked around. Only then did he realize that the light which had seemed so bright was actually rather dim. The equipment in the mess was covered with light grey cloth, and the air had a stale smell to it. "Let's get going," he said finally. "I want to see who's left here."

"I still wish I had some weapons," Stancell said as he followed Bedford across the room. "My *gendo* skills are pretty rusty."

"We're here to seek and save, not destroy, Chief." Bedford held a finger to his lips, then opened the door and peered cautiously into the corridor.

Now the fun really begins, Stancell thought as he followed Bedford out of the mess. They had come back to save whoever was left from the danger on level eighty-seven. Now Stancell hoped he and the Syndic wouldn't be the ones needing saving.

This way.
—You sure, Issy?—
Yes.
The further they had come through the complex the faster they had moved. Kalissae was surprised that they had seen no evidence of the Security Guard, and worried too. If the Guard had left already, that meant . . . Apprehension clouded her thoughts. Suppose it was too late? She hesitated as a small shiver of fear ran through her.

Issy was forced to make yet another biochemical adjustment as her fear released new hormones into her body. *Trust me,* he said as reassuringly as he could.
—I do. Otherwise we wouldn't be here.— Kalissae smiled to herself with a flash of irony as she moved down a narrow service hallway that cut across the complex on level nine. *Here* was a very special place.

Bedford and Stancell used a leapfrog system to work their way up through the levels of Euphrates. Each took a turn at moving ahead, leaving the other to watch the rear. They moved up to level eleven, zigzagged across it, and found no signs of any other presence. Moving swiftly and quietly, they worked level ten the same way. Still they saw no one.

Stancell took the lead as they came out of the stairwell on level nine. Bedford watched with appreciation as the big man moved efficiently down the corridor and ducked into a service hallway.

Kalissae struck out blindly at her attacker. Her scream was cut short when he pivoted the full weight of his body and slammed a huge fist into the aortic center of her chest.

Issy fought for control.

Stancell recoiled in horror as Kalissae slid down the opposite wall and slumped to the floor. Before he could react further, Bedford was past him and down on one knee next to her unconscious form.

"I didn't . . . I couldn't . . . ahgh," Stancell stammered as he moved to kneel opposite Bedford.

It was all too much for Issy. Kalissae's body was sending out chemical shock waves to protect her. But in order to protect himself, he had to retreat. He sensed Bedford's presence, but there was no way to make contact. Later, he thought as he slipped inside himself. Later.

"What happened, Chief?" As Bedford asked the question he put his hand on Kalissae's neck to check her pulse.

"Is she all right?"

"She's alive, but her pulse is weak. What happened?"

Stancell looked very shaken. "It all happened too fast. We ran into each other and an instant later I hit her. Are you sure she's all right?"

"No, dammit," Bedford snapped. "We've got to find a better place to check her out."

"Around the corner."

"Good. Help me get her up. Then I'll carry her, and you lead the way."

"I'm sorry, Syndic. I really am."

"Me too, Chief. But it wasn't your fault." He felt very protective as he held Kalissae in his arms. "Let's go."

The room Stancell led them to a short distance down the main corridor had obviously been abandoned in a hurry. The previous occupant had left some personal things behind, including a rumpled blanket on the sleeping foil. Bedford laid Kalissae down as carefully as he could, then pulled the blanket up to her shoulders. Stancell hovered over them like an anxious mother.

"Where can we find a medkit, Chief?"

"There should be one by each elevator bank."

Bedford straightened up and looked at Stancell carefully. "Are you all right?"

"I guess. Just a little shaken, that's all." He looked down at Kalissae and the frown on his face deepened. "Look, Syndic, I'll go look for a medkit. You lock this door behind me, and don't open it unless you're sure it's me." He looked back at Bedford and continued. "It may take a while, but don't give up on me."

"I've got faith in you, Chief. Be careful."

"You too." With one more glance at Kalissae, Stancell left.

As soon as the iris snapped shut behind Stancell Bedford flipped on the lock. He sighed as he pulled a chair up next to the foil and checked Kalissae's pulse again. It was regular, but not as strong as he thought it should be. He started to pull his hand away from her neck, then stopped and let it relax. Her pale green skin twitched under the light touch of his fingers. Almost absently he stroked her neck to soothe the twitching.

Issy was right, he thought. She is beautiful.

Two emotions surged through him in connected waves. Sorrow at the loss of Issy was followed by compassion for this beautiful woman, a compassion so strong that it overtook the sorrow and washed it away.

Her body shivered as though responding to his thoughts, and for an instant her eyelids flickered, opened, and closed again. In that same instant static buzzed Bedford's brain, static that called to him, drew him closer to her in some inexplicable way. Then it was gone, and he shook his head to clear it of the strange sensations the buzzing had left behind.

Issy withdrew into himself again. His attempt to reach Bedford had hurt. There was no other way to describe the sensation. It was one thing to project himself into Kalissae's mind from the ore pocket, and quite another to reach out from a living being. Ruefully, Issy admitted to himself that he could not do it, at least not while Kalissae was unconscious. He would have to wait.

*   *   *

The first medkit locker he checked was empty. Stancell shook his head. Without thinking he punched the elevator call button so he could check the lockers on adjacent levels.

Damn you for a fool, he thought. He stepped past the elevators and entered the service shaft. Climbing as quickly as he could he heard the elevator go past him as he stepped out on level eight. He pushed the up and down call buttons on level eight, reentered the shaft, and climbed down past nine to ten. Maybe that'll confuse anyone tracking the elevators, he hoped.

The grim look on his face eased when he found the medkit in its locker beside ten's elevator bank. He started to reenter the service shaft, then thought better of it. Better to track across ten, take another set of stairs, and track back through nine to where Bedford and Kalissae were waiting for him.

Stancell turned quickly and headed down the corridor. He could take a shortcut through the Castel storage room and be back with Bedford inside of fifteen minutes. A small smile crept to his face.

It was premature. Halfway across the Castel storage room, with his image reflected a hundred times off the highly polished cylinders, a voice froze him in his tracks.

"Hello, Chief."

Stancell quickly looked around and saw a hundred reflections of Rosenthal beside his own. Rosenthal held a laser pistol easily at his waist. In one of those crazy rushes of thought that sometimes come to men under stress, Stancell wondered which of Rosenthal's images would shoot him. "Well," he said with as much control as he could bring to his voice, "what are you waiting for?"

"Some answers to some questions."

He still couldn't pick out Rosenthal from his reflections in the dimly lit room. But it didn't matter. If Rosenthal fired, all the images would fire at the same time. He would meet his death at the hands of a hundred Rosenthals. The thought almost made him laugh. "What questions?"

"Some very simple questions, Chief," Rosenthal said as he stepped out from the crowd of his reflections.

Bedford dozed heavily in the chair beside Kalissae's restless form. Too much exercise and too little sleep had finally caught up with him. He had wanted to stay awake, knew he should stay awake, but fatigue had drugged his body and he could no longer fight its effects. His breathing was slow and regular, his mind, dreamless.

Kalissae screamed.

For one brief instant a monster had filled her dreams. Rising from the innocence of unconsciousness, she could not connect the monster to herself. She screamed, and with the scream woke herself and Bedford.

Seconds after Kalissae violently sat up, the sleeping foil stabilized under her. Her pale silver eyes were wide open with remembered horror. Now she was awake and thinking beyond the horror, searching for a peace she knew must come.

Beside her Bedford struggled out of his warm cocoon of sleep. Her scream had plucked the silky threads of his lethargy, triggering a dormant thought: Danger! Adrenaline flowed to his brain. Resting synapses fired. Jagged tears appeared in the chrysalis of darkness. His world trembled. Yet even that was barely enough to drag him back from the borders of sleep.

He is tired, Issy said unexpectedly. *Be gentle with him.*

—I will, my friend. I will,— she said subvocally. Bedford had stopped rubbing his eyes and was staring at her with a blank look of surprise.

"Kalissae, uhmm, Manager, are you all right?" He leaned toward her and held out his hand as though seeking reassurance.

She put her hand in his, aware of how awkward it felt. "Yes, Bedford, I think I am. But I'm not sure—"

"—what happened to you," Bedford finished for her.

"Exactly." Kalissae gave his hand a gentle squeeze, gratefully withdrew hers, and folded it carefully in her lap with its mate. What stirred in her had no name in any of the languages she understood. It was greater than affection, greater than love. With Issy's memories had come an intimate knowledge of Bedford's life. No one but Issy could know him better than she did. No one but Issy could feel closer to understanding him. But the knowledge and understanding and intimate memories combined in a swirl of emotional turmoil that would not settle for her.

"You and Chief Stancell ran into each other. I think both of you must have reacted instinctively because he said he was hitting you before he even realized it was you." The brightness in her eyes seemed fixed on him in a strange way that made Bedford self-conscious about his empty hand still resting on the foil. He leaned back away from her and crossed his arms over his chest, trying to look natural, and wondering at the same time why he felt so uncomfortable. *Fatigue*, Issy would have said. And he would have been partially right.

"Anyway," Bedford continued, "we got you out of the hallway and into this room as fast as we could. Chief Stancell went looking for a medkit. I volunteered to keep watch over you, but, uh . . ." He turned his head slightly so he was looking just past her. "I'm afraid I fell asleep. Sorry." The odd brightness in her eyes annoyed him. "You're sure you're all right?"

Be careful. Go slowly.

—I will, Issy,— she snapped in irritation. The residual sensations of awe she had felt after her union with Issy were wearing off. Kalissae felt an odd sense of comfort with the new relationship, a sense of oneness which allowed her to express an opinion divergent from his. "Yes, Bedford, I'm quite all right. It was just a nightmare."

Tell him I am here. Tell him—

—Hush! You said to be careful, and I—

I know, but—

—No buts, Issy. Let me do it my way. I can't cope with your chatter while I'm trying to talk to Bedford. Please?—

Very well, Issy finally said. While he trusted her, that was not the reason he gave in. Had he been inside Bedford he would never have tried so much force, never have disregarded Bedford's right to decide which course of action they would take. Kalissae deserved the same consideration.

"Bedford, there is something I need to explain to you."

Bedford watched with fascination as the brightness in her eyes shifted tones and intensity while she took a long pause. Then she glanced down and back up as though making a decision. The brightness seemed steadier, but less intense.

"In fact, there are several things that need explaining to you," she said as she stalled a little longer. It was going to be harder than she had thought to explain anything without revealing Issy's presence almost immediately. Maybe that was the best way.

"But, I'm going to have to give it to you a little out of order, so—"

"I think you'd better lie down," Bedford said quietly as he rose from his chair. "I think that blow to your head hurt you more than you think it did." Her inability to formulate her thoughts was not a good sign.

"Nonsense. Now sit down, or I'm going to get up." She didn't like him hovering over her. It gave her irrational impulses.

Reluctantly Bedford sat back down in his chair.

She wasn't sure what she was trying to protect Bedford from. After all, she expected Issy to transfer himself back to Bedford as soon as they could get back to eighty-seven. But she *knew* his reaction was not going to be good.

"Rosenthal locked me up in my quarters... me and Malvin, actually. But Malvin was in shock by that time. He had given up. They had sealed us in and I think I was ready to give up myself."

"So how—" Bedford bit off his own interruption. "Sorry."

"I'm coming to that. Like I said, I think I was ready to give up. Then I thought I was going crazy. I started to hear voices, or a voice in my head." Even now, as much as she had accepted Issy and the burden he brought with him, she shuddered at the memory of that moment. Impulsively she reached out for Bedford's hand, and when he responded she cradled it in both of hers. There was something natural about the way it rested there.

"But I was not going crazy. Bedford, it was Issy who was talking to me."

Bedford started. "Issy? How? Where is he? What—" His emotions flooded faster than his tongue could express them.

"I don't know how," Kalissae rushed on. "He just did it, and then we did an O.P.R. on the door, and I met him down on level eighty-seven, and then—"

"You met him? You mean he's down there now?" Suddenly Bedford was excited.

"No. He's here." Kalissae touched her head and saw the confusion spread across Bedford's handsome features. "I mean he is here, inside me, now. He said he would die if we did not merge. He's been through a lot since he left you, Bedford." She knew she was saying it badly, but it all seemed to come out at once.

"I don't understand. You really let Issy merge with you?"

Tell him you had to.

"Issy said to tell you I had to."

Bedford pulled his hand away from hers and leaned back in his chair. It was hard to believe what she had told him, yet there was absolutely no reason to doubt she was telling the truth. So Issy had gone away, and come back, and found Bedford gone, and merged with someone else. But now they were in the same room again. "I'll bet you're ready to let me take him off your hands," Bedford said with a low chuckle.

I have to stay with you for now until we get back—

–I know.– "Yes, I am ready to get rid of him," she said

half-truthfully. "But we all have to go down to level eighty-seven before he can transfer."

"Why?"

"Because. . ." On his face she saw more than a question. There was also pain and disappointment. But she couldn't really tell him why they had to wait without taking up too much time. "Because Issy has to be close to the ore pocket." That term was no longer accurate, but she had to use it with Bedford.

"Do you know what that ore pocket really is?" he asked. Before she could answer, he continued. "It's some kind of automatic trap that can activate itself and destroy a whole mine. Worse than that, it consumes people."

"We know," Kalissae said quietly.

"What do you mean, *we know*?" Bedford was startled by his own vehemence. Why was he angry? And why at her? And why did she say Issy wanted to delay their reunion?

"Don't shout at me, Bedford Odigal. I know because Issy is inside me and *he knows*."

Gently.

"Shut up, Issy. Your ex-partner is exercising his poor manners again."

So are you.

The strangeness of this conversation suddenly struck Bedford as amusing, and a small grin spread on his face.

"What are you grinning at?"

"Us," Bedford said easily. "I'm shouting at you. You're shouting at my symbiont—who is now your symbiont— who is obviously giving you internal directions. Well, doesn't it—"

"Seem like we ought to try again? Yes. But as soon as Chief Stancell gets back, we all need to go down to level eighty-seven and get this straightened out." Kalissae knew it was going to be far less simple than that. She also knew there was no way to explain it to Bedford.

He will understand soon enough.

—But will he accept?—

Will you?

—Don't you think I have already?—

Yes. And when the merging is complete, so will Bedford.

Bedford stared at Kalissae as she tilted her head and looked off into the distance. He knew she was talking to Issy. What he didn't know was why that made him angry. Then when she nodded with a little smile, he knew why he was angry. Jealousy had been behind his other emotions. He felt a very strong affection for her. But that smile, that smile which he knew was a response to something Issy had said to her, that little smile made him want to slap Kalissae's face.

FOURTEEN

"Baalz!" Stancell yelled as he jumped behind the nearest Castel cylinder.

Rosenthal fired instinctively. Then just as instinctively he dropped to the floor. Above his head the deadly beam of light reflected off the highly polished cylinders in a lethal web of ricocheting energy. His right arm burned with pain.

Stancell was afraid to move under the pyrotechnic display. But he was more afraid to stay still. He wormed along the floor on his belly toward the door on the opposite side of the storage room. By the time the reflected laser fire dissipated, Stancell was close enough to jump up and run for it, the medkit securely in his hand.

The few seconds it took for the door to cycle open seemed like an eternity. When the iris finally flared Stancell scrambled through bent at the waist and ran as hard as he could for the stairs.

Rosenthal fired an unaimed shot at the Chief's fleeing form and missed. The bolt of red energy struck the door's controls with a popping sizzle and the iris clanged shut.

"Damn!" he cursed as he slowly pulled himself to his feet. Then he cursed again when the locking light over the door came on.

Suddenly a deep pain cut through him. It took a few seconds before his QuietSun training stilled it in its place. There was no time for pain. Not while Stancell roamed free in the mine.

Commander Lanse controlled his anger and used it to work for him. But it still threatened to break loose at any provocation. "So you panicked," he said disdainfully to the young squad leader on the vidiscreen, "like children running from shadows."

The squad leader dropped his gaze. "Yes, sir," he said quietly.

"I can't hear you, Thumpton."

"I said, Yes, sir."

"Proud of yourself, Thumpton?"

"No, sir."

"Want to redeem yourself?"

He looked back up. "Of course, sir."

Lanse let a sneer curl his lip. He only wished that Rosenthal could see him in action. "Think you can control your men, Thumpton? Or do you need my help?"

"I can do it, sir."

Anger and shame mixed on Thumpton's face, and Lanse noted them with satisfaction. "Good, Thumpton, you go to work on your men. You make sure they understand that if they don't follow orders this time, there will never be another chance. You think you can do that, Thumpton?"

"Yessir!"

"Then you do it, because when we go back to Euphrates you and your men will be leading the way."

"Yessir!" Thumpton saluted smartly.

Three crews to go, Lanse thought as he casually returned the salute, then turned away from the vidiscreen. If the remaining mutinous crews were listening to his conversa-

tion with Thumpton, they ought to volunteer to go pick up
Rosenthal . . .

Suddenly it occurred to him that it was taking a lot of
time to bring the Security Guard back into line, and that,
in fact, Rosenthal might not approve at all. There was no
more time to waste.

"Syndic Odigal! Quick! Let me in!"

The door flared open and Bedford stood in the entrance-
way staring at Stancell. "What the hell's wrong wi—"

"Inside, quick." Stancell pushed Bedford back and spun
around as soon as he was through the door. He punched
the controls, and the instant the iris closed he activated
the security lock. With a sigh he turned back to Bedford
and slumped against the door. "It's Rosenthal. He's gone
crazy. Tried to kill me."

"Okay, Chief. Slow down and catch your breath. Then
you can tell us what happened." Bedford took Stancell by
the arm and led him to the chair.

Stancell started when he saw that Kalissae was conscious.
"Manager! Are you all right? I'm terribly—"

"I'm fine, except for a little knot on my head. Where
did you see Rosenthal?"

"Down in the Castel storage room on ten. I was taking
a circuitous route after stupidly punching for an elevator."

"And?"

"He took a shot at me when I tried to get away from
him."

Retreat to level eighty-seven.

"Issy says we should go back down to eighty-seven."

"Issy?" Stancell looked confused.

Bedford felt another twinge of jealousy. "My symbiont is
currently residing in Kalis—MZ Borish-Major." As he
switched his gaze to her he felt more vulnerable than
when Issy had been missing altogether. "Does he say
why?"

"I know why, and I think he's right. Besides, that may be the safest place to hide from a QuietSun."

"You mean there's a QuietSun here too?"

Kalissae suddenly realized how much more she knew about what was happening than Bedford did. "Rosenthal is a QuietSun . . . and a genetic one at that. I saw his tatoo just before he locked me and Malvin up."

"Why didn't you tell me that before?"

"Because there were more important things to tell you before."

Harder things, Issy added.

—Yes.— "Anyway, that's when we found out that Rosenthal is a QuietSun."

"Then the Security Guard . . ."

"Is under his leadership," Kalissae finished for Stancell.

"But they all left. At least all their ships did."

It was Kalissae's turn to be surprised. "You are sure?"

"Positive," Bedford said firmly. "Which leaves us with the question of why Rosenthal is still here."

The moment of silence which followed Bedford's question was broken only for Kalissae. *We should go now*, Issy urged.

"He obviously won't blow up the mine until they come back for him," Kalissae said quietly. "Now is the time to get down to eighty-seven and . . ." Bedford was staring at her in a strange way as she let her sentence trail off.

"And what?" he asked.

"I can't explain it. I mean, I know, but I really can't explain it. But it is important that we go down there as quickly as we can."

Bedford didn't like it. If Rosenthal was planning to destroy Euphrates, the best thing they could do was get back to *Lady Victoria* and launch out of here. What's Issy up to? he wondered with a bitterness that surprised him.

"We can't forget Rosenthal," Stancell said with a glance at the door. "No telling where he is right now. If we take the elevator down to eighty-seven, we're going to give ourselves away."

"That settles it." Bedford was grateful again for Stancell's reasoning. "Level eighty-seven will have to wait."

No. Make him understand. Tell him about—

–Hush.– When she turned to Bedford, defiance burned in her silver eyes. A pale blue flush filled her cheeks. "We have to go to eighty-seven. If you want Issy back, it is your only chance."

"I don't believe it."

"I don't give a damn what you believe, Syndic Odigal. What I tell you is the truth. We're going down an—"

"But Rosenthal—".

"We'll take our chances, Chief. But you do not have to come if you would rather not. What happens on eighty-seven will not concern you."

"ODIGAL! I know you're in there!" Rosenthal's voice came clearly and distinctly through the thin plasteel door. Suddenly they were faced with a more immediate problem. "Open the door, or I'll burn it open."

Instinctively Bedford put himself between Kalissae and the door. "Chief? How long will it take him to do that?"

"You've got ten seconds," Rosenthal called again.

"If his pistol's charged, not very long."

"Five seconds, Odigal!"

"Open it, Chief."

Reluctantly Stancell flipped off the security lock and pushed the button. A second later the door flared open.

"So, we meet again, Syndic Odigal. And with your friends, I see." Rosenthal stood back from the open door with the laser pistol held casually at his hip in his left hand. The pain showing on his face was explained by his right arm. It hung burned and limp at his side with the hand tucked into the laser's holster.

"Shall we return to your ship?"

A wounded animal, Bedford thought, an animal who might kill them at any moment. "Do we have a choice?"

"You could die. I'd be more than happy for you all to die here. However, I'm afraid I need your assistance for a while, so the answer to your question is, no."

"We'd rather die, Rosenthal," Kalissae said suddenly as she stepped from behind Bedford.

Stop it.

A flash from the laser pistol barely missed Kalissae and made her jump.

Rosenthal laughed grimly. "You can die if you want to, Manager, but I need the Syndic for now."

"Bring the medkit, Chief," Bedford said quietly as he stepped toward the door. "Looks like Sr. Rosenthal will need that too."

"Yes, but not until we've left this place."

They filed out single file, Bedford, Kalissae, and Stancell, all under Rosenthal's watchful eyes. He had pushed the pain in his arm back to an aching throb, and he would have liked nothing more than to have killed them all and been done with it. But he would have to save that pleasure for later.

As they waited for the elevator which would take them up to the surface level, Issy and Kalissae carried on a furious dialogue which ended when he said, *If the chance comes, take it.*

"That's how we understand the rules, sir," the face on the vidiscreen said.

Commander Lanse cursed to himself. Under the narrowest interpretation of the rules, Malotte was probably right. Lanse did not have the authority to order them back within the blast zone. But this was no time for narrow interpretations. If Rosenthal was still alive, he would expect Lanse to pull the Guard together and get back to him regardless of the methods necessary to do it. He turned back to the screen with the most impassive expression he could muster.

"You have five minutes to change your mind, Malotte. Talk to your people. If I don't have your answer by then, whatever happens will be your responsibility." He flipped off the vidiscreen without waiting for a reply.

"Prepare to fire on the *Titen*," he said calmly to the tactical sergeant.

"Preparing to fire," the sergeant said automatically, but the look on his face said that firing on one of their own ships was anything but automatic.

Lanse hoped Malotte and his crew would capitulate. But he suspected they would not. If they refused to give in, he wanted everyone else in his command to see exactly how swift and sure the punishment for a mutiny could be.

He had given them every chance. Now they stood between him and the completion of his job. Five minutes was more than generous. Rosenthal probably wouldn't have given them any time at all. He probably would just have blasted them from—

"No response, sir," the communications officer said in a strained voice that broke into Lanse's thoughts.

"Very well. Fire control?"

"Ready, sir!" the sergeant barked.

"Fire at will."

Two bright green pillows of light shot from Lanse's cruiser and hit the *Titen* fore and aft. There was no giant explosion, no fireworks, no violent destruction followed by only random debris. Instead, the *Titen* twisted slowly against the void as a transverse radial crack spread around her hull and peeled the cruiser open ever so slightly. Nothing of any consequence came through the crack, nothing except the fine, frozen droplets of what had been *Titen*'s internal atmosphere.

Everyone on the bridge watched the grim scene with total fascination. Finally Lanse broke the silence. "Excellent, Sergeant. Secure from battle stations, and prepare to return to within detonation range of *Euphrates*."

He was pleased with the way things had turned out. He had maintained discipline at the cost of only one ship. Now he could take his little task force to fire-point-E, send in one of the cruisers with Thumpton's team to pick up Sr. Rosenthal, and once they had safely returned, they could blow *Euphrates* into memory and be done with this business.

"Course set and under way," the navigation officer said.

Lanse settled back in his command chair and prepared to enjoy the short trip back to Euphrates. Yes, he thought, this has all turned out very well indeed. I can't wait to see Sr. Rosenthal's face after this. He should be pleased. Very pleased. And grateful in some concrete way.

Issy, you must hurry. Her voice wavered with anxiety. *I cannot last much longer like this. My unit has detected a belligerent presence, and I will be forced to act. Please hurry. I want to live.*

The words were spoken softly. Even though Tyene doubted that Issy could hear her, she felt compelled to say something, to try to communicate with him rather than give up hope. He must return for me, she thought. He must, before my duty demands that I stay and do again what I have done so many times before.

Issy! she screamed into the emptiness of the mine. *You must help me! You promised!*

The ore pocket glowed with a new, flickering, blue life. The darkest seams of level eighty-seven were bathed with light. The belligerence was coming closer. Automatic systems switched on other automatic systems. Tyene's words were lost in the crackling of the dome around her. She knew time was running out.

"Now, Syndic, get this ship moving." Rosenthal stood slumped against the command module bulkhead, barely able to keep his laser steady. Only willpower and anger held him up against the pain and fatigue which tore at his body like hungry scavengers. "I said *now*, Odigal."

Bedford glanced quickly at Stancell and Kalissae, then returned his gaze to Rosenthal. "I think you should do something about your arm. You'll never withstand the takeoff—"

The sudden burst of fire grazed Stancell's left forearm.

As he spun instinctively away from it, he tripped over his own feet and fell to the deck. "Great Holy Gunson, damn!" he yelled as he grabbed his arm and glared angrily at Rosenthal.

"No more talk. You get this ship off the ground, Odigal, or the greenie will be next. And this time I'll shoot to kill."

Kalissae ignored him and went down on one knee beside Stancell. Her sharp, blue canines were bared in a snarl. "Beast," she said under her breath. Stancell shook his head at her. The wound was very minor. She looked up at Rosenthal with utter disdain. "So kill us all," she growled. "Then try to get off this mine."

Don't push him. Tyene needs us.

"Enough." Bedford's single word got everyone's attention. "Kalissae, you and Stancell strap in over there. Rosenthal, you can strap in right where you are. There's a jump seat in the bulkhead. Just pull that orange lever."

Without waiting to watch them follow his instructions, Bedford turned back to the controls and finished the preliminary start sequence. Only then did he turn to make sure they were all seated. "No more laser fire," he said to Rosenthal. "You breech the hull, and *Lady* will shut down all her systems until we fix it."

Rosenthal nodded slightly, but said nothing. He could not strap himself to the jump seat without putting his laser down, and he was not about to do that. Nor was he going to let anyone get close enough to do it for him.

"Ready," Bedford said calmly. Then he hit the switch marked FULL STOP. The *Lady*'s engines responded immediately.

With a slight smile that momentarily overrode his pain Rosenthal said, "All right. I think I can handle things from here." He waved Bedford away from the command chair, then slowly changed places with him. "Strap in," he said. As soon as Bedford did, Rosenthal allowed himself to relax slightly and glanced at the readings on the board.

Bedford gave Kalissae an exaggerated wink.

Moments later Rosenthal hit the launch button. *Lady*

Victoria rose smoothly to a height of ten meters. Then she slammed back down to the landing apron. Smoke poured out of the command console.

Bedford released his straps and dove across the module toward Kalissae and Stancell.

Rosenthal fired wildly into the overhead.

Kalissae and Stancell had their straps off by the time Bedford reached them. To their surprise he dove through a small hatch between their acceleration couches. Kalissae was the first to follow him. Stancell barely got his legs in the narrow tunnel before the hatch snapped shut at his feet. A short crawl turned into a downhill slide that dumped them one on top of the other into a small padded sphere.

"Where the hell . . ." Stancell asked as he untangled himself from the other two.

For a brief instant Bedford was extremely aware of Kalissae pressed up against him. Then Stancell pulled her off, and Bedford stood up. "Escape pod," he said as he reached for a small, recessed handle.

He yanked it, and another hatch opened. "We'll crawl through the pod and out into the suit bay. Then we each grab an emergency suit and make a run for the mine. *Lady*'s not going to be flyable for anouther hour or so."

Rosenthal fired at demons in the smoke-filled command module. Suddenly an icy wave swept through his brain. It was more than smoke. It was gas.

He rolled out of the chair and onto the deck. With a ragged, jerking crawl he moved across the deck toward the main door. Talons of self-control dragged him along. Years of training dominated his movements. The desire for revenge fueled his determination.

The knuckles of his good hand felt the edge of the door. With grim resolve he pulled himself to his knees and hit the door button with the muzzle of his laser pistol. It slid open silently, and a rush of smoke flowed past him. Just as he tried to move through it, the door halves started to close.

He pressed his good fist against one side of the door. It paused for a second, then with a pop it started to close again. As he twisted to get out of its way, his limp right arm flopped out of the holster and between the closing halves. The door crunched shut with a protesting whine.

No one heard Arter Rosenthal's scream.

"Why not take the X-Nineties?"

"There are plenty of those in the mine, Chief." Bedford zipped up the emergency suit and checked its oxygen bottle. "What we need to do now is get out of here."

"And get down to level eighty-seven."

Yes.

"That too," Bedford said with a smile.

Kalissae returned his smile with a sudden warmth, then finished closing her own suit.

It took the three of them almost fifteen minutes to make the short trip from *Lady Victoria* back to the main entrance lock because Bedford insisted that they stick close to the walls instead of crossing the open space. The emergency suits were not equipped for communications, but Stancell and Kalissae understood that he wanted to stay out of view just in case Rosenthal could see them.

Once in the mine they quickly shed their suits and headed for the elevators. Bedford felt a strange, new excitement. He was going to get Issy back. That would make him an even match for Rosenthal. Might even give him an edge over the QuietSun.

Hurry, Issy. Tyene's voice echoed through Issy and into Kalissae's brain.

We're coming. We're coming.

Five minutes after the elevator began its long descent to level eighty-seven, a lone figure staggered into the mine.

His movements were slow, like a man teetering on the brink of massive traumatic shock. The right sleeve of his emergency suit was empty.

Once the lock cycled and its internal door opened, the man laboriously unzipped the seals of his thin, plastic coverall. Each simple function seemed to take forever, but finally the crumpled emergency suit lay at his feet like the sloughed-off skin of some deadly orange creature.

Rosenthal forced his brain to work. Willpower had gotten him this far. Willpower had made him cut off his useless arm and cauterize it with the laser pistol. Willpower had held him conscious long enough to pump painkillers into his veins along with a tiny supply of the stimulant that he always carried with him.

He had suited up and staggered to the mine in a daze of repressed pain and raw edges. But now he would have to call on his willpower to keep him alive.

It wouldn't have to be for long, just long enough for him to turn Euphrates into a smoldering ball of molten rock. He would detonate the nuclear charges by hand.

The Syndic had gotten the best of him twice now. There would not be a third time. Not for any of them. Willpower would see to that.

FIFTEEN

"Fire-point E . . . Mark!" The navigation officer spit the words out in a terse, staccato voice as he watched Euphrates come into range on his scope.

Commander Lanse was deep in private reverie, and it took him a few moments to respond to the information. "Secure from cruise and maintain position," he finally said as he pulled his mind away from thoughts of the prestige he was about to acquire by rescuing Rosenthal.

"Communications, contact the surface and get Sr. Rosenthal on the blinker. Operations, prepare a shuttle for immediate departure to the mine's surface locks. Security, I want Thumpton's squad, fully armed and ready to leave in five minutes." He had gone over what he had planned to do so many times that the orders fell out of his mouth like a computer printout.

With each set of instructions the activity level inside the cruiser went up a notch. The crew paused only briefly as Lanse gave his last order. "Weapons Control, begin preliminary countdown to detonation."

Lanse relaxed and listened to the buzz of swiftly moving

men and equipment as the ship reacted to his commands.
It won't be long now, he thought as he stared at Euphrates
through the forward view screen, not long until that little
speck of dust won't exist anymore.

"Stay back." Bedford thrust his hand out to prevent
Stancell and Kalissae from leaving the elevator compartment.
"Where's all the light coming from?" he asked as he
blinked his eyes and tried to adjust his vision to the bright
glow which washed in from the corridor.

Kalissae kept her eyelids firmly clamped shut, but the
intensity of the light was so strong that it forced its way
through the thin layers of her skin. She felt like she was
looking right through a star filter into the heart of her
cells.

It is the ore pocket.

"It is the ore pocket," Kalissae repeated aloud. "It was
glowing when Issy joined me, only not this brightly."

"Okay." Bedford managed to regain partial vision by
squinting. "What does *Issy* want us to do now that we're
here?" He still didn't like having to talk to Issy through
Kalissae. He felt cheated. And besides, too much could be
lost in the translation, too much which could mean the
difference between understanding and not.

Before Kalissae had a chance to respond, Stancell broke
in. "I don't care what that thing has to say. I think we
should get out of here."

"Noted, Chief, but we really don't have any choice if
Issy says differently." Bedford turned to Kalissae. "Well,
what does my symbiont say we're supposed to do?"

"*Your* symbiont," she began—then she paused. Her
eyes were finally adjusted to the light, and she could see
Bedford's frustration expressed in a thousand little ways on
his face. Damn him anyway, she thought. I can't help it if
Issy came to me and not him. I can't change the fact that
he has to talk to his Ancient through me. I can't make—

*We must go to the ore pocket immediately. It may be too
late already. Hurry, Kalissae. Hurry.*

Issy's words shattered her frustration. There was a
poignancy in his request that made her understand Bedford's
obvious emotional jealousy. "We're going to the ore pocket,"
she said flatly as she stepped out of the elevator. Without
waiting to see if they were following her she headed down
the corridor.

"Kalissae? Wait a moment. Stop." Bedford's pleas had
no effect. "Wait. Let's at least all go together." He breathed
a curious sigh of relief when she stopped a few meters
down the corridor and turned back to where he stood just
outside the elevator.

"All right," she said, "but we have no time to waste. Issy
is in a hurry." And so am I, she thought as she turned and
resumed walking down the tunnel toward the flashing
glow.

Bedford motioned to Stancell, and they moved to catch
up with Kalissae. As they pulled along side of her, Bedford
said, "I want Issy back as much as you want to be rid of
him, but that's no reason to be careless."

Kalissae stopped walking and stared at Bedford. "Look,
maybe I don't want to give him up. Maybe I like having
someone inside me to talk to, someone whose motives I
can appreciate and understand." She was surprised by
what she was saying, but she continued without hesitation.
"Issy wants to get back to you. You want Issy back. But
you can't stall every time I relay his messages because you
think I'm not telling you exactly what he wants. That's
not . . . not love."

Her last word caught him cold. Bedford stood speech-
less for a second, wondering what she meant. Love?
During his long relationship with Issy that particular
expression of what they felt for one another had never
been used except in a brotherly way. Somehow he knew
that Kalissae's meaning was different. There was a slight,
almost hidden nuance to the *way* she said it, a delicate

thread of emotion which spoke of love between a man and a woman.

"You're right," he said without further argument. Then to give himself time to think he added, "Let's get going." As they walked the last stretch of the tunnel, he silently speculated about whether Kalissae Boristh-Major really knew what she felt for Issy. He also wondered what Issy felt, and what *he* thought about these strange circumstances.

"What the . . ." Stancell stopped abruptly at the end of the tunnel and shielded his eyes from the naked blaze of the ore pocket. Bedford and Kalissae stepped to either side of him, but because of his split-second warning, they were able to avoid the temporary flash-blindness.

"The walls," Bedford said. "Look at the walls."

All around the interior surfaces of level eighty-seven the intense radiation from the ore pocket had caused small deposits of iridescent minerals to glow. The tiny pinpoints of light twinkled with every color in the visible spectrum. Because of the moisture which was ever-present in the lower levels of Euphrates, the irradiated particles seemed to flow together on the damp walls in a cold, pyrotechnical waterfall.

A sudden chill ran up Kalissae's spine. Quick flashes of what she had seen during her last encounter with the ore pocket made her shudder. She hadn't noticed the glowing walls before, but she knew from the random, indistinct shadows that danced across their shiny surfaces that the pocket itself was alive with images. "What now, Issy?" she asked aloud, glad that the light was too bright for her to look directly at its source.

We must attempt a transfer. You must press yourself against the ore pocket. Then Bedford must do the same.

Kalissae started to relay the message, but Issy stopped her.

Wait. That is not all. The pocket is very active and a transfer will be difficult. Our success will depend upon you and Bedford being in as close physical contact as possible.

That shouldn't be any problem, Kalissae thought as she started to relay the message again.

Naked.

Her mind abruptly choked off her voice. —What? Do you mean we have to— -

Yes. Clothing will only impede the process, slow my flow from you to Bedford. Do you understand? It is NECESSARY. And time is running out.

—But— -

Please, Kalissae. You must trust me again.

When she looked at Bedford, she knew the nervousness showed on her face. Inside she was a whirlwind of conflicting emotions. But one overrode all the others. She trusted Issy.

"Issy says . . ." Kalissae paused and took a deep breath, then plunged on. "He says we must take off our clothes and come into full contact with each other as we touch the ore pocket. It's necessary for him to successfully make the transfer." Before Bedford could protest, she quickly added, "I don't like it any more than you do, but we don't have time to argue about it. Chief, would you mind moving down the tunnel?"

"You're crazy. You're both crazy." The weariness in Stancell's tone said as much as his words. "I'll wait down there, if that's what you want, but not because I think it's a good idea—because we're in this together." Without another word he turned and headed down the tunnel.

Stancell's outburst had given Bedford a moment to think. What was Issy up to? The absence of clothing couldn't make all that much difference, could it? Or was this really Kalissae's idea, some kind of perverse Pflessian way to . . . to what? "I think we should do what Issy said."

"We don't have a choice," Kalissae said as she turned her back to Bedford and started undressing.

Hurry, Issy prodded when he realized that Kalissae was taking her time getting out of her clothes. Then he wondered what they would think if they knew that what he had told them to do was not for the reason he had given.

"I'm ready," Bedford said as he avoided looking directly at Kalissae. He was eager to get it over with. Yet strangely he wanted what he felt to last a little longer.

Hold each other close and step to the ore pocket.

They did it in reverse. Stepping to the ore pocket meant they would have to clamp their eyes shut, which would save them both some embarrassment.

They held hands without saying a word and walked tentatively toward the ore pocket, each with eyes firmly shut, each with the free hand out in front of them. When they touched the pocket, a high frequency tingle ran through their bodies.

Together, Issy commanded.

They both heard the command and drew into each other's arms with their sides pressed against the pocket. Bedford trembled slightly, and Kalissae pulled him tighter against her. Moments later they were engulfed in fiery brilliance.

The stiff, half-curled index finger of Rosenthal's left hand reached out and stabbed at the button marked S-twenty-three. It made contact on the second attempt, and the small video screen just above and in front of his head flickered to life.

Recon-plan-execute, recon-plan-execute, his brain kept stammering over and over again. The words and what they meant were like an indelible watermark imprinted on his subconscious by years of harshly reinforced training.

Recon-plan-execute. He punched S-twenty-four, but the security cameras on that level didn't reveal what he was searching for. A powerful, hate-filled pulse of vengeance welled up in him, but he beat it back down with his three word litany. Recon-plan-execute, recon-plan-execu—

A sudden burst of radio chatter interrupted his thoughts and dragged his tired eyes away from the surveillance screens. In his confused state he quickly dismissed what he had heard as nothing more than an audio mirage, a self-induced trick of the mind which he could ignore. He shook his head to get rid of it. But as he turned to activate the cameras on S-twenty-five the static-cluttered sound came again.

"Helical Security cruiser *Poyst* calling Euphrates control. Request Sr. Rosenthal respond immediately. Over."

The voice came through the transceiver in a high-pitched whine, but Rosenthal understood. He moved stiffly to the subspace communications console and keyed the transmit switch. "This is Rosenthal." The rough, cracked sound of his voice shocked him. They're too late, he thought as the *Poyst*'s radio operator came back on the air.

"Sr. Rosenthal, please hold for a moment. Commander Lanse needs to speak to you." There was a long moment filled with spitting subspace interference. Then a voice boomed from the speakers.

"Commander Lanse reporting for duty, sir. We will send a shuttle to pick you up immediately. Are you in any danger?"

Rosenthal didn't know how long it took him to answer, but in his mind the decision seemed swift and logical. "Commander, you will cancel your pickup vessel and commence detonation procedures immediately."

"Sir?"

"Blow this place up, dammit! That's an order, Commander, or didn't you hear it?"

"Yessir, but—"

Anger boiled through Rosenthal's mind like hot steam through the vents of a volcano. He disciplined each word out of his mouth so that there could be no misunderstanding. "I will brook no questioning of my order, Commander. I want this mine destroyed. Now!"

He paused for a moment and let the hammering in his temples subside. "Set your chronograph to eleven-point-five-zero, and activate on my mark. Ready?"

There was a short pause, then Lanse said, "Ready, sir, but won't you please let—"

"MARK! Now get off this channel and leave me alone."

Rosenthal slammed his hand down on the transceiver with so much force that sparks flew from the panel, followed by a puff of dirty yellow smoke. The panel went dead.

When he turned away from it, a malicious smile cracked Rosenthal's face. "Ten minutes, Odigal!" he screamed. "Ten minutes and I'll meet you in Hell! You *and* your damned precious ore pocket!"

"I've got you now!" Rosenthal's words screeched through the loudspeakers of level eighty-seven with a sound like unoiled bearings protesting under load. "You're going to die, Chief. You're all going to die."

Stancell snapped his head in the direction of the sound. That was Rosenthal's voice. He was sure of it. But Rosenthal should have been dead.

"Prepare to be incinerated, you fools!" the dead man's voice screamed.

"Syndic! Manager!" Stancell called as he ran toward the ore pocket. He slackened his pace as he approached the end of the tunnel. The light from the ore pocket had diminished considerably, but it was still very bright. A quick glance around revealed no one. Then a familiar shadow flickered near the pocket. "Syndic?"

"Yes, Chief."

"Did you hear that?"

"We heard it." Bedford stepped out of the shadow with Kalissae beside him.

"What happened? And what are we going to do?" Stancell dropped his eyes as soon as he saw them clearly. They were both still naked.

Kalissae answered the first part of Stancell's question. "It didn't work. Issy couldn't make the transfer. The ore pocket is in some sort of lockout mode which prevented him from entering it and—"

"You've got six minutes, Odigal, six minutes of life left." Rosenthal's voice dissembled into a long, howling laugh.

"What are we going to do?" Stancell asked again. At the

moment he could not have cared less about whether Issy had made the transfer.

"Issy says the ore pocket will protect us," Bedford said. Then he turned to Kalissae and added, "And Issy loves us enough to make good on his word."

Kalissae smiled. She was no longer embarrassed to be standing totally naked in front of Bedford. The experience with the ore pocket had changed all that. The pocket had expanded around them and burned away all their inhibitions in its unrelenting light. Their minds had been stripped bare for each other to see. How could clothes mean anything after that?

Issy must have planned it that way, she thought. He must have wanted them to know the capacity for intimacy they held for each other. He must have wanted them to realize that a deeper relationship was possible. That was what Bedford had meant when he said Issy loved them enough to protect them.

"Four minutes!" Rosenthal's voice gurgled with madness. His words were barely understandable. But their effect was heightened because of that.

"I hope you're right, Syndic," Stancell said with a shiver. "But in case you're not . . ." He dropped to his knees and prayed silently to the gods of his youth.

Kalissae grasped Bedford's hand and squeezed it tightly as she watched the Chief. The warmth she had felt since touching the ore pocket with Bedford had disappeared. She wanted to be held, but it was Bedford who said it first.

"Hold me," he whispered.

They held each other, both trembling slightly as the time ticked away. There was nothing for them to say to each other, nothing they could do to alleviate the uncertainty they faced, nothing but hold onto each other as though nothing *else* in the universe mattered.

Issy tensed as the last remaining seconds passed swiftly. Tyene had said she could stop the explosion. Tyene had said she would protect them. He had trusted her, and in doing so had directly committed his friends to whatever came of that trust. He knew that now was no time for doubt, but he couldn't help wishing it was over with.

Tyene? There was no answer. He could not reach her. As the last second snapped past he braced himself for the worst.

Nothing.

Four minds on level eighty-seven strained to detect the first signs of an explosion.

Still nothing. Tyene had done what she said she would do.

As the time moved past the point where the detonation should have occurred, loud, half-relieved, half-hysterical laughter broke out on level eighty-seven. For the moment they were all safe.

Stancell was the first to say anything intelligible. "It worked! That damned symbiont of yours did it!" He jumped up from his knees and slapped Bedford on the back, smiling and laughing at the incredible fact that they were all still alive.

In the joyous frenzy of self-congratulations that followed, Bedford took Kalissae's face in both his hands and kissed her. It was a short, light press of his lips to hers, but it was enough to shock both of them. For one long moment everything stopped. Neither of them moved, nor spoke nor dared to alter this special addition to their feelings.

Stancell broke the mood. He didn't mind watching them so much as he worried now about what would happen next. If they wanted to make love to each other, it would have to wait. "If I know Rosenthal, he's going to be down here any minute to try to finish what the explosive failed to do. We've got to be ready for him."

"A trap," Kalissae answered as she stepped reluctantly away from Bedford. "As soon as he enters the main tunnel we can grab him."

"First things first, Manager."

Kalissae flushed when she saw him point to the pile of clothes on the floor. She instantly felt embarrassed and foolish. They had been so taken up by the events of the past fifteen minutes that they had stopped thinking about their nakedness. Stancell had brought them back to a different reality.

"Thanks, Chief," Bedford said with a half-chuckle. "It wouldn't look right for us to attack Sr. Rosenthal without our clothes on, would it?"

"Suit yourself, Syndic." Stancell grinned at his own pun, turned away, and looked back down the tunnel toward the elevators. His mind immediately went to work on how they might best trap Rosenthal.

Bedford bent over the pile of clothes, feeling suddenly exposed and cold. He sorted them quickly and handed Kalissae hers. As she took them without looking directly at him, a small shiver ran through him. "Chilly," he said.

"Yes," she answered with a small smile he couldn't see.

See, I told you he is basically a nice man.

Kalissae refused to answer Issy. There was too much she had to sort out for herself before she could cope with what she had been through. And right now there wasn't time.

Rosenthal crushed his clenched fist into the faceplate of the chronograph just before the single, narrow sweep hand reached the second time mark on its finely calibrated dial. Splinters of broken glass lacerated his knuckles, but he continued to grind his bloody fist into the bowels of the ruined instrument.

He was past feeling any pain. His mind had completely collapsed into a heap of biological rubble once he realized the explosives had not gone off and would not go off. After a few mindless seconds one word rose from the wreckage of his brain—Vengeance.

The two-syllable term wavered on the edge of what little sanity he had left like the final, self-destruct program to some doomsday computer. Vengeance. Vengeance. Vengeance.

Arter Rosenthal turned from the smashed chronograph

intent on executing with lethal perfection the last supreme command his mind would ever give. He would destroy Bedford Odigal, or die in the attempt. Vengeance gave no quarter.

Issy let himself drift. The trap for Rosenthal was set. There was nothing further he could do but wait until it was sprung. He focused his energy away from Kalissae and into himself in an attempt to understand why he had not transferred to Bedford. It was true that the ore pocket's level of activity had made it more difficult for him to enter, but he knew he could have overcome that. What had really happened was that he had decided not to leave Kalissae.

Why? The question nagged at him in a thousand ways. He loved Bedford, and he knew Bedford loved him. But he could not leave Kalissae. More had changed than the way Bedford and Kalissae felt about each other. The experience with the ore pocket had changed *him* too, a change he was not sure Bedford would either like or understand... especially when it came to Tyene. Tyene. Tyene, the keeper of the—

—Issy? What's the matter?—

Nothing.

—Yes there is, I can feel it.—

I am sorry, Kalissae. I did not realize my concern might be affecting you.

—Can you tell me about it?—

Yes, I think I should. When I prepared for the transfer to Bedford, something happened, something which—

"Odigal!" Rosenthal's voice boomed down the corridor into level eighty-seven. "Odigal! Come out and face me like a man!"

Bedford tensed his muscles, ready to spring the moment Rosenthal entered the main shaft. Kalissae stood behind him ready to follow his move. Stancell waited on the other side of the tunnel.

"Odigal! Come out where I can see you!"

There was a brief pause before the sound of Rosenthal's footsteps came echoing into the silence. Each of them knew in their own way that they were dealing with a madman, a QuietSun gone past the insanity of his training. Each of them shuddered inside with the knowledge. The confrontation would be lethal.

SIXTEEN

Rosenthal's crouched form crossed the invisible barrier that separated the main tunnel from the entrance corridor of level eighty-seven. As he half-staggered into the open, his shadow splashed across Bedford's face, acting like a trip wire, triggering an instantaneous release of pent-up energy to Bedford's legs. He lunged out of hiding with his head down and flung his body in a full broadside of muscle at the QuietSun.

Rosenthal sensed the attack too late. Stunned by the speed of the charge, he looked up just as Bedford's head slammed into the middle of his stomach. The momentum of Bedford's body threw him to the ground. A deep gutteral growl burst from the pit of Rosenthal's pain.

He jerked himself over to his back with a moan just as Stancell pounced on him. A quick, defensive thrust of his good left arm slammed into the Chief's pectoral muscles. The sound of cracking ribs was muffled by Stancell's swiftly exhaled breath.

Rosenthal laughed insanely as he scrabbled to his knees. "Him! I want him!"

Bedford knew who he meant. "Take care of Stancell," he yelled to Kalissae as he moved closer to Rosenthal.

The QuietSun was trying to rise to his feet when Bedford gave him a pivoting kick on his armless right side. There is no honor in mortal combat, he thought as his foot smashed into the bloody stump.

Rosenthal's body recoiled from the kick, and he spun on one knee. He caught Bedford's ankle with his left hand and shoved upward with a hard sweeping motion. Bedford landed on his buttocks with a hard crack, and Rosenthal used Bedford's leg to jerk himself to his feet.

"Prepare to die, Syndic."

Bedford heard Kalissae scream and rolled away from Rosenthal at the same time. When he tried to get to his feet his head spun and his ankle screamed with pain. He looked up just in time to see Kalissae land a well placed kick behind Rosenthal's knees.

Bedford's eyes widened in disbelief as the QuietSun collapsed in his direction. Rosenthal fell directly on top of him before he had a chance to move out of the way. Almost instantaneously the madman grabbed him by the throat.

"Die, Syndic," Rosenthal rasped. "Die!" With one powerful, pistonlike stroke Rosenthal slammed Bedford's head against the ground.

The world spun away. Agony clutched Bedford's throat and his chest. He struggled, not only against Rosenthal, but also against some dark force which pressed against his brain.

No! a female voice cried. *No! No! No!*

The voice broke out of the darkness of his mind and screamed in his ear. As Rosenthal choked off his air supply, strange, euphoric feeling came over him.

Bedford, the voice said, *I will not let you die. Through ssy I have known you. We will live together.*

Like a fire which did not burn, energy raged through Bedford. Violent winds tore away his thoughts. Crackling charges filled his brain. His body jerked and moved in spasmodic contortions that he could not feel. Bedford was lost in the black vale of unconsciousness.

Kalissae stared in shocked disbelief. When she had kicked Rosenthal, the reaction had thrown her down. By the time she got to her feet Bedford and Rosenthal were caught in a fiery red light that expanded and glowed until it burst with a loud explosion that deafened her and knocked her down again.

Tyene, Issy answered in response to Kalissae's unasked question. *Tyene is with Bedford. I had worried that she might not be able to help when the time came. The pull of our history is strong, but she has overcome it.*

The fireball burned before her. "Bedford!" she screamed.

He will be safe . . . if . . . if he can take the strain of her knowledge. She is like me but very different. She has taken the power of the—

A loud wail shattered the sound of Issy's voice, a terrible, piercing sound that drove even Issy himself into that special place in the mind reserved for the last moment of existence.

The wail was echoed by moans from Kalissae and Stancell.

Bedford suddenly felt Rosenthal's mass diminish in inverse proportion to the increase of energy. It was as though he were feeling the scene and watching it from a distance, at the same time.

Rosenthal, the QuietSun, the man who had dictated the life and death of so many people, was being compressed into smaller and smaller increments of space-time. The process continued unabated, an irreversible geometric progression which stretched into infinity, reducing everything that was Rosenthal and everything that Rosenthal was by a factor of point-five until he was no more.

In the end, only his scream remained behind, a hollow nerve-rasping howl from the soul that shredded the air of level eighty-seven. When the scream faded away, no physical evidence remained to indicate that Arter Rosenthal had ever existed.

It is done, the voice said in Bedford's brain.

Through her tears Kalissae watched the fireball disappear.

Bedford felt a sudden surge of comprehension, a wave of understanding which brought him to the brink of consciousness. —Who are you?— he asked before the wave of energy crested and he fell back into the darkness.

Tyene, the keeper of the law, the one who wishes to become a part of you. Peace, Bedford. Peace.

Bedford listened, but did not hear, for the roaring surf of alien dreams had curled itself around him and pulled him under.

Commander Lanse stared dumbfounded at the bank of instruments as they continued to click and whir, inexorably following their separate paths away from confluence.

Nothing had happened! he thought as his eyes checked and rechecked the thin red setting marks on each of the half-dozen demolition controllers. Everything read the way it was supposed to, but nothing had happened. "What the hell's wrong with these things?" he asked the electronics specialist.

The specialist hesitated for a second before answering. "I don't know, sir," he said in bewilderment, "but look at this." His finger quivered as it tapped the clear faceplate of a gauge that read zero-zero-point-zero.

"And?" Lanse didn't really understand what all the dials and digital readouts indicated. He just knew what their proper settings should have been.

"That, sir, is the net thermo-nuclear potential of the charges which were set on Euphrates. Or at least it should be."

"Are you telling me it's zero?"

"Yessir. At least that's what it says."

Lanse's brain went into high gear. "Instrument failure?"

"Possible, but not likely, sir. We use a simple modification of the Geiger-Edwards system. Besides, it does explain why the charges failed to detonate."

Maybe, Lanse thought. But it did not explain who had

done it, or how the physically impossible had been accomplished. Or why. Suddenly the superstitions which had partially caused the mutiny seemed less crazy. But that was nonsense.

"What about a transmission break?" Lanse asked, hoping the specialist would give him a reasonable technical explanation for the lack of detonation.

"No, sir. We used the standard three-circuit triad method. All circuits show Class-A readiness."

The specialist's positive tone removed any doubt from Lanse's mind that something unexplainable had happened on Euphrates. His training taught him that the unexplainable often went hand-in-hand with the dangerous. It was time for him to make a decision.

They could attack the mining complex using conventional weaponry, or they could run. Running was not part of Lanse's vocabulary, not the reason he had taken so much effort rounding up the remnants of the Security Guard. He had brought them back to do a job, and the last voice contact they had with Sr. Rosenthal left no room for interpretation as to what that job was. He had ordered the complete destruction of Euphrates even at the cost of his own life. That order would be carried out.

"Secure from demolition stations and prepare to close on the planetoid."

"Sir?"

"You heard me, Guardsman. We're going to finish this thing. Now move."

Chief Stancell looked around through eyes and brain wrapped in the soft warmth of painkillers. He lay with his back propped against a small crate just to the right of the entrance tunnel. Kalissae sat a short distance in front of him tending to Bedford's prostrate form. Beyond her on the far side of the tunnel, the ore pocket continued to give off eerie waves of flickering light.

All is so peaceful, Stancell thought as the narcotic in his

veins blocked the remaining traces of pain from his injury. He fought his growing drowsiness, wanting to enjoy for a little longer the feeling of relaxation, the feeling of well-being that had been missing since *Lady Victoria* had been attacked.

"How is he?" he asked out of a genuine concern for the Syndic's health. He liked Bedford Odigal. Besides, conversation would help him stay awake.

Kalissae's hands were busy testing the tightness of the support bandage she had wrapped around Bedford's ankle. When she looked up in response to Stancell's question, she gazed at her unconscious patient's face, and not the Chief's. "He seems to be all right. The ankle is just sprained, I think."

"That's good." Stancell tried to focus his eyes on Bedford's head, but found it impossible. "Do you think he'll come out of it?" he asked as he let his vision wander again.

"I don't know, Chief. Without the proper diagnostic instruments . . ." Kalissae let her voice trail off. Issy had tried to contact Tyene shortly after the fight with Rosenthal, but he couldn't get through, couldn't find out whether Bedford was seriously hurt or not. They would all have to wait until he regained consciousness before they would know if he was all right.

Kalissae rose and moved over to sit beside Stancell. "How are you doing?" she asked as she tried to get her mind off Bedford's condition.

"Fine. Just real, real fine." Stancell gave her a silly grin. "You know, I could get quite fond of that stuff you gave me. It makes everything so pleasant."

She returned his smile with as much of one as she could muster. "It's great stuff, isn't it? Why don't you let it work and try to get some sleep. I can take care of things while you rest."

"Nooooo, no, no. I'd rather talk."

Kalissae smiled again at how much the drug had loosened up Stancell's normally serious personality. "Okay, what do you want to talk about?"

He pondered for a moment about what they were all going to do next, but quickly let the subject slip from his mind. That requires me to make decisions, he thought. And decisions require too much sobriety, the chemicals in his bloodstream added. "Let's talk about . . . about . . . that." He pointed at the ore pocket.

Kalissae's look of amusement faded. "What about that?"

"I don't understand. I don't understand any of this at all. I know I should have caught on by now to what all this . . . this, uh, stuff that's been going on means, but . . . humor an old pitman. Just exactly what is that thing?"

Stancell's expectant gaze was soft, but his question bored through her like a sharp needle, puncturing the thin, clear envelope in her mind that contained the information he asked for. But as the facts poured out to the edge of her tongue, she hesitated.

Tell him. He deserves to know.

—But how can I? I don't understand it all myself.—

So? Tell him as best you can. Even I do not comprehend all of it. Did that stop me from sharing my history with you? Did that prevent me from being totally honest with you?

—Well . . . no.—

Then tell him. I will fill in where I can.

Kalissae felt Stancell's eyes on her. He stared, his eyes blinking softly, his face full of distant anticipation. "The ore pocket is actually an alien power nodule, a sort of high energy military bunker," she said.

"Hell," he said quietly. "I was afraid of that back on Tigris. It's the same thing, isn't it?"

"Yes, but this one's still active."

Stancell flopped his head back against the crate and stared at the smooth, rock ceiling alive with its tiny points of light. "How's it work? Who built it? Why?" The questions slurred across his lips. Then an image of what they had found inside the egg on Tigris shattered his euphoric mood.

"Why did it kill all those miners?" he asked as he

brought his head back down and glared at her. There were some things that even a powerful painkiller could not mask. Anger was one of them. Stancell was still outraged by the loss of so many of his friends, so many people who had died without cause.

Kalissae looked away, unable to endure the pain she saw in his eyes. —Issy? How do I tell him it was unavoidable? How do I explain that the Tigris disaster was the result of Seren design, not random chance? Issy, I need help.—

The truth. Tell him the truth.

"I don't want to hear that creature's explanation," Stancell snapped when he realized she was talking to Issy. "I want to hear how *you* can justify what happened." The effects of the drug were weakened by his anger. Pain tugged at his broken ribs with cruel fingers.

Kalissae saw him wince as he gently probed his chest. "Do you want another injection?" she asked as she reached for the medkit.

"No." He motioned for her to stop and winced again. "I want an answer."

She had to respond. "It couldn't be helped, Chief," she said finally. "These bunkers were built by an ancient race, a race so old that they had forsaken their physical bodies and existed as small, coherent, self-sustaining configurations of electromagnetic energy. They call themselves Serens, and we're sitting on what was once the extreme edge of their intergalactic empire."

"Get to the point," Stancell interrupted. "All this is very interesting, but it doesn't explain why Tigris was destroyed." He felt disconnected from Kalissae's words, separated by a veil of static which radiated from his pain.

"You have to know what they were in order to understand what happened to them."

"All right. Go on then. But you'd better give me one of those things." He pointed to the medkit. As soon as Kalissae pulled out a clear, plastic-wrapped syringe, he added, "Make it a half dose. I don't want to be too dopey."

After giving him the injection, she sat facing him with

her arms wrapped around her knees. She glanced briefly at Bedford, then continued her explanation, wishing all the time that Issy would join in. "The Serens originally constructed their power domes as stasis chambers for their abandoned bodies, a form of insurance in case they chose to return to their corporeal way of life. By the time some of them chose to do that, it was too late. They returned and found the domes had reduced their bodies to little more than giant heaps of—"

"Isoleucine." Stancell completed her sentence in a flat, objective tone. "So the galaxy has been eating from the graveyards of dead aliens." He shuddered with a small exhalation of pain. "No wonder Rosenthal's superiors wanted this place destroyed. If the news of that got out, there'd be hell to pay."

Kalissae felt like she had gotten past the hardest part and wondered if Issy was helping her organize her thoughts. "After the Serens discovered their mistake, they converted the domes into bunkers to protect themselves from the reason they had decided to return to corporeal existence. They were threatened by biologically based sentients. Intelligent beings with physical forms had the one thing the Serens did not, the ability to experience their surroundings through tactile senses.

"We don't realize how lucky we are. We can see, touch, smell, taste, and hear our environment. Put yourself in the Serens' position, Chief. What if the only way you could get the sense of a place was to view it on a monochrome video monitor?"

Stancell grunted in reply. The second dose of painkiller was finally taking hold.

"Anyway, after untold centuries of having only that type of input, the pull, the *richness* of biological sensations became too much for them. Their civilization began to deteriorate, to be absorbed and integrated into the species along their borders who still had physical bodies.

"And a schism developed in their society. The borders shrank, leaving behind domes like these here and on

Tigris, outposts redesigned to stem the tide of Seren dissolution."

"But it killed a whole mine full of people...good people." History still didn't answer his question.

"And saved our lives. Why do you think the bombs didn't go off?"

Stancell turned his head and spit. "Hell of a trade, three lives for hundreds. How do you know that thing won't kill us in the end?" He thrust an accusatory arm in the direction of the ore pocket. "Or have you forgotten that we're biological too?"

Kalissae hesitated.

Tell him what I am. Tell him about Tyene.

Issy's words pushed down the fear which had caused her to pause. "Because we're in contact with a...with two Serens. They won't hurt us."

A chill, alien wind blew through Stancell's mind. He stared at her in disbelief. Two Serens? One in the ore pocket, but the other... His jaw slackened as an answer formed slowly in his mind. "Issy?" Was that it?

"Yes."

A thick, grey numbness descended on Stancell like a heavy fog which reached all the way inside and touched the very marrow of his bones with its cold, wispy fingers. The Syndic's symbiont? Could it...no. Issy was now part of Kalissae. Or was it in both of them? Or... The confusion mixed with the painkiller reminded him he was in no condition to fight the situation even if he wanted to. He wondered why he had joined with Bedford back on *Lady Victoria*. What was their ultimate goal? The Syndic had warned him there would be things he might not understand, things which would seem to contradict...

Kalissae left Stancell to his thoughts. He needed time to work things out for himself. It was hard enough for her to understand, and she was privy to Issy's history.

Stancell's mind wouldn't clear. He had a hard time believing that some race he had never heard of was worth all the death and destruction which had occurred. Maybe

Rosenthal was right. Maybe this mine should have been blown up. Maybe they should destroy... Destroy. That word stopped him.

More destruction? Was that what he wanted? Was that the way for the galaxy to grow and prosper? The distant pain in his body answered *no* to that line of reasoning. But then, what was the Syndic's eventual purpose? And what was Issy's?

"Chief," she said when she saw the questioning look in his eyes. "I know all this seems so senseless, so... empty of compassionate reasoning, but believe me, the Serens, at least the two we know, are not evil creatures. I don't know why the ore pocket on Tigris did what it did. Maybe it felt threatened, attacked by the sudden increase in population there. But something triggered its defensive mechanism. Tyene..." She paused for a moment, realizing she had not told Stancell about the other Seren. "Tyene is the other one, the one who lives in this ore pocket."

Kalissae glanced quickly at Bedford who still lay unconscious. "At least I think she's still in the ore pocket."

Stancell caught her meaning and stared at the Syndic. "You think this Tyene may have entered him?"

"It's possible, but we won't know anything until he wakes up." She heard the concern in her voice. *Wake up* was a euphemism. Bedford was not asleep, he was unconscious. For all she knew he could be in a coma and might never *wake up*, never be there to tend and nourish the feelings which had budded between them. The external muscles around her aorta tightened.

"Anyway," she said as she turned back to Stancell, "Tyene controls the power of the bunker, the dome, the ore pocket, whatever we're going to call it. She told Issy its destructive force can be channeled, directed against specific targets."

"Rosenthal," Stancell said hoarsely. He had seen what that destructive force could do.

"Yes. She protected us." And Bedford too, she added to

herself. But did Tyene protect him enough? If she didn't, I'll, I'll... Kalissae was surprised by the anger in her reaction. It confused her. What would she do if Tyene had hurt Bedford? What could she—

Her thought was broken, erased forever by the sounds of Bedford stirring.

The water was warm, and deep, and salty in a familiar way. The Orange Ocean? No, this was different. It was like the Orange Ocean, but it wasn't.

His thoughts were going in circles. Bedford searched for a memory which would tell him where he was. At the same time he pulled his arms and kicked his legs with hard straining motions to stay afloat. He was tired, very tired. But he knew he had to maintain a certain momentum to keep from being dragged further down into the whirlpool which turned him slowly round and round.

Above there was light. It illuminated his position on the inward slope of water like a faint beacon. The light was his goal, the place he had to swim to. He kicked and pulled harder.

Finally, after what seemed like hours of exertion, he began to rise. Once the upward journey started, he rose faster and faster toward the light.

"Kalissae?" Bedford asked as he bobbed to the surface of his sweat-drenched dream. "Kalissae, are you there? Are you all right?"

"I'm here," she said as she patted a piece of astringent-soaked cloth on his forehead. "I'm here." Even though she was still worried about him, she could not keep a broad smile from her face. His first word had been her name.

"Is he going to be all right?" Stancell had managed to move over beside her and was looking at Bedford.

"He seems to be coming around. Give him a few minutes."

As if on cue, Bedford's eyes popped open. Then a slow, weak grin spread across his face. "You know," he said hoarsely, "I'm getting tired of finding myself waking up from one traumatic experience after another."

Kalissae took away the cloth. "How are you feeling?"

"Tired. Weak. Hoarse, as you can plainly hear. But I think I'm okay."

"You look awful," Stancell said without thinking.

"You don't look so good yourself, Chief. What happened?"

Stancell and Kalissae both started to answer at once. Then both of them stopped talking. "Go ahead, Manager. You have more energy than I do anyway."

"Where do I begin?" she asked with a broad smile. Then when she realized what the beginning should be, her smile disappeared. "I suppose I should start with Rosenthal."

It took Bedford a moment to put Rosenthal in perspective. He sighed as he realized he was going to have to get another part of his life secondhand. "Rosenthal," he whispered.

The Helical Security cruiser *Poyst* took the lead position as the rest of the vessels under Lanse's command drew themselves into a classical Quad-V formation. Once the formation was set, he ordered his captains to bring all weapons to bear on the forward quadrant.

The Security Guard was going to destroy a deserted mining planetoid which could offer no resistance. Lanse frowned. Euphrates was a no-risk target. It would be good practice for the crews, and it would fulfill his last order to destroy it, but there was something missing.

"Set your weapons to fire at five-thousand-meter intervals," Lanse ordered on the ship-to-ship communicator. "We will advance at point-hex-ought-one-five. REPEAT, point-hex-ought-one-five. No random fire, gentlemen. You will keep your sensors aligned with the *Poyst*'s target beacon."

Confirmation of his orders flashed on the overhead

display. He motioned to his fire-control officer to stand ready. "Very well, I will fire one burst for luck, and we will begin." There was a short pause, then Lanse said, "Fire."

A sparkling ball of green energy spewed out of the *Poyst*'s center fire-port and described a two degree arc through space as it rushed toward the main superstructure of the Euphrates mining complex. *Poyst*'s detection instruments registered a slight up tick of energy when the explosion took place on the surface. But no one noticed. The Quad-V was coming up on its first mass-fire position.

SEVENTEEN

A shock wave rippled unevenly down through the levels of the Euphrates mining complex. The target of the first burst of fire from the *Poyst* had been the top sections of the central shaft which ran all the way down to the bottom of the mine. The blast had shattered the small, jutting superstructure that held various communications towers, navigation beacons, and microwave receiving dishes. The damage there was total, but did not penetrate into any of the lower levels.

The shock wave did.

Bedford jerked himself up into a sitting position as soon as he heard the first low rumble. Kalissae had just finished explaining to him what had happened, and they all cocked their heads in silence as the rumble got louder.

The sound came again, heavier, stronger, accompanied by gentle, uneven vibrations.

"What the hell is that?" The Chief's question was directed at Kalissae. Bedford was on his feet now, staring up at the smooth, twinkling ceiling of the shaft.

Her gaze joined his. "I don't know. Sounds like explosions."

A feeling of stark terror welled up in her throat as she wondered whether all the bombs had been deactivated.

"Sure does," Stancell said. He still sat on the floor, unwilling to rise and risk more pain in his chest. "Look."

Bedford and Kalissae glanced at Stancell, then to where his outstretched arm pointed. They stared for a moment in disbelief, trying to deny in their minds what their eyes saw. It was a futile effort.

"It's growing," Bedford said finally. "The ore pocket is growing." He cut his eyes to Kalissae and saw that she was no longer looking at the pocket. Her head was tilted slightly, and Bedford knew why. What was Issy telling her? And where was Tyene, an unconscious memory asked as it uncovered itself in his mind.

She must act. It is the law, Issy said as he tried to make Kalissae understand.

Her retort was fast and angry. –Whose law? The Serens'? Tell her to stop before any more of us die. The power of the dome will kill us.–

I cannot stop her. But it is not you the dome is preparing to absorb. You have nothing to fear. You will be safe.

–Not us? Then who?–

The belligerents.

–What belligerents?– Kalissae spat the question at him. She was tired of all the riddles in Issy's answers.

The dome is programmed to absorb any belligerent who comes within range of its sensors and commits an overt act of aggression.

–Theeran?–

Yes. But now Euphrates is under attack from outside by someone, someone the dome was designed to protect against.

Kalissae's mind was a whirl of questions. Why didn't the dome take the laser drill crew? Why didn't it attack—

Her thoughts were interrupted by a clanging sound. There was no telltale rumble, no warning, just a tremendous ringing caused by the first mass-fire volley as it smashed into the upper levels of the mine.

It sounds like a giant bell, Bedford thought as he stared

first up at the ceiling and then down the tunnel toward the elevators, a carillon ringing its own death—

"Issy says we're under attack, and now I believe him." Kalissae stepped closer to Bedford, then inexplicably she grabbed the material of his tunic and yanked.

Her quick movement caught him off guard. The force of her pull combined with his loss of balance, and he fell to the floor several meters behind her. "What's the idea?" he asked wide-eyed and surprised at how strong she was. Then he saw.

Head-sized chunks of rock came crashing down from the ceiling to the place where he had stood.

"I didn't have time to yell," Kalissae said as she reached for his hand to give him a pull up.

Go to the Lady Victoria.

Bedford got to his feet and brushed off his tunic. "We've got to get out of here," he said to Kalissae. Then he turned to Stancell who had covered his head when the rocks started falling. "Are you all right, Chief? Do you think you can travel?"

"Issy says we should go to the *Lady Victoria*. He can't reach Tyene."

"I'm not going anywhere," Stancell said quietly. His broken ribs grated bone on bone every time he moved.

"We could carry you." Bedford looked at Kalissae and added, "Hell, this Pflessian muscle-woman could probably carry you all by herself."

Stancell smiled. Then with a more sober expression he said, "Sorry. I'm afraid my ribs would never make it. I'd just as soon not settle my estate gasping for breath from a punctured lung." He gingerly adjusted his position to place less strain on his injured side. "But don't let me stop you. Get out of here!"

Kalissae glanced at Bedford, then back to Stancell. "At least let us try, Chief."

"No." Stancell waved them both away. "It's *my* decision this time, Manager, Syndic. This something I give the orders on. Now get out of here before it's too late."

Bedford stepped toward the Chief, but was stopped by a groaning, ripping sound from above. The shaft quivered visibly under the strain of the intense bombardment, and more rubble fell from the ceiling of the tunnel.

"Please, save yourselves. The mine is starting to break up, and you don't have much time," Stancell said once the rumble of the attack subsided.

"Oh, Chief..." Kalissae looked at Bedford for an answer. Issy had told her that Tyene would protect them from whoever was attacking the mine, but he couldn't rule out possible death or injury from falling debris. He said go to the *Lady*, but Stancell couldn't go. She knew that. There were no easy choices.

A brief wave of melancholia swept through Bedford once the course of action became obvious. He and Kalissae would have to leave. Without Stancell. "Is there anything we can do?"

"Just go."

"I won't forget you, Chief, and if—"

"There isn't time for that. Now get going."

Bedford took one long, last look at Stancell, then motioned for Kalissae to come with him. "See you after all this is over," he called over his shoulder as they walked toward the elevators.

"Yeah. I'll fill you in on how that thing works," Stancell said softly. Bedford and Kalissae were already out of range of his voice. "Good-bye, Chief," he heard them yell as they disappeared into the access corridor.

As soon as they were gone, he looked at the ore pocket and wondered if Friesh had felt any pain when it happened. He doubted it, not if the Tigris pocket had grown as fast as the one here. At its present rate he estimated he had at best three or four minutes to live, three or four minutes to become an unwilling part of... what had Kalissae called it?

It didn't matter now. As Chief Stancell watched, the ore pocket spat, and popped, and grew, impervious to his thoughts, intent only on doing what its designers had so carefully prescribed for it.

* * *

"All, fire!" Lanse said in his best command voice. Then he turned with a smile to look at the status board. So far he was pleased. Most of the mine's upper structures had been reduced to twisted wreckage. He was sure a few more hits would overload the self-sealing limits of the complex. Once internal pressure was lost, their weapons would be more effective. Euphrates would collapse in on itself like some monolithic creature killed by a perfect brain shot. The plasteel, concrete, and synth fiberboard would be swallowed whole by the very pit they now held together.

It was easy, he thought. Then a haunting little voice which afflicts all military minds added, *maybe too easy*.

"Prepare to commence rapid fire," Lanse said, trying to appease that little voice. There was no sense taking any longer than they had to. "Continuous barrage will start on the next scheduled mark. Slow to point-double-hex-one-one."

He scanned the readiness instruments and saw that they had less than six minutes until they reached the point where rapid fire would be most effective. Six minutes, he thought, six minutes and we can go home.

Bedford extended his arm and grasped Kalissae's hand, pulling her up and over the cracked edge of the elevator doorway with one hard yank.

Too much, Issy said as she flew up with such force that she almost knocked Bedford down.

"Sorry. I overestimated your weight." He gave her an embarrassed look.

"Thanks a lot."

He didn't mean it that way.

"I didn't mean it that way."

Kalissae smiled. "You and Issy must have gone to the same school of interpersonal relations." Bedford's puzzled look made her smile broaden. "Never mind," she said. Then she took a good look around. "Do you think we'll be able to make it?"

Bedford slowly scanned the area. They had been lucky, lucky the elevator had stopped halfway across the entrance to this level, lucky they had only fallen ten meters or so when the cables had snapped, and lucky neither of them had been injured. But, he thought as another shock wave came roaring through the mine, it looks like our luck has run out.

"We don't have enough time to reach the surface on foot. The damage is light here, but it can only get worse as we go higher. And there's no guarantee once we get there that we can get out, or that *Lady Victoria* is all in one piece." The thought of damage to *Lady Victoria* angered him even further.

He looked back at the useless elevator and sighed internally. "I think we should try to get back to Stancell."

Kalissae offered no protest or argument. Bedford was right. At least at the bottom of the mine they might be safe until the bombardment stopped. If they were still alive then, that was more hope than they had now. —Issy?— *Back down.*

"Issy agrees. We can go this way."

Bedford followed her to a narrow door marked AUTHO-RIZED PERSONNEL ONLY.

"Won't the Chief be surprised," she said grimly as she paused to unlock the door. "I hope he doesn't get too angry at us for spoiling his private show."

"Some show," Bedford muttered as he walked through the doorway into a hallway lit by dim red lamps. His eyes adjusted quickly, and soon were they walking at a rapid pace down a series of zigzagging, ladderlike stairs. At level seventy-two he did some fast calculating and estimated they were still one hundred and fifty meters from level eighty-seven, and Stancell, and—

The thought of the ore pocket triggered a reaction that surprised him. —Tyene?— he asked subvocally. He was amazed he had used that form of communication to call anyone other than Issy.

—Tyene?— he asked again. He let his mind flow with

what he felt. The powerful sensations which welled up inside him were almost like an affinity, an awareness of someone like Issy who was not Issy. But how? Why? Tyene was in the ore pocket. Still, he felt pressed to call on her.

–Please, Tyene, we need your help. I understand and agree, but we need your help now.–

"I agree?" he asked as he bumped into Kalissae's back. "What are you talking about?"

They were there. He didn't know how he had managed to walk blindly without falling, but somehow his feet had carried him down the stairs on their own. "Uh . . . oh, nothing. I was just thinking aloud."

She looked at him curiously, wondering what could have so occupied his thoughts at a time like this that he wasn't watching where they were going. "You sure you're all right?"

"Yes," he answered absently.

"Then let's get back to Chief Stancell." Kalissae paused before opening the door to level eighty-seven. She didn't believe Bedford. Something was wrong. –Any ideas, Issy?–

When Issy did not answer, she pushed open the door. Every nerve in her body tingled as the light from the ore pocket streamed into the stairwell. For the first time she felt Issy stir within her as though he was seeking to hide himself. –Are *you* all right?– His answer sent a thrill of excitement that ran through her unlike anything she had ever experienced.

Bedford pulled back from the door as soon as the light hit him, but quickly regained his self-control and followed a short distance behind Kalissae. As he left the darkness behind, he could not help but wonder what he had meant when he said, "I agree." Somehow he knew the time had come for him to find out.

Tyene felt the ageless machinery of the dome strip away the final, self-restraining safety devices in preparation for the ascent. The automatic functions were complete. The controls waited for her to take command of the dome. Like an eager, well-trained beast it was poised in anticipation of her final adjustments, which would unleash its massive powers.

Selectivity, she thought as she ran effortlessly through the maze of options the dome presented her with. Selectivity was the key. It was the reason she was here, the reason she had spent so much time separated from her own kind . . . alone.

For a brief moment she wondered how the dome on Tigris had lost its selectivity. Had its keeper finally gone mad? Had the keeper died? She had no way of knowing. That keeper, the last of her living neighbors, had voluntarily cut off contact with her . . . how long ago?

Tyene thought of the millennia, the infinite number of moments which stretched back so far into the past that she had trouble remembering the time when she had agreed to commit her life to the dome and its mission. It seemed so distant, so inconsequential, especially after she had lost contact with the Council, and through them, with her people.

But now, as she watched the three humanoids standing just outside the margin of her fortress, and realized with a strange sense of anticipation and fear that her loneliness was about to come to an end—NOW she felt that time itself had constructed its own justification, that the random meeting with Issy had been made inevitable by the length of her wait, if by nothing else.

She was proud of what her race had been able to do by stretching its lifespan until it approached immortality. With limitless time all the events with small probabilities came within reach. Events were unpredictable, but with time, and time alone, any event might come to pass.

Issy, she said, threading her words through the growing storm of energy which surrounded her. *It is time.*

"Loo—" Stancell's word was swallowed up by the electrostatic embrace of the ore pocket. He tried to warn the others, but it was too late. The pocket's expansion was almost instantaneous. It had engulfed everything on level eighty-seven before his mind even realized that it was coming.

Kalissae had tried to warn Bedford, but found herself unable to move. The swirling, ethereal clasp of the dome's power held her firmly in place, suspending her body like a marionette hanging inanimate from some puppet master's wall. She could see and hear everything around her, but it was impossible for her to add or subtract physically from all that was happening. At the same time she felt exhilarated by it all, an exhilaration she knew was Issy's.

As the dome took on a thicker, more opaque quality, she wondered where Bedford was. Had he been absorbed into this flowing mass of flickering energy and . . . life? Yes, life, for Tyene was here too, guiding the power of the dome and preparing herself for the transfer.

—Issy, I am frightened,— she said as the molecular tension of the dome crystalized around her, —frightened for him.—

A surge of energy hit Bedford's body as soon as the flaming edge of the dome overtook him, a familiar energy, one he had experienced before. He saw Stancell and Kalissae frozen in place in front of him. He called to them, but they didn't move. Quickly he moved closer and called again. In the light of the dome they seemed blinded and deaf.

—Tyene? Are they safe?—

Do not fear, Bedford. They will not be harmed.

Her voice was clear now, so clear that he knew what must be happening. —Why can't they see or hear me?—

Because you now move at the natural speed and in the same dimension as I. As we speak, only the space-time equal to a few nanoseconds has passed. Enough for now. I must leave you and attend to the process. Peace, Bedford.

—But . . .— He knew she was gone. Loneliness caught him up in its net. He had never given much thought to the idea of loneliness. He had never been alone. Issy had been his constant companion since before he could remember. Now, as he marveled at the intricacy of the dome's interior, separated from Issy, and separated from Tyene, and cut off from Kalissae and Stancell, he knew for the first time what it meant to be alone. And being alone, being singular after a lifetime of being plural brought home to him an almost unbearable sense of tragic despair.

Tyene had said that a conversation which took minutes in the world outside the dome only lasted a few nanoseconds in her natural state. He knew she was old, probably as old or older than Issy. But when he applied the minutes-equals-nanoseconds factor to any rational concept of her age, he discovered something about time and loneliness that he had no words or images with which to convey.

It was almost impossible to grasp in terms of her loneliness just how long she had been here. Long enough to have given up hope, he thought. And to have died from the sheer weight of millennia spent without companionship. The fact that she was still very much alive amazed and somehow excited him. But his eagerness would have to wait. The dome had started to move.

"What's that?" Lanse jerked forward in his seat and stared at the *Poyst*'s main view screen.

The navigation officer made a quick check of his console, then turned to his commander and said, "Probably just some debris thrown up by our barrage. At this distance it's still not very big on my trac—"

"Not that, you idiot. That!" Lanse hit the ten-x magnifier on the screen's controls and jumped out of his command chair. "Don't your instruments detect that thing?" he asked nervously as he stepped closer to the screen and pointed his finger at the oversized image of Euphrates.

A look of shock came over the navigation officer's face as he stared at the object Lanse was pointing at. May the Gods help us, he thought as he quickly turned back to his console and saw that all it registered were the random blips caused by pieces of wreckage from the mine. "No, sir. My instrum—"

"Son-of-a-... That's impossible! How could a Panz-Rol sucker-ship be coming out of that mine?"

The navigation officer's face flashed from shock, to puzzlement, and finally to fear. What the hell was Commander Lanse talking about? That wasn't a Panz-Rol war machine. It was a tripedal Hoop lizard, the biggest one he'd ever seen—and the only one since he had almost been killed on Styl by a Hooper one-hundredth the size of the monster which was crawling out of the mining complex.

Suddenly the intership communication channel buzzed with activity as each of the cruisers in the Helical flotilla began reporting what they saw. Each captain broke in over the voice of another, quickly overloading the circuits with disjointed snatches of frightened conversation. Each swore to the fact that some different lethal menace was coming up out of the mine, and within moments Lanse realized that panic had taken hold of his command.

"Get control of yourselves!" he screamed into his transceiver. "We've got to stay calm. IN FORMATION, prepare to warp out. COORDINATES, delta seven-six-niner-niner—Dammit! It's a trick! We've got to stay in formation!"

Lanse watched in horror as one of his ships broke from the Quad-V and tried to turn away from Euphrates. The cruiser hadn't gone more than a thousand meters when the Panz-Rol vessel lashed out with its gigantic central tentacle and sucked the cruiser in.

It was over so quickly he didn't even have time to warn them. "Get us out of here!" he yelled to his navigation officer.

The young Helical navigator did not hear his commander's voice. His mind was too mesmerized by what he had just seen. What surely must have been the largest Hoop lizard in the galaxy had effortlessly swung itself up from Euphrates and snatched one of their cruisers. Snatched and swallowed it in less time than it took to draw a single breath.

Bedford stared with intense interest through the crackling walls of the dome. But like a man staring through the obscuring veils over the entrance of a Filentt harem chamber, he understood the need to remain silent.

The spherical shell of energy in which he stood bored up through the solid rock of Euphrates as effortlessly as a spaceship moving through the empty parsecs between star systems. There was no noise, no strain, no vibration. The dome simply cut a path to the surface as though some unknown law of physics dictated that it should happen this way.

Like an air bubble through water, he thought as the dome finally broke through the crumbling crust of Euphrates. It had come up near the landing pad, and Bedford thought he saw *Lady Victoria*. In an instant it was gone. Seconds later Euphrates began to shrink away from him like a misshapen slamball.

Suddenly the dome stopped. It held itself a stationary distance from the mining planetoid, and Bedford shivered with unexplainable anticipation. Within moments the dome started to swell. Strange sensations contorted Bedford's body, and he swelled with it.

Relative size became meaningless. Ships with the markings of Helical's Security Guard flashed past, but the dome was expanding so quickly they barely registered in Bedford's mind. Euphrates shrank rapidly away to a small, inconspicuous point of odd light against the backdrop of space. Still the dome expanded.

Just as he wondered how long the dome would continue to expand, it stopped. Its pause was longer this time, as though the sense of urgency which had activated it was gone.

Bedford gazed around in wonder. Deep space surrounded

them. Nebulae passed casually before them. Solar systems no larger than the tip of his finger paused for his examination, speckled with the dust motes of planets. And on those planets, beings and civilizations of every description and philosophical persuasion went about the business of their existence.

For the first time in his life he truly understood that the universe was one vast pool, a cosmic entirety in which relatively short-lived creatures were separated from one another by infinite distances of space and time. But those same creatures were indivisibly joined by the thin, abstract thread of sentience.

The panorama was almost overwhelming. Bedford wondered how the Serens had been able to capture this essential truth about life in the universe. He wondered how they knew that the thread of sentience could be so easily broken. And how they ever hoped to protect it.

Suddenly the significance of the dome opened like a bursting seed pod and scattered answers to his questions throughout his consciousness. A feeling of satisfaction welled up inside him. But as each new kernel of knowledge flowered in his thoughts, one nagging paradox grew beside them and threw a dark shadow over their growth.

If the Serens had been wise enough to grasp the real danger, the unity-threatening menace posed by belligerent species, what had gone wrong? What had happened to cause the power domes to fail? And why had the Serens lost their collective presence in this part of the universe?

A slow, sweet, vibrato hum drew his attention away from his speculations. The dome was shrinking. Fast. Yet, as he watched the millions of stars outside the dome run together in blazing swirls of light, he could not help but wonder what lay ahead.

The puzzle of the Serens pulled at him. It was an attraction that appealed to his deepest curiosity. He wanted to know the answers, wanted to know them so badly that everything else in his life seemed only basic preparation for this moment.

He made his decision without effort, and reassurance flooded through him like a warm nurturing tide. With a great sense of contentment he let his mind rest.

EIGHTEEN

Chief Stancell felt slightly dizzy and disoriented. The ore pocket had returned to the bottom of the mine. Though his mind told him it was impossible, he knew he was standing again on level eighty-seven. Once the pocket deposited him in the exact place he had been before, it shrank away and half-buried itself into the side of the tunnel from where it had come. One last spitting tendril of bright blue light signaled an end to its luminescence. Then it took on the dull grey sheen of the egg he had seen on Tigris.

"Did you see what that thing did?" he asked more as a test of reality than as a question directed to anyone.

"Yes." Kalissae's response was hushed. "It disintegrated them, crushed those cruisers into dust like . . . like they were miniature ceramic toys and not real ships."

It took Stancell a few moments to register Kalissae's voice. "No," he said finally as he turned to look at her. "It absorbed them, soaked them up like drops of water into a sponge."

Bedford smiled as he watched a puzzled expression

come over their faces. They had seen different things, things that had been conjured up from their separate memories, things that made what had happened seem plausible. The truth was that they were both correct. "Are you two all right?" he asked as he stepped closer to them.

Kalissae turned her questioning gaze toward Bedford.

I have recovered.

"Issy and I seem to be all right."

"Me too, but don't ask me how it's possible." Stancell made a quick physical check of himself as though to confirm what he already knew. "What did you see, Syndic?"

Bedford paused before answering. What had he seen? Not anything like what they had described. The destruction of the Helical Security Guard ships had taken place so fast that his memory carried only a flickering image of the annihilated cruisers. "I saw..." he said hesitantly as he looked first at Kalissae and then at Stancell. "I saw the cruisers disappear. But more importantly, I saw the reason, the overriding rationale for the Seren power domes."

They both stared at him in incomprehension. Then almost in unison they said, "What?"

He knew they deserved an answer, but he wasn't sure he could put what he knew into words. Bedford searched his mind for the right terms, but even the rich nuances of a language like Galactic Standard were pitifully inadequate. There was no way to express—

It is even beyond my comprehension, Bedford.

The sound of Tyene's voice did not surprise him. Yet when it came, it sent a thrill through his body. The rush of pleasure elicited in him feelings of cohesiveness with her that were both intellectual and sensual. —Please, go on,— he said after a brief, silent pause.

I don't remember why the domes were built. I do not remember the reason I committed my life—not my personal reason, anyway. After a while the habit of maintaining vigilance justified my presence there. Yet one thing is still clear to me after all this time. It is only a word, a single clue as to the purpose, a solitary concept which burns at

*the center of Seren logic and justifies all you have seen.
The domes were constructed as a barrier against the one
thing which threatens us all: entropy.*

"Entropy?" Bedford asked aloud. Before he could ask
Tyene to be more specific, he noticed that Kalissae had
suddenly dropped her head. Issy, he thought as he stepped
quickly over to her and grabbed her arm just as her legs
gave out.

—What's wrong, Issy?— she asked weakly. Bedford's one
word had triggered a frightening sensation in her. For one
long moment her body's involuntary functions, breathing,
heartbeat, muscle control, had all paused. And in that
moment she had known it was Issy's reaction, not her
own.

"Kalissae?" Bedford eased her into a sitting position on
the floor and sat facing her, holding her hands. "Kalissae—"

A tingling pulse of energy in their hands brought her
eyes up to meet his. She clasped his hands tighter. Thrill-
ing waves of power flowed between them. They were
bound together in a timeless moment. Issy and Tyene
were communicating.

The two Serens spoke in a strange, nontemporal form of
speech, a language which neither Bedford nor Kalissae
could decipher. It was a language Issy had not used for
millennia, the ancient mother tongue of the Serens.

Their private conversation seemed very brief. When it
ended, Bedford and Kalissae looked up and saw Stancell
standing over them with a puzzled expression on his face.

He stared at them like they were some strange new life
form, but his look expressed curiosity more than anything
else. "Okay," he said as soon as he saw the look of
awareness return to their faces, "will one of you be kind
enough to let an old pitman in on what's going on?"

They both started to answer, but Kalissae edged Bedford
out. "Have you ever met an old friend, someone you
haven't seen in a very long time?"

Stancell nodded and said, "Yes?"

"Well, Issy and Tyene have just had such a reunion in a

conversation that would not have been possible without
the physical reality of our bodies." She glanced at Bedford
and continued. "While they were able to communicate
before, this is really the first time they were able
to . . . experience one another, to know each other on
something other than an intellectual basis."

"So what did they say?"

"We don't know," Bedford and Kalissae said simultaneously.

"Great. Now I suppose—"

"But we did get a strong impression of what they talked
about," Bedford said. "How would you like to take a trip,
a journey which might answer all our questions?"

Stancell cocked his head, took a deep breath, and
sighed. What was the Syndic asking? he wondered as he
glanced back to the ore pocket. "There's really only one
answer I want." He pointed to the grey bulk of the
deactivated dome. "What's the purpose of that thing?"

Bedford looked at Kalissae then back up to Stancell. "I
only have a partial explanation. It was apparently built to
destroy any belligerent species it came into contact with,
to prevent any aggressive race from exploiting the peaceful sentients in the galaxy . . . maybe the whole universe. I
don't know any more than that. Neither do Issy and
Tyene."

"And Tigris? They certainly weren't aggressive."

"I don't have all the answers, Chief. They probably did
something over there which activated the dome. And
Tyene thinks there's a good chance the Seren inside was
either too weak to control the dome's selectivity, or that
she was dead." Bedford saw a look of sadness cross Stancell's
face, and stood up, pulling Kalissae with him.

"Chief," he said as he stepped up to Stancell and put his
hand on the Chief's shoulder, "I feel the same sense of loss
as you do. Too many people died here, and most of them
were innocent victims trapped in the web of violence that
Rosenthal started."

"That's another thing I don't understand. What was
Rosenthal after? Destroying the mine didn't make sense

unless he knew what we had found inside the pocket on Tigris."

"Shavas-Korp," Kalissae said suddenly. They both looked at her questioningly. "One of Helical's minor competitors for Isoleucine mining. They went out of business very suddenly and very mysteriously—and Rosenthal as much as admitted to me that he and his superiors had taken care of them."

"But why?"

"Because an investigation into the accidents Shavas-Korp had experienced would have caused too much trouble. Or maybe they did know where the Isoleucine really came from. I don't know why. But I do know that Rosenthal didn't need much of an excuse to do what he did."

Stancell shook his head. "So Rosenthal tried to blow up Euphrates for political reasons, just to avoid what the revelation might do to Federation politics."

"Yes," Bedford answered for her, "and in a way he succeeded. But look, Chief, you never gave me an answer. How would you like to take a long trip with us?"

"What trip?" Kalissae asked before Stancell had a chance to respond. "And what did you mean about Rosenthal succeeding?"

"They're both really tied together." Bedford pointed to the inert ore pocket. "The power dome has gone dormant because Tyene is inside me now. Ask Issy what that will mean when the Federation authorities finally get out here to see what happened."

"I don't have to ask Issy or Tyene or any other critter, Syndic." There was anger in Stancell's voice, and he made no attempt to hide it. He was tired of being the forgotten fifth side to their little quadrangle.

"I'm sorry, Chief. What I was going to say was that when the Federation gets here, it will be our word against the evidence. The power domes are nothing more than Isoleucine pockets now."

"But what about all the death and destruction? Surely they will realize that what we tell them has to be true?"

"Remember, Rosenthal was a Federation agent. He was trying to cover up the facts about what the ore pockets really are." Bedford paused to let Stancell think, then added, "No, Chief, I'm afraid the Federation will be more than happy to say we are all insane and be done with it. *And us.*"

He is probably right, Issy whispered to Kalissae.

His voice seemed slower and more pensive than before. "Chief," she said as she took Bedford's free hand, "if we stay, we're liable to end up locked away somewhere where no one can get to us. Or worse . . ."

Stancell knew what she meant by "worse", but he still didn't understand—"This trip . . . just where are you going?" His voice showed more interest and less anger.

"I'm not sure."

"Neither am I," Bedford added. "We'll let the Serens guide us as best they can. But one thing I am certain about, Chief. We've got to contact the Seren race before the Federation expands blindly into them. You saw the results of that here. We must try to prevent it from happening again. And Kalissae and I are the only people we know of uniquely qualified to make the next contact."

"Because of your symbiosis with them?"

"Yes."

Stancell took a long, hard look at his two companions. We've been through a lot together, he thought as he watched their expectant faces. But I'll never be as they are now, never be anything more than a delaying factor to what they do. And that could be fatal to us all.

"Tell you what," he said as he smiled at them. "Let's see if we can get *Lady Victoria* ready for space, and I'll give you my answer then."

Kalissae knew that Stancell had already made his decision, and a glance at Bedford told her that he knew also. Bedford spoke first. "Chief, how would you like to be a Free Syndic?"

"Thanks, but I'd rather play this one on my own," Stancell said in a strong, quiet voice. "It's time I took a little of the responsibility for this mess onto my own shoulders. This old miner still has a few tricks in his kit bag, and there has hardly been a bureaucrat born I couldn't get on the right side of." The thought of a confrontation with some smart-assed bureaucrat gave him a small reason to smile. "Besides, you'll need a little cover if you expect to be far enough away from here so they won't be able to follow you."

"I only thought you might like some judicial weight added to your position."

"Syndic, as of this moment I'm resigning as your Deptenens. If there's one thing I've learned after all these years, it's that people will cater to an old pitman's idiosyncracies more than they ever would to someone with your kind of title. We really run things out here. We make the orders work. Or didn't you notice that?"

Kalissae allowed herself a brief laugh at the truth in what Stancell had said, and somehow that broke the tension between them. Bedford and Stancell laughed with her.

"We'd better get to work," Stancell said. He motioned to the stairs. "But I want you to do me a favor before you leave."

"Anything."

"Could you please thank Tyene for me." They waited for him to continue. "My ribs," he said as he unraveled the bandage from around his chest. "Somehow she was able to heal them while we were inside the dome."

Bedford reached out with both hands and lightly touched Stancell's face. "Tell her yourself," he said as his fingertips made contact.

Stancell did not know what Bedford was talking about. Then it happened. —Thanks, Tyene,— his mind said in a way that gave him more understanding of what a symbiotic relationship was all about than any book full of explanations.

The grace is yours, Stancell heard a clear voice say.

Bedford took his hands away and the three of them walked slowly out of level eighty-seven for the last time

*   *   *

Chief Stancell stood in front of the only functioning view screen in the Euphrates communications center and watched the visual readouts as the *Lady Victoria* rose slowly from the landing pad. "Good luck," he said into a small comset he had loosely draped around his neck.

"Thanks. And good luck to you, my friend." The sound of Bedford's voice was made deeper by the damaged speaker through which it came. Kalissae's good-bye followed, and then the speaker went silent.

As the *Lady*'s image shrank in the view screen, Stancell wondered what they would find out there. Would Issy and Tyene remember enough to guide them to that place in the universe where the Seren race still existed? Would they be able to avoid what had killed so many people here and on Tigris?

He tried to imagine what it would be like to run headlong into an area of space where there were thousands of ... of what? Ore pockets? Power domes? He had come up with his own name for the alien creations, a name dredged up from his memory of something he had read once in a history book.

"Cenacles," he said softly to the ghosts who now dwelled in the quiet emptiness of Euphrates. "You were all taken into a Cenacle, taken to offer others salvation." Stancell wondered if that long dead savior would have understood what he meant. That man too had tried to save his people.

When he refocused on the view screen, the *Lady Victoria* was no more than a pinpoint of light. Moments later it disappeared. For the first time he realized how much he was going to miss Bedford and Kalissae. He would have to face the bureaucrats on his own, but they faced a far greater challenge.

It's up to you, he thought as he turned off the view screen. *It's up to you to make these deaths have some meaning, some positive impact on civilization.*

❂   ❂   ❂

Bedford waited until they were well clear of Euphrates before he asked Tyene what coordinates to set on *Lady*'s navigation computer.

I must consult with Issy, she said after she had searched Bedford's mind for residual clues Issy had left behind.

"Kalissae," Bedford said as he turned to where she was strapped in the communications chair.

She came to him without a word. Silently she reached out and took one of his hands in hers.

The flow of information came almost instantaneously. Numbers and alpha codes rattled through Bedford's head so fast he had a hard time keeping up. Finally the burst of data ended, and he punched the last set of digits into the computer.

Two things struck him as *Lady Victoria* responded to the instructions. First, he did not recognize any of the coordinates he had entered. And second, Kalissae still had a grip on his hand, a grip which tingled with sensuality.

"Issy?" he asked in an odd tone.

"Is the course set?" Kalissae asked.

"Yes, but—"

"Then come with me." She pulled him from his chair, out of the command module, and down the companionway to his cabin.

"I don't think—"

"Then you shouldn't," she said as she pulled him into her arms and tilted her head.

"Are you sure?" he asked gently.

"Yes," she whispered as she brought her lips close to his. "Now shut up, and kiss me. We've ALL been waiting a long time for this."

ABOUT THE AUTHORS

WARREN NORWOOD lives in Fort Worth, Texas. He is the author of three previous books, collectively known as *The Windhover Tapes*, entitled *An Image of Voices*, *Flexing the Warp*, and *Fize of the Gabriel Ratchets*. A fourth *Windhover Tapes* book, *Planet of Flowers*, will be published by Bantam in early 1984.

RALPH MYLIUS presently lives in Dallas, Texas after a three-year sojourn to Saudi Arabia during which time he was the controller for a large corporation. When not writing, he works on his two ancient B.M.W. automobiles. He and Warren Norwood have been close friends since their junior high school days. *The Seren Cenacles* is his first novel and he is now at work on other book projects.

The remarkable saga of Gerard Manley and his sentient spaceship *Windhover* concludes in this stirring volume.

Gerard, his wife ShRil and their daughter CrRina have made the journey to the planet Brisbidine to study the strange flora that covers each of its eleven continents. There, they will make a remarkable discovery about the flowers—and will be propelled into the heart of danger as the perils from Gerard's past come racing up for one final confrontation.

On the following pages, you will read some of the exciting opening scenes from THE WINDHOVER TAPES: PLANET OF FLOWERS. The mystery of the flowers and the memories of Gerard's past will begin to unfold as well as the threat two people pose to Gerard and his family. All of these stories will interweave to form the breathtaking conclusion to *The Windhover Tapes*.

In a postpartum fit of perversity Chizen Dereaviny had named her son Hopeman. Then as though wanting to deny the blatant meaning in his name she referred to him thereafter as Hap.

Now Hap was fourteen Standard years old and Chizen wondered if there was hope for either of them in the future. They were headed to the colony planet, Brisbidine, under a special clemency ruling handed down by the commissioner of emigration on Sun's March.

There had been many applicants ready and willing to give up their hard lives on Sun's March for a freer life on a remote planet outside of any galactic control. But for unknown reasons she and Hap had been singled out, and Chizen had been told to report to the commissioner of emigration.

She had gone to her meeting with the commissioner with some trepidation, wondering if she had revealed the secrets of her past by some inadvertent word or action and would soon be told that her name had been stricken from the list of acceptable applicants. Much to her surprise, the commissioner had been cordial and even somewhat defferential toward her. After they had worked their way awkwardly through the amenities of hostess and guest, Commissioner Dusea had told Chizen that she and Hap had been granted emigration rights. They along with a small group of others from Sun's March would travel to Brisbidine aboard the freespacer Rowlf.

The right, of course, had been subject to a condition, but it was a condition so simple that Chizen had accepted it immediately. She was to carry with her a sealed directive, a directive which Commissioner Dusea herself claimed not to know the contents of. Upon arrival on Brisbidine, Chizen was to break the seal, read the directive, and do her best to fulfill its terms. If she would swear on her honor to do that, she and Hap were free to board the *Rowlf* and leave Sun's March and Ribble Galaxy forever.

As the huge pioneer transport, *Rowlf*, had made its way slowly from system to system picking up volunteers Chizen had been tempted more than once to break the seal on the directive and find out exactly what it said. But as she had sworn on her honor to do her best to fulfill its terms, so she had sworn on her honor not to open it until they were planetside on Brisbidine. And honor was something Chizen had come to understand during her exile. She would wait to read the directive as she had agreed to do.

"Eat time, mother," Hap said as he poked his head into her cramped cabin.

"Go ahead. Shortly I will join you."

"Eating with the team?" he asked, referring to the rec-team she had joined and which was leading the ship's competition in four of its six chosen sports.

"No. Not until tomorrow."

"Shall I wait for you?"

His handsome face reminded her constantly of his father. "No. Eat with your friends if you wish." He left without comment, and she thought how unlike his father that would have been. Odd memories scrolled through her thoughts for a moment or two before she automatically cut them off.

That part of her past was gone. She was a pioneer now, destined to build a new life for herself and Hap, a life free from any entanglement with what had gone before. Except for that directive, she thought with a glance toward the small personal locker where she had safely locked it away.

*   *   *

"Gerard!" the voice screamed.

A bloody hand reached out for him. A sea of agonized faces moaned in the background.

"Gerard," the voice screamed again. Its face spread in fury. Its eyes bulged wildly in their sockets. "Gerard!"

He awoke with a start. It was Fairy Peg.

The dream was unexpected, but not new, and it was no longer a nightmare. His nights of horrid dreams and fragmented memories of Fairy Peg seemed mostly behind him now. The treatments he had received from Chief Headfoot at Jelvo U. had eased the pattern of his dreams and helped him live with them.

Fairy Peg and Ribble Galaxy were part of a past he was gradually learning to forget. He would never know whether or not he had actually betrayed them and caused the deaths of hundreds, maybe thousands of people. But he was learning to live beyond even those thoughts, learning that whatever he might have done could not, and must not destroy his new life.

ShRil pulled him close. "The dreams again?" she asked in a sleepy voice.

"Yes."

"Are you all right?"

"Yes."

"Can you go back to sleep?"

"Yes."

"Good."

She wiggled a little and relaxed against him, the sounds of her breathing quiet and reassuring. Gerard shut his eyes and tried to relax, waiting for the heaviness that would pull him down to sleep.

He drifted. His eyes rolled back in his head. A face appeared. With a start he opened his eyes. ShRil mumbled and twitched beside him.

It had been Fairy Peg's face, but not Fairy Peg's face. Whose? He shut his eyes and tried to recapture that face from the depths of his memory.

It was Fairy Peg's face, but hard years and toil had written their history in lines across her furrowed brow and wrinkles in the corners of her eyes. It was a worn face, a tired face, a face pulled down at the corners by having frowned more than smiled. It was a face he fervently hoped he would never see again.

Once more he drifted. Thoughts tumbled lazily through his mind. Words echoed back at him, from another place.

Hap had bribed the handler for a seat assignment beside one of the shuttle's few windows. Now as they pulled slowly away from the *Rowlf* he wasn't so sure he had spent his credits wisely. Everything was upside down. Brisbidine hung at a forty-five-degree angle above them with the *Rowlf* partially obscuring the view. The shuttle had no artificial gravity, and Hap's stomach twisted and turned in unhappiness. But he was determined to enjoy himself.

He glanced quickly at his mother and saw that she had taken the drugs offered her and seemed to be sleeping peacefully. Hap would never have made the descent asleep. He had no idea when he might get to space again, and he didn't want to miss a thing. As he stared out the port he forgot about his stomach and lost himself in the wonder of what he was seeing.

Chizen was not asleep. She had taken the drug, but only enough to help her overcome the nauseous feelings that always came to her with weightlessness. For the moment she was pleased that Hap was enjoying their descent and she was unwilling to spoil his pleasure with her concerns. He would have to face the problems of their new life soon enough.

Watching him made her feel better. He was like his father in many ways, especially in his looks and his naive acceptance of the twists and turns life had presented to him. She started to shut off her thoughts about Hap's father then consciously decided to let them flow.

He was dead now. Chizen knew that, but knowledge that he had died did nothing to lessen the vividness with which she could call his image into her mind . . .

strong, brown-haired, with a broad face that blushed easily . . . oh, how she had tried to impress him, tried to make him see her for herself.

She remembered the night of Hap's conception, the night she had come to him with the full knowledge that she was at her most fertile, the night she had offered him a moment's reprieve from his misery and he had taken her into his arms . . .

Anger burned through the memories which followed that night.

It was too much. Chizen shut the memory down again. Then she vowed once more to keep that memory buried. This was the beginning of a new life for her and Hap, and they would be better served if she left the past well behind them and concentrated on what they could make for themselves on this new world.

"It is agreed then? The Constant will meet aboard this ship four cycles from now and make the journey to Cosvetz. Are there any who do not wish to participate?"

"Perhaps I should not go."

"Why, Gatou-Drin? We understand that Cosvetz is your idea and that you are biased accordingly."

"Thank you, Askavenhar, but—"

"You have an obligation to be there, Gatou-Drin."

She paused for a moment, the pleasure apparent in her multifaceted eyes. "Very well. I will come."

"Any others?"

There were none. Spinnertel left as quickly as he could without appearing to rush. As soon as he was back aboard his ship he downed two quick liters of his favorite tranquilizer, a mixture of alcohol and the oily essences of several rare herbs. He needed to relax, and he needed to think. But for the moment the relaxation was more important.

He had been humiliated in the Constant, and there was nothing, absolutely nothing he could do about it.

He poured himself a third liter of the spicy alcohol and reclined on his favorite contoured mat.

Damn the Verporchting, he thought, then smiled ruefully to himself. He had created the Verporchting as a counter-ego, an innocent opposite, expendable and amusing, useful for stirring up a minor tempest here and there. But the last reincarnation had shown too many mutations and too much independence. It had annoyed Spinnertel and he had arranged a convenient and—he thought—final death for it.

Now it appeared he would have to get rid of another one. But he would have to do so without jeopardizing his status in the Constant, however little that status might currently be worth. He would have to find the most ingenious way. Then maybe those old stuffed-heads, Askavenhar and Gracietta, would grudgingly acknowledge that he was a force to be reckoned with.

Somewhere through the fourth liter Spinnertel fell asleep.

"There it is," Carson said simply.

The patch, as Carson referred to it, filled the open space below them. Gerard estimated it to be roughly one hundred and fifty meters in diameter and from their perspective on the edge of the low cliff, the flower colony's geometrical layout was clearly visible. "Do they all look like this?" he asked.

"All I've seen. Same shape, same colors, same umbrella plants on the edges. Amsrita measured eight or ten of them."

"Why wasn't that in her reports—or your reports?"

Carson looked away from them and ShRil thought he was not going to answer. When he turned back there was an odd look in his eyes and a softness in his voice that surprised her.

"She said not to. Said we had to be careful what we told and that telling too much was just as bad as telling too little. Made me promise—later, when I had to write them for her . . . that I'd only say what had to be said to get others to come here. I promised . . . but, well, you might as well know it now if you haven't figured it out for yourselves. I didn't want no one else to come here."

He had turned back away and the last sentence was almost whispered. ShRil put her hand on Gerard's arm and shook her head. When he arched his eyebrows in question she touched the corner of one eye with a forefinger and tilted her head toward Carson.

Gerard understood. Carson was crying. The fact that ShRil was physically incapable of shedding tears made her understanding of Carson's emotion no less real. But why was Carson crying? Was it because they had stirred up his emotions about Amsrita? Somehow Gerard didn't believe that. He was beginning to think Carson was a little unstable. Yet he had no logical explanation to offer for Carson's tears other than sentiment. They would have to wait until Carson was ready to tell them.

"Sorry," he said finally with his back still to them. "Didn't mean to let go like that." He wiped his face on the dark cloth of his jacket then turned to face them. "You got to understand, if you can, that what I told you is true. Those flowers are killers. There's no way to get rid of them all, but that doesn't mean that we've got to put up with them any more than we have to. I hate them. It'll come the day when you'll hate them too."

"I still don't understand," Gerard said quietly. "If they're so bad, why wouldn't you want someone to come in and study them, and find a way to help you get rid of them permanently?"

Carson's eyes showed red around the edges, but his gaze was steady and his voice firm when he answered Gerard. "Can't do that either. Amsrita understood it and tried to explain it to me. Has something to do with the whole planet. They're all over it, you know. Eleven major continents and every one has its colonies of flowers. They're necessary here, part of the ecology, and more than that too . . . maybe."

"Something else that was not in the report?" ShRil asked.

"Weren't no place in them for that 'cause, well . . ." His voice cracked slightly, but he shook his head with an odd jerk and cleared his throat. "Let's sit." Without waiting for them he brushed the loose debris off a long, knee-high, black rock and sat down. Gerard and ShRil sat next to him.

"See, at the end Amsrita wasn't making much sense most of the time. Told me to put down lots of things that didn't fit together. I wrote them down, but I didn't put them in the reports. Then after she died . . . well, I did something pretty stupid, I guess. I burned those notes. Didn't want to have them around. Didn't want to be reminded of what she'd been through."

"And did not want anyone else to know?" ShRil added softly.

"Truth," he said, giving her a little smile. "But I shouldn't have burned them."

"Because there was something in them you now think might be valuable?" Gerard offered.

"Yes. And because you two could've read them, and maybe understood better how dangerous the flowers are if you could see what they did to her mind."

The pair stood out from the other greenies in subtle ways which Geljoespiy detected easily. She carried herself with a certain graceful set of her shoulders and a tilt of her chin that spoke for a level of living denied by her clothes and belongings. He not only looked the right age, but also had the same broad face and wide-set eyes as his father. They were almost definitely the two Gel had been told to watch for.

Gel could not guess the reasons behind his mentor's interest in these two, nor did he wonder about fathers and unclaimed sons. He would keep the boy and his mother temporarily at his place as requested, and attempt to win their confidence and trust. In the long accounting of what he owed Letrenn that small act would not begin to make repayment.

"You two," he said to the chosen pair, "move your gear over to that blue skimmer over there."

Chizen looked carefully at the small, dark man who had spoken to them. "Are you the administrator?" she asked.

Gel laughed. "Don't have any administrators around here, lady, at least not like you mean. I'm just doing my turn." Without Junathun's help, he thought. "You'll be staying at my place until you decide what it is you want to do. Then we'll set you up with a place of your own or find you more permanent quarters. Now get your stuff over there. I've got to get all these people sorted out and assigned before it's too late to move them." Gel turned away without waiting for a reply and began to visually assess the rest of the group the shuttle had dumped in his sector.

Chizen watched him for a moment then said, "Come on, Hap. Let us do as he says for now."

"I don't like him, mother."

"You do not have to like him or anyone. But for the time being we have little choice but to follow his directions. Do you want to sleep outside tonight?"

"Might be fun."

"Will be cold. Move."

Hap moved. It took them three easy trips to carry their meager belongings from the assembly area to the blue skimmer the dark man had indicated. Without waiting for instructions, Hap opened the small cargo hatch and loaded their four duffles and two personal lockers neatly into the available space.

"He keeps a clean skimmer, anyway," Hap said as he closed the hatch. "Looks pretty old, but . . ." He let the sentence go when he realized that his mother was paying no attention to him. She was staring back toward the assembly area lost in some thought of her own.

The late afternoon sun cast long shadows from the volunteers and pioneers sorting them out in the assembly area. A skimmer full of people had pulled up to the edge of the area and caught Chizen's attention. One of those people looked familiar. She could not be sure but . . . She shaded her eyes and squinted hoping in some way to cut the hundred meters between them and make a positive identification.

Her hand shook. Her breath stopped. For a moment her world stopped with it. Then the skimmer turned and moved away taking its mysterious passenger with it.

Chizen let her hand drop to her side with a shaky sigh. It was impossible. He was dead. There was no way he could be here on Brisbidine. No way. An arm encircled her shoulders.

"Are you all right, mother?"

"Oh. Yes, Hap. I, uh—"

"Maybe you'd better sit down."

"Yes, maybe I should. The trip down seems to have gotten to me. I feel a little dizzy."

They sat beside the skimmer and Chizen took deep breaths of the strange air laden with its warm scents of growing things. But she could not tear her thoughts away from that vision of a man in the distant skimmer, a man who looked anything but dead.

Gel and his wife had fed Chizen and Hap well and made them as comfortable as possible in their small house. After a long monologue during which Gel had extolled the virtues of Brisbidine, Essenne had finally insisted that their guests be allowed to get some rest.

Chizen waited until Hap's breathing evened out in the healthy rhythms of adolescent sleep and the sounds from the other rooms had stilled. Then she turned on the small glow lamp beside her bed and stared at her personal locker.

Resting securely near its bottom was the directive. She had been too busy to think about it since they had landed. Then the shock of seeing someone who looked like Hap's father had pushed the directive further from her mind. Now she couldn't stop thinking about it.

She slipped quietly out of bed, wrapped the blanket around herself against the chill, and sat on the floor in front of the locker. It's dark, travel-worn surface looked somehow warm and reassuring to her in the dim light, but she hesitated to open it. As much as she wanted to know what the directive contained, she didn't want to know. Finally, after several false starts she centered her thumb over the lock-plate and pressed.

Moments later she had the directive in her hands. She closed the locker and climbed back into bed. Lying on her stomach she broke the seal on the thin box and slowly opened it. With a shiver she pulled the blanket tight around her and read the message she had carried half-way across the universe.

The directive was written on the inside of the box itself. Disbelief, anger, and confusion fanned the fires of her memory as she read the words then watched them slowly fade as some self-destructive mechanism in the box destroyed the message. Nothing could destroy it in her mind. It would always be burned there in the indelible fire of emotion.

Sister,
Gerard Manley lives. He who betrayed Ribble Galaxy survives. He is said to be going to the planet Brisbidine. If you would restore your good name and honor, you will kill him. We await verification of his death.

OUT OF THIS WORLD!

That's the only way to describe Bantam's great series of science fiction classics. These space-age thrillers are filled with terror, fancy and adventure and written by America's most renowned writers of science fiction. Welcome to outer space and have a good trip!

FANTASY AND SCIENCE FICTION FAVORITES

Bantam brings you the recognized classics as well as the current favorites in fantasy and science fiction. Here you will find the most recent titles by the most respected authors in the genre.

☐	23365	THE SHUTTLE PEOPLE George Bishop	$2.95
☐	22939	THE UNICORN CREED Elizabeth Scarborough	$3.50
☐	23120	THE MACHINERIES OF JOY Ray Bradbury	$2.75
☐	22666	THE GREY MANE OF MORNING Joy Chant	$3.50
☐	23494	MASKS OF TIME Robert Silverberg	$2.95
☐	23057	THE BOOK OF SKULLS Robert Silverberg	$2.95
☐	23063	LORD VALENTINE'S CASTLE Robert Silverberg	$3.50
☐	20870	JEM Frederik Pohl	$2.95
☐	23460	DRAGONSONG Anne McCaffrey	$2.95
☐	20592	TIME STORM Gordon R. Dickson	$2.95
☐	23036	BEASTS John Crowley	$2.95
☐	23666	EARTHCHILD Sharon Webb	$2.95

Prices and availability subject to change without notice.

Buy them at your local bookstore or use this handy coupon for ordering: